HORRORICANE

HORRORICANE

Edward Newton

A
Grinning Skull Press
Publication
PO Box 67, Bridgewater, MA 02324

The Skull logo with stylized lettering was created for Grinning Skull Press by Dan Moran, http://dan-moran-art.com/.
Cover designed by Jeffrey Kosh, http://jeffreykosh.wix.com/jeffreykoshgraphics.

Published by Grinning Skull Press, P.O. Box 67, Bridgewater, MA 02324

ISBN-13: 978-1-947227-71-2 (paperback)
ISBN: 978-1-947227-72-9 (ebook)

DEDICATION

For Treina, Kobe, Gage, Oliver, and Bennett

ACKNOWLEDGMENTS

Thank you to Florida, for three years of research on storms, sunshine, and beautiful beaches.

def. hurricane
hurr·i·cane
ˈhər-ə-kān/
noun
1: a tropical cyclone with winds of 74 miles (119 kilometers) per hour or greater that occurs especially in the western Atlantic, that is usually accompanied by rain, thunder, and lightning, and that sometimes moves into temperate latitudes
2: something resembling a hurricane, especially in its turmoil

0"

[Leo]

Leo's laboratory is a mess. What would his mother say? Surely curse him in Japanese because that's what she's good at. Galileo Enomoto is good at something else. He's *great* at something else. When it comes to science, Leo is a *rockstar*.

The rest? Well, the rest sucks.

"C'mon, Leo," Arianna complains. "It's Friday, for Chrissakes. Let's wrap it up and get out of here."

"Out?" Leo asks, pausing for a moment from looking for the last printout that he put...somewhere. "Like for drinks?"

"Whatever shakes your maracas, dude," Arianna says. Then she catches his meaning. "Oh, you mean, like me and you? Are you shitting me? My boyfriend would kill me if he ever saw me out with another guy. Or you."

She says it like she isn't sure if Leo is a guy or something else. His face turns red and he goes back to looking for the report. "You can go. I'll finish up here."

"We're partners," Arianna sighs like she just told her family she has cancer.

"Yeah, partners." Arianna hadn't contributed more than a full help-

3

ing of boobs to their work so far. But at the end of the day, Leo has as much chance of experimenting with her physiology as Arianna has in mastering paleotempestological reconstructions. "Go on. Don't worry. I've already got your name on our report."

Arianna leans across the desk where she's been sitting for the last half an hour, scrolling through social media. Her cleavage is on full display today. It looks like her breasts are ready to party for the weekend. She lets him get an eyeful, gives him a knowing grin, and thanks him before she skips out the door.

Leo finds the paleotempestology report tucked between an electronic tablet and his clipboard charts and remembers he was distracted when Arianna dropped her lipstick and bent over to pick it up, her top *allllllll-most* spilling out from the straining black lace bra. Damn gravity never seemed to work quite right when you needed it to. This afternoon, science had let him down.

The entire east side of the UCF laboratory is a window, blinds drawn. Leo checks the weather app on his phone to see what it's like outside instead of walking over and looking for himself. He is trained to trust technology over his own eyes. Bytes and binary don't lie, but visual input may be corrupted by any number of variables.

It isn't supposed to rain until overnight. But the weather in Florida works like a science geek and smooth moves—can't ever quite figure out what's next. Leo certainly doesn't want to get caught in a rainstorm. He's wearing a white polo shirt today because he forgot to do laundry all week, so he couldn't allow himself to get soaked in a downpour; he would look like a sorority girl in a wet t-shirt contest. His man-boobs aren't quite as big as Arianna's tits, but his hairless chest could be mistaken for feminine under the translucent material. His room-mates are planning a weekend party that starts tonight, and Leo refuses to walk through a dozen girls showing off his strangely oblong aureoles. People are shits, and Leo doesn't want to give them a reason to throw their shade in his direction.

The app still promises no rain until after midnight. That gives Leo another few hours to crunch research numbers. His semester assignment is a mammoth research project about using the past to predict the future in a paper co-authored by Arianna. (It doesn't matter if her name is on it or not. She wants to be a meteorologist on a local newscast. That means being photogenic rather than scientific.) Meteorology is guessing the future—his mother often teased that astrology is as respectable a science as meteorology. His father sometimes taunted Leo about studying "meteors." "Awfully specific," he would jibe. "Like studying only comets." Once, he spent an entire afternoon joking about the Avon lady being a "cometologist."

As it happens, paleotempestology *is* a rather specific field of study. Leo studies past tropical storm data. He also collects information from the job site following every hurricane. He charts the past to indicate future storm patterns. Field research takes him onto atolls and into marshes, trudging through coastal lakes to gather samples and data from over-wash deposits. Leo primarily concentrates on oxygen isotopes as reflected in coral, tree rings, and even in fish bivalves. All this research indicates the frequency of the storms and can be predictive of tomorrow's inclement weather.

Leo likes working in the laboratory more than working in the field—he's more comfortable analyzing data rather than collecting it. The information gathered by himself and others in the program is entered into a database and correlated into a record covering storm events over several millennia. In theory, Leo and the other paleotempestologists ought to be able to come up with a model to someday accurately forecast tropical storms.

They'll be able to predict hurricanes.

Predict the *future*.

Outside, the wind howls like a wolf baying at the moon. The sound seems mournful—as if the state of all things has saddened the world. Why wouldn't it be? The world is a shitty place. Leo sometimes wonders if he took up paleotempestology not to determine *if* the ultimate storm is coming but to predict *when*. Humanity has pushed the planet to the brink of a breakdown. Pollution, overpopulation, global warming, the rape of natural resources. Soon, the world will push back.

5

Leo isn't trying to save the world or discover some useful warning; instead, he's trying to discern an expiration date so he can determine how much longer before this suffering ends. The world's suffering. And his own.

He thinks about Arianna, somewhere with her boyfriend, laughing and showing off her chest. He thinks about any girl, anywhere, everywhere but right here. There are sixty thousand students at UCF, yet Leo has been lonely ever since he arrived in Orlando. The world is ending, and he's fine with that. Let's get it over with.

"How long you gonna be?" asks a janitor popping his head into the room.

Leo looks away from the charts hanging on the wall. The janitor is way past retirement age, maybe eighty even, old as hell and bent over like a wilted palm tree. The old man squints across the room as if unsure whether Leo is a student or a teacher, male or female, man or mannequin. The janitor seems surprised when Leo answers.

"Not long," Leo says. "I want to get out ahead of the rain."

"Might be too late," the janitor replies. "Gonna start any second now."

Leo rolls his eyes as the janitor turns and trudges away. What does this old man know about the weather? He certainly didn't check the app before commenting on the forecast. Leo had another few hours before the precipitation is due to arrive.

Leo turns back to the data. Vague. Disparate. Incomplete. Indecisive. Like a message written in the sand after the tides have scrubbed at the shore. The data could mean a hundred different things. It suggests the next storm could arrive in a hundred years or a few weeks. The one thing science says for sure is Central Florida isn't going to see a hurricane tonight. Too bad, since Leo would love to see Arianna's night completely ruined by natural disaster.

He checks the instruments along the wall opposite the windows, machines attuned to the world outside these four walls. He notices the needle on the barometer is moving fast enough that he could *clock* it, like it's ticking off time instead of millibars. It's at 31.2 inches and falling. Fast. He has never seen it drop so precipitously. The weather app said he had until after midnight, but as the pressure drops right before Leo's very eyes, he suddenly doubts technology. That makes his stomach instantly queasy. If you can't trust machines, then who can you trust in this world?

The elderly janitor had warned Leo the rain was coming. Maybe something could be said for old-fashioned *observation*.

Leo goes to the window and looks outside. Palm trees blow in the wind. Clouds gather overhead, big gray puffs that blot out all the sky Leo could see. Lightning reaches from one roiling thunderhead to another before the rumble rolls across the sky. There had been no major storms brewing in the Atlantic lately—the hurricane season is over. It *should* be over. But this looks like there's a storm on the horizon. A big one. Leo examines the air pressure again. Already under 29 inches. And still spiraling fast.

.01" (trace)

[Amaris]

Amaris Azmi is seventeen, but she's all ready to set sail solo, say *namaste* to her siblings, and put her parents in her past. They wouldn't understand. They wouldn't let her do what she wanted to do. The only word they know is "University," and Amaris isn't going to freaking college. With a name like hers, she's not destined to get a Bachelor's in mind-numbing Physical Therapy like her mother wants her to. "Amaris Azmi" is going to look *epic* on the top of a blockbuster summer movie poster.

Epic!

"What're we doing here at Disney if you're leaving tonight, Amaris?" Ryan asks.

Ryan fidgets nervously. She's the one who will lie to Mr. and Mrs. Azmi for the next two days. She must cover for Amaris until she's far enough away from Orlando that they won't come after her. She might be almost eighteen, but "almost" isn't the same as being a legal adult. Amaris needs a head start.

"Two reasons, Ry," Amaris says, smiling ear to ear. Her heart is racing, her skin tingling. The excitement makes her pee herself a little. She has never been so eager for anything in her whole life, not any

Christmas, not getting her puppy Mr. Waggles when she was ten, not that amazing night she spent with Scott Masters last October. *Nothing!* "First, my parents track my phone, so I'm gonna answer one last call and let them hear the Disney noises in the background and see my location here and now. Say 'goodnight' and 'I love you' and all that crap. That should cover it for tonight. You take my phone, and you cover me for a couple of days. Phone audio glitches out, so you text them something from me—you make excuses."

"Yeah, I got it," Ryan says, sounding miserable. "But what's the other reason we're here?"

"The Beast," Amaris announces like it's the premiere of her very own blockbuster movie in the near future. "One last time."

It had always been *their* ride. Amaris and Ryan. Since they'd been tall enough to both get on the coaster. It was third grade, and Amaris had finally hit the mark they'd made on her bedroom door jamb. They'd begged their parents to take them to the park, and Amaris's father had accompanied them on the attraction for the first time. It had been thrilling, a feeling that came in second to everything after. Even the night with Scott Masters. They had ridden the Beast a dozen times that day.

So now Amaris and Ryan wait in a line that's long and slow-moving. There's a quartet of boys who pass them regularly in the serpentine queue, the hungry pack eyeing the teen girls with every pass. One wears a black leather jacket despite the balmy December weather, and Amaris wonders if he has a motorcycle and what it would take to make him drive her to California. In the end, she decides that she doesn't want to sleep with him, and he probably wouldn't accept anything less in trade.

"Are we going to make it?" Ryan asks, looking at the gray clouds gathering in the distance, forming a disconcerting cyclonic pattern.

"We have to," Amaris answers. "This is my last wish for Florida. I want to ride the Beast before I go."

"The weather doesn't care whether you get to go on it or not, Am," Ryan says.

But the line moves forward, and no announcement comes that the attraction is suspended as Amaris and Ryan get closer and closer to the

Beast. They know the turns of the queue by heart, and this is the final run-up to the ride. The boys who'd leered from the line get on the Beast, all of them screaming like babies cutting teeth as the coaster starts moving. One more set of riders in front of Amaris, then—

"Due to inclement weather, this ride is shutting down for the safety of our guests," comes the disheartening announcement. A collective groan issues from the crowd, interspersed with a smattering of four-letter words. "Please proceed to the nearest exit."

Sometimes the suspension of rides in Disney lasts for a few minutes, but Amaris knows this weather will shut down the Beast indefinitely. And she needs to get the hell out of Orlando. She and Ryan make their way to the exit as instructed.

The sky is overcast, and Amaris stares up at the thick clouds as a smattering of raindrops falls. One can always count on random rain to ruin any plans in Orlando. She scowls at the sky as if nature gives one crap about her sullenness, then turns to Ryan with a pouty face.

"Looks like I'll have to get a raincheck on our last ride, Ry."

"Once you get to L.A., I don't think you're ever coming back, Am."

"Then you can come to see me in Cali. We have a Disney there, too, y'know."

"I know," Ryan sighs. She stares at Amaris like it's the last time she's ever going to see her friend, and Amaris doesn't even notice in the moment. But she'll look back on this convo soon and she'll wonder if Ryan is still alive. Soon enough, Amaris will understand these next moments will have been their last moments.

The girls take shelter in a souvenir shop selling stuffed versions of every conceivable character, eyes all glaring at Amaris. A poster on the wall advertises the Tomorrowland attraction with the caption, "Where tomorrow is today." The clerk slides a bin containing umbrellas out to the main entrance, indicating they don't believe the precipitation will be a passing shower. Bottles of water fill a refrigerated bin by the door, trapped H_2O taunted by the free-falling raindrops outside. A hole in the ceiling of the shop lets through an anemic *dripdripdrip*.

"I'm going to call Mom," Amaris says. "You ready to back me up?"

"I guess," Ryan agrees unenthusiastically.

"Do your part. I'll do the talking."

"You'll start the lie. But then I have to keep it alive."

Amaris glares at Ryan as the phone rings once. Ryan has already agreed to this arrangement, so it's bullcrap that she's now heaping guilt on Amaris about it. If Ryan hadn't wanted to lie, Amaris had a half dozen other girlfriends who she could've convinced. She doesn't have time to deal with Ryan's waffling.

Amaris hears her mother's voice before she even answers the phone, but it's in her head and from the past, from earlier this year, after Amaris had told her mom she wanted to go to Los Angeles and be an actress. "This is America, Amaris," her mother had said. "They're living in Hollywood, not looking for Bollywood." Her mother had been right about one thing; this is *America*. It isn't the racist place her mother grew up in anymore, especially in California. A dreamer with Indian ancestry has as much chance at making it as any white girl.

Her mother answers after the first second. "Amaris?" Like her caller ID isn't showing Amaris's name and displaying the face from Amaris's third birthday with her face full of strawberry frosting and playing the ringtone that's the theme song from *Tubbytots* even though Amaris hasn't watched it since she was in kindergarten. Yet still, every time, her mother answers like it's a question.

"Hi, Mom," Amaris says, putting as much excitement and happiness into her voice as would be expected when one's at a place like Disney. "It's raining a bit, so I thought I'd call and touch base before we hit the rides again. I don't know if I'll have another chance before you get to bed."

Her mother's a nurse and works at 5:00 a.m., in bed by nine every night.

"Well, text me when you get to Aryanna's house," Mom says. She can't ever call Ryan "Ryan" because her mother is convinced it's a nickname for boys. Her mother is *so* last millennium. Everyone born in the twentieth century is like that. "Rain, you say? Did you bring a slicker?"

A *slicker?* Mom won't even say a swear as mild as "darn," and yet she uses terminology that somehow sounds dirtier than even a snappy "moth-er-fucker." Who the hell doesn't call it a *raincoat?* Someone born when phones still had cords, Amaris supposes.

"We're in a souvenir shop. We'll stay under shelter until it passes. Can't be much longer," Amaris says.

As soon as the conversation ends, whether rain or shine, Amaris is getting the hell out of Disney. She has five hundred dollars on a pre-paid Visa card, money put on there by her grandmother throughout the last two years' worth of birthdays and holidays. She also has two hundred in cash from working at Molly's Diner and stashing her tips over the last few weeks. Finally, she has some funds in her PayPal account from stuff she had sold to friends the last few days—extra clothes, shoes, make-up, electronics. Things she isn't taking to L.A. And she's never coming back.

After a stilted conversation, Amaris says, "All right, Mom. Gotta go."

"Okay, sweetheart. Be careful. I love you."

"Love you, too, Mom," Amaris mumbles and disconnects. "All right, Ry. Stick around the park for a couple of hours. Here's ten bucks for some snacks. Text her tonight. Cover me for tomorrow with some texts from my phone and maybe call her once and tell her I fell asleep or whatever. Try on Sunday, if you can, but she'll start to get suspicious. It'll fall apart sometime Sunday. But I'll be on the other side of the Mississippi by then."

Ryan looks miserable, but Amaris can't let her off the hook. This is the only option now. "I guess this is goodbye."

Amaris hugs her friend. "Come see me in Cali."

Then she turns to the rain. Sprinkles. Making the world a haze, like the scene before her is a dream that isn't fully realized. An idea that might turn out bright and sunny or could as easily stay gloomy and gray. The structures of Disney look undefined, as if Amaris is watching something as it fades, a painted picture washed away by running water. A curious effect, one that portends an unformed tomorrow. Amaris takes it as a sign.

She steps forward into the rain, and she doesn't look back.

.25"

[Carlos]

Carlos Licha paddles out from the beach off the coast of New Smyrna. The swells are pretty good today—lately, conditions haven't been conducive to catching some serious waves. At sixty-five, there are some days when his body might not agree with his surfin' spirit; such some days aren't today.

He takes a moment out on the water. His suit fits ankle to neck; the cool December water is a nice contrast to the bright sun warming his black attire. He loves the smell of it, the wax on his board mixed with the salt water and the musky scent of sea life, and the sound of the crashing waves on the sandy shore and the slap of water all around him and the whisper of the wind in his ears. If he could live right here off-shore...

But he couldn't. Man wasn't meant to be entirely aquatic. Evolution-arily, Carlos is out of his element. No gills. No fins. No blowhole. The salt water feels fine for a while but would deteriorate his skin after pro-longed exposure. Nothing to drink. Food is elusive without the right adaptations to hunt in the water. Man has been made for land, so why does Carlos feel such affinity to the sea?

Because the ocean is a capricious lover, taunting him with its charms before rejecting him outright. Even the waves push him in, then try to send him back to the beach, expelling him from the watery world where he doesn't belong. This lifelong love affair with the sea has always been a one-way relationship.

Carlos exhales, making a wish to be a fish, but that wish would never be granted. There's no magic in the real world. The days are entirely predictable.

Carlos used to come out here every day. Half his life while living in Florida and the first half back in Puerto Rico. Always the ocean. Carlos and the sea. His older brother, Diego, had been all about work and success and power—Diego had become a multimillionaire by age thirty-five. Carlos and Diego had argued whenever they'd been together about working hard versus living the easy life. Then Diego was diagnosed with terminal cancer, and all the money in the world couldn't save him. He'd bequeathed Carlos a house right on the beach and a monthly stipend enough so that Carlos never had to work again. Diego had left Carlos a short and simple message in his will: "You were right." Carlos had just turned thirty when Diego died.

That was half a lifetime ago. Carlos has never had a real job ever since. He gets up in the morning and surfs or sleeps late and surfs or goes for an evening surf. Carlos has been in the water nearly every day for all these years. Only hurricanes have kept him out for an entire day. He is as much a staple of the beach as the shells along the shoreline or the sight of a cruise ship along the horizon.

But lately, there have been aches and pains, and getting out on the board has sometimes been a trial rather than a blessing. Like hard work rather than living the easy life. Age is catching up to him. He has taken a day or two here and there and skipped surfing. He still swims or walks along the shore, but sometimes he leaves his board behind. The tide of his life is going out.

But not today. Today, he feels good. The waves are nice. He had been up and out early. Now he feels the tug and push of the current, urging him to take the next wave, take the next wave, take the next wave. But he knows which one to take. He knows enough to wait for the right one. He lets one after the other pass. Because there's always a next one. And a next one. Until it's the one he wants to ride.

He times it perfectly without thinking, then he's upright and moving, a man walking on water, defying the natural order, giving the sea one massive middle finger by rising, rising above, and being a master of the moment. The ocean is powerful and mercurial and cares not one whit for Carlos any more than the next partner who dares dance the dance for a while. But in those few seconds, Carlos is in control, and the ocean has met its match.

Then a wave crashes and he's underwater. The moment had been glorious but, as always, short-lived. The ocean never fails to remind Carlos who is a god and who is a mere man.

Mere man.

Carlos treads water offshore, deep enough to stay submerged but near enough to see the people stretched out along the beach. It's December, and the combers are limited to locals out for a walk and penny-pinchers who found an off-season deal on the Internet. He doesn't feel the affinity for his fellow man that he does for the ocean all around him. But the sea doesn't feel the same about him. The waves push him forward, away, like a piece of food stuck in its craw.

Carlos turns to swim back out as a smattering of rain drums his board. There wasn't any precipitation in the forecast today, but then the weather in Florida has always had a mind of its own. He could still surf in a quick shower, but the skies have become more ominous than a momentary passing system. Out east, he sees lightning flash across the sky, cloud to cloud, and cloud to sea. He isn't going to surf in a lightning storm.

The occasional annoying tourist would sometimes ask if he were worried about sharks. "Leave 'em alone, and they'll leave you be." Implied was that the same rules ought to apply to man. But lightning? Lightning will kill you any day of the week.

Carlos feels something in the water. Is it the tingle of a current from a lightning strike far offshore? The ambient static charge of the coming storm? The vibrations of the raindrops across the endless stretch of water? It feels like something else. Like the quiet hunger pangs of the entire ocean.

He looks around. The waves go up and he's in a trough, the world blocked by water. There could be something nearby. Something over the next crest. Or something swimming beneath him right now. That is always the situation out here in the sea. What you can't see. It never bothered Carlos before. He never worries about maybes. But maybe...

There's something else in the water.

He imagines a school of sharks acting irrationally, stirred up by the unnatural electrical storm. Supercharged by the unexpected weather. The waves raise him toward the top of a crest. Higher. Higher. He sees a shark fin nearby. Too close. Then another. Another. A dozen. He has never witnessed a group of predators all concentrated so near the shore at one time. The sharks are acting oddly. Carlos reaches the apex and jumps on his board, catching the wave, letting the sea take him toward shore and away from the frenzy of sharks.

Leave 'em alone and they'll leave you be.

The wave crashes in the shallows, and Carlos is safe from the shark-infested depths. He gazes back as a dozen fingers of lightning shatter the sky. Seconds later, thunder rolls over him in waves of bass. The clouds offshore turn in a meandering rotation. Carlos has seen his share of hurricanes and lived through a handful. He has always stayed, never evacuated. He knows how the storms come and go. They form with plenty of warning, somewhere other than right off the Space Coast of Florida. This spot is *never* where they originate. And he knows damn well that there were no hurricanes out in the Atlantic when he suited up this morning.

So, what is he looking at?

Like the birth of some great new force, he witnesses the contractions of nature. The process of something new being unleashed upon the world. Mother Nature is in labor, and this is what it looks like when she's fully dilated. Something original is straining to come forth, something the whole world isn't prepared for.

Something different.

Something disquieting.
Something wrong.

.50"

[Rabe]

Rabe sits across from a hot babe. The restaurant is five-star all the way. Most of the dudes are dressed in suits and wearing ties, but Rabe is playing his part. He wears rope after rope of gold chains, an Orlando Magic jersey, keeps his cap on with the logo from a record label turned askew. Rabe rocks a pair of Jordans. Everyone whispers, wondering if he's a famous rapper.

Carla is practically bursting the seams of the little red dress. Rabe plans to see it hanging from a chandelier before the night is over, but that's not until after dessert. After more drinks. He has all weekend to enjoy Carla, and it's only Friday evening.

"This is such a fancy place," Carla says. "Y'know, Rabe, we coulda had dinner anywhere."

"Not for our first time together, Carla. We been talkin' so long on-line, I feel like I know you better than I know myself, but I ain't *seen* you, baby. I want the whole world to see you. See *us*."

She smiles. That's working. She's already putty in his hands. He'd been working it for months, and now it's the weekend of payoff. Rabe's been sending Carla sexy selfies since they first connected online. When he told her he'd be in Orlando to talk to media reps about his upcoming album release, she agreed to meet him for the weekend. The whole fucking weekend.

"Everyone's wonderin' who's the big spender," Carla coos, clearly enjoying the attention.

"Black man with big bucks," Rabe replies. "They think I gotta either be a rapper or play ball."

"Everyone's gonna know your name when the album drops," Carla sighs. "L'il Angeni gonna be a *playa*."

"That's yummy," Rabe says.

"Yummy as hell," Carla agrees.

The waiter comes and asks for their order. Rabe expects the man to intimate that a black couple dressed as they were should be at a club instead of a fancy eatery and wouldn't know their chicken tikka masala from their saltimbocca. Maybe Carla doesn't, but Rabe orders for both of them, and she gazes appreciatively across the table. The waiter nods politely, the consummate professional, and excuses himself.

"So..." Carla starts, leaning forward and giving him a look that says he can do any damn thing he wants to do to her. "I wanna hear some of your rhymes."

Rhymes? Right. Rabe looks across the table, and Carla stares at him expectantly with her mouth open just so. The words don't come to Rabe now, but L'il Angeni must be able to drop some lyrics when the fans are asking, especially if he expected this particular fan to be naked within the next couple of hours.

"Pretty damn. Hella slam. Walkin' words to the bedlam bedroom. Woke to booty and workin' pootay, makin' sizzle and swizzle drizzle, wash and rinse that saucy whistle."

Carla's gaze glazes, and Rabe swears she climaxed right there in the middle of this five-star restaurant.

An explosion cracks outside, and Carla shakes off her adoration, her eyes growing wide and worried. "Fuck was that?"

"Harmless thunder," Rabe assures her. "Storms rip through Orlando every other day, fast and furious and without warning. Lasts for a minute, then gone again."

"I hope that's the all in Orlando that lasts for but a minute," Carla says coyly as the waiter returns with drinks in an awkward moment of bad timing.

The waiter asks if they need anything else, but what Carla needs isn't on the menu. Rabe dismisses him, and the waiter disappears. Carla smirks, her cheeks flush. Rabe wishes they could skip right to dessert, take the chicken to go, and rush back to their suite. He wants her more than he's ever wanted anyone. The buildup has already been months of virtual flirtation.

But a couple more hours of anticipation will enhance the experience. The future always arrives before you know it anyway, so Rabe reins in his lust and revels in the foreplay.

The lights flicker, then the whole restaurant plunges into darkness, and for one moment, Rabe wonders if he just died. Aneurism. Heart attack. Bullet to the back of the head. Victim of some East Coast rap war mixed up with mistaken identity. Li'l Angeni doesn't have any enemies, but maybe someone else is trying to make a name in the hip-hop world. Maybe Rabe is on their turf. Maybe Rabe is caught with his hand in the wrong cookie jar. Maybe dead is better than living until Monday.

Because as much as he anticipates tomorrow and the next day, he dreads the ever after. Next week. The week after. The year after. Because Carla won't be there after the weekend. Carla is his present— she doesn't have anything to do with his future. His past dictates his future.

The pitch lasts a second. The lights come back on, and a crack of thunder follows, announcing its presence after the effect has already passed. Carla appears worried. He reaches across for her, and her hand finds his. The present will last for a while longer. Maybe not long enough, but better than not at all.

The chicken tikka masala arrives, and the taste is a prelude to a perfect night.

"Ever been overseas?" Rabe asks as he finishes his chicken. Carla is only half finished.

"Are you goin' on a European tour?"

"No. I mean, not yet. Just wonderin'."

"Shit, this as far from Detroit I been since Mama took us to Cedar Point when we was sixteen."

Rabe nods. What kind of rapper asks a smoking-hot woman with sweet tits about foreign shit? After arranging her flight from Detroit and coordinating everything for a whole weekend, one wrong word could fuck it up without anyone getting properly fucked.

Outside, the wind begins to blow.

The wind whips along the street out front, driving the rain at an awful slant. Luckily, the restaurant is in the lobby, and their suite is upstairs. There's no reason to go out outside.

He considers the darkness again. The lights going out. Someone sneaking up behind him. A ruthless badass with a big-ass gun. Bitin' bullets. Spittin' slugs. There's a rap song in there somewhere, but Rabe certainly isn't the one to put it together. He doesn't know writing rhymes from surviving hurricanes.

He's a husband and a father.

He's an insurance salesman from Omaha.

He's certainly not a rapper. He isn't Li'l Angeni. Never will be.

Rabe is not even really Rabe.

He's a liar and a cheater.

.75"

[Cass]

Cassandra Ming had used her feminine wiles to get into the front row at the news conference because, of course, she was going to. *If I can cut the line because the dude thinks I have a nice ass, then let him stare and show me to my chair*, she thought. The octogenarian reporter from some *print* publication standing beside Cass is old enough to know better, but he gazes at her with a pervy intensity and a glance at her backside.

"Easy, Jimmy Olson," Cass sneers. "I'm not into wrinkles."

The old man scowls and says nothing. He's holding a *notepad*. Made of *paper*. And a *pencil*. A *wooden* pencil. He's going to write down something that someone will print and no one will read. Dinosaurs making cave paintings on the walls. He probably even knows how to spell words without autocorrect!

What would he do if he learned Cass is trans? Does a fossil like this guy know what that even means? He appears to have been the right generation to cheer on Caitlyn Jenner in the 1976 Olympics. He must have a general understanding, but Cass assumes he holds onto his archaic gender pronouns and dated normative binary definitions with the same gumption as he grips that *wooden pencil*.

Cass Ming is a reporter for the *Blahblahblahg*, a consortium of online avatars bringing truth to the masses in short blurbs under a hundred characters, *including* emojis. It's a stepping stone to bigger, better blogs. She's gonna be Big Time, so as never to become an old Dino like the Bengay bastard beside her.

The State Representative from the 10th District right here in Orlando steps out on stage and strides confidently to the podium. Marcus Roquefort has represented Orlando for six years. Young at thirty-six, he's nevertheless ambitious and intuitive. French-Canadian by birth, his dark skin and purposeful mustache make him look as Latino as any of the non-politicians working much harder jobs all around the metro area. He speaks Spanish as fluently as he speaks bullshit—as slick as the rain-soaked sidewalks beyond the tent area in the middle of the park. He's here to announce his candidacy for the United States Senate.

"Thank you all for coming out in the inclement weather, although this is par for the course around Orlando, right?" he starts with a characteristic smoothness. "I've been proud to represent the good people of—" Blah. Blah. Blahg.

Cass has heard it all before. Everyone has. There's nothing new under the Florida sun or anywhere else on this borrrrrrrrrrING planet. Politics has been going on as long as Cain battled Abel to represent the district of Eden as the favorite son. Pricks with dicks. Wielding rocks has turned to slinging mud (mostly), but the intent is still to crush the opponent. Nowadays, sticks and stones don't hold a candle to the power of words. Words can hurt a lot worse than knives or guns. Cass can decimate an entire career with a single accusation.

Some targets more easily than others.

Representative Roquefort tells the crowd he's gunning for the open Senate seat. Health care, climate change, immigration, all the right notes. He smiles as he talks about the plight of Floridians, and he smiles as he speaks of deportation, and he smiles as he opines about the recession. It's all very happily tragic, and he plans to fix it all. With a smile. And a mustache. "Send me into the swamp because I know a thing or two about wrangling gators…"

Blah. Blah. Blahg. Cass uploads the announcement she had prepared in advance. Under a hundred characters. Half of them emojis. Most of them are smiley faces, sunshine-colored caricatures of Marcus Roquefort. Empty information fed to the masses like pablum. That isn't the real story.

Representative Roquefort has answered a dozen questions while Cass posts her article and bides her time. Empty sentiments parlayed in pastel, politically perfected soundbites. For a French-Canadian impersonating a local Latino, the man knows his way around vanilla. He had even referred to the popular queer reporter from local KYQQ by their preferred pronoun of them/they/their. He is batting this ball right out of Champion Stadium!

Cassandra raises her hand, pushes out her chest, and tilts her hips suggestively. There had been a time in her life when that would've gotten her ass kicked. Now her ass gets Cass called next by the future Senator from Florida.

"Cassandra Ming for the *Blahblahblahg*," she advertises. "In the age of information overload and disinformation defense, how would you address illicit rumors if directed at you or your family?"

"My family is strictly off-limits in my campaign, Miz Ming," Representative Roquefort replies like he's reading off a TelePrompTer in his mind. "Politics nowadays has become too personal and, unfortunately, unprofessional. I aim to instill civility back into the political discourse."

"You would take the same tact against your opponent, then, if the hat was on the other head?" Cass presses. "The retiring Governor has already announced her intention on also running for the Senate. What if your organization came across actionable information against, say, the Governor's husband? You would sit on it? Dismiss it?"

"That would be within the purview of the free press, Miz Ming, not politics. The separation of fodder and facts is a fascinating topic and one I would be happy to discuss further after the press conference, if you like."

Cass nods, and Representative Roquefort moves on. Other questions. More scripted answers. But none will pique his curiosity like Cass had managed. Every time his eyes sweep the crowd of reporters for additional questions, his gaze stops on her, a short stutter that surely no one else even notices. But Cass knows. She has him, like a bug stuck in honey, maybe hopelessly fallen into a trap, but oh what a sweet predicament.

Geriatric Jimmy Olsen watches her with his old eyes, cataracts making her wonder if he can even see anything besides the pink blur from her form-fitting dress. But the smirk on his leathered face suggests he knows exactly what's going on between Cassandra Ming and Marcus Roquefort. He has probably seen a lot of shit in his day. Then he shrugs. Makes a note. On paper. With his pencil.

Cass pays the old coot no mind. Even if he reports something about whatever he thinks he knows about Representative Roquefort and a flirty reporter, no one is going to read it anyway.

1"

[Edd]

Eddale Farder watches the *dripdripdrip* from the ceiling, a runnel of spittle hanging from his bottom lip perfectly mimicking the leak coming from between seams opening in the sagging drywall. The basement has been falling into disrepair for the last few months, and he's been hounding his mother to get it repaired, but she claimed her medical bills had to come before his comfort. They won't start denying her access to health care in America because of a past-due bill, but he might die from falling drywall if the ceiling comes down on his head.

The water will fill the bucket soon, and he's not even close to finished with his campaign. He's going to have to get up before he finishes the game. *Goddamnit.* Does his mother know what she's risking by letting this problem go? Does she realize she's jeopardizing a whole world because she can't properly manage her finances?

"Jessiqua, head around back and cut off their escape!" shouts the squad leader in Edd's ear.

Edd's buxom avatar wears combat fatigues featuring short-shorts. He makes her skedaddle around the bombed-out bunker and sets up position in a narrow pass between a concrete wall and a steep butte. Any bastard tries to get through, Edd will have Jessiqua's delicate digits squeeze the trigger and perforate the piss-diddlers.

The bucket grows fuller. His game becomes essential. Without Edd, his team would fail and the battle would be over and the whole strategy could be in jeopardy, which might affect the outcome of the war and the future of all furkind.

Jessiqua isn't just a woman—she's a genetic hybrid of woman and rabbit with voluptuous white ears extending like twin antennae, whiskers twitching whenever she's feeling frisky, and a cottontail sexier than the sweetest human ass Edd has ever seen. When VR becomes his reality instead of this bullshit that's really reality, then he plans on marrying Jessiqua and living his remaining years in bunny-humping bliss.

Until then, she's a badass digital soldier trying to free all furkind from the oppressive rulers of Humana. A squad of gene-purists is coming up the ravine

"Like shooting fish in a barrel," Edd tells his squad, aiming.

"Hey," scolds Jawzz, a half-boy/half-shark.

"Hay?" admonishes Miss Turrid, half-human/half-stallion.

"Sorry," Edd apologizes, shaking his cottontail to give Jawzz a little tease. He likes it when the other furkind get flustered by Jessiqua, even if he never lets them put a paw on her. "I'm gonna perforate some smoothies."

Smoothies. Humans who are without fur. Edd pities them as he aims.

The bucket overflows, a thin flood spreading across the linoleum floor.

"Aw, shit," Edd curses, making some chat monitor in another basement somewhere else on this small world flag him for indecent dialogue. Kids can play this game—extreme violence is condoned and the furkind can copulate (albeit in scenes more reminiscent of barnyard fornication than online porn), but dropping a scatological four-letter word elicits the ire of some sixteen-year-old prick probably still sucking at his mama's teat. Some half-human/half-calf.

Edd pulls off his headset and puts down the controller, grabbing up a towel off a hook and trying to dam the damn spill before it soaks into his game system. He grabs the bowl from last night's popcorn, only the old maids left for dead at the bottom. Edd picks up the full bucket, more water slopping and spilling. "FuckFuckFUCK!" He slides the popcorn bowl under the leak and carries the pail into the bathroom, dumps it down the drain. By the time he gets back to the bowl, the old maids have overspilled and are setting sail across the basement.

The leak has become a waterfall.

"Maaaaaaaaaauum!"

The water is going to short out his game system.

The war will be lost!

Then the lights flicker, fail, plunging Edd into absolute darkness. If the leaky ceiling hadn't ruined his campaign, the power outage would've finished it. The weather wants to doom the world one way or another. In the darkness, there's no Jessiqua or Humana or smoothies. There's Edd and the howling wind and driving rain—nature versus man. Beyond the darkness and the walls is chaos: endless, ugly, and hungry.

"Maaaaauuuuuuuum," he calls again.

No answer. Neglect. Had Mom fallen asleep in front of *Wheel of Fortune* again? What time is it even? Did she go to the grocery with Gertie Gregland? Mom wouldn't have braved the rain and wind. Is she ignoring Edd, finally tired of his constant caterwauling?

He fishes in his pocket and pulls out a smartphone, the dull glow illuminating the wet. The sound of another leak springing up comes from somewhere in the shadows beyond the perimeter where Edd's light can penetrate. He flips on the flashlight, a bright LED stabbing the darkness of the basement.

Water drools down from a bowed section of the ceiling, bubbling like an upside-down loaf of bread rising in the oven. Edd imagines it's filled with water like a bulging bladder, a soaked section of drywall not so dry anymore. "Shit," he hisses, and there's no moderator to scold him this time. He feels like a sailor in a sinking ship.

He trudges toward the steps, stopping to scoop up his console as he passes the sofa. He could recover from losing his controllers and the flat screen and the speakers—those are limbs he can live without.

But Edd needs to rescue the brain. He must save the passwords and all his upgrades built into the console. He tucks the brain into a waterproof backpack and slings it over a shoulder. Then he heads up and out, abandoning the ship.

"Maauuummmmmmm!"

Upstairs, it's dark. The only sounds are the splashes of more leaks. The whole house is full of holes. He points his phone flashlight at the recliner where his mother is always sitting, and she's gone. He searches the house, but there's no one else home. Her purse is missing. She must've left without telling him. Or maybe she *had* told him, and he'd been too engrossed in saving furkind to hear her.

Nevertheless, who the fuck is going to do something about these leaks?

1.5"

[Renata]

Renata Sánchez waits for her name to be called. She stares out the window at the rain. It's starting to pour. The forecast hadn't predicted torrential rain, but Florida forecasters are notorious for being wrong. Like she'd hoped was the case when the doctor had forecasted her future in seven months. Ren hadn't believed it at first. The doctor had to be wrong. *Had* to be.

The weatherman had been wrong.

The doctor had been right.

Renata didn't tell the father. It's none of his damn business. He hadn't bothered to call after their weekend getaway to the Keys, so she didn't bother to call when she found out the birth control they'd been using hadn't worked. This is Ren's choice and her choice alone.

Ren sits all by herself. She asked her best friend to come along, but Mava had something come up at the last minute. Renata faces the future alone. Two very different paths that can go two very different directions, right now, right here. She has already picked the path. She knows where she wants to be in seven months.

Her phone sounds off, her ringtone a Drake lyric filled with expletives. She gets snarky looks from two or three other pregnant women lined up in a row. Like waiting in the queue at Disney. Taking turns on the roller coaster of life. Ren glares back, certain none of these bitches are such devout Christians that an F-bomb would taint their delicate sensibilities.

"What is it, Cybill?" Ren barks into the phone. "I told you I didn't want to be disturbed."

"It's Mister Parker," Cybill stutters. Surely the last thing she wanted to do in the entire universe was call Renata Sánchez this afternoon. "He's asking about the Clemente file. He said he wants it on his desk *pronto*."

Pronto? Is that a dig at her Latino heritage? Parker is always a *tilde* away from saying something completely racist. One of these days, HR would escort him out the door, and he can try to find a job working retail somewhere. But today isn't that day. Today, Ren must get the fucking Clemente file on his fucking desk. *Pronto.*

"My appointment shouldn't take very long," Ren guesses. She's never done this before. "I'll be back at the office immediately afterward. Tell him the file will be ready before I go home for the night."

"This weather," Cybill mutters worriedly. "Will you be able to get back to work?"

Ren stares out the large front window into the rain. The sky seems to promise more of the same. But everything can change in a moment in Florida. The sun can be shining by the time this is all over. Wait five minutes, and everything can be very different than what it is now.

"Everything will be fine, Cybill. Tell Mister Parker I'll get it done."

She puts the phone away. Ren wants this appointment over with. She has important things to get finished. Renata Sánchez is on track to become Vice President of Curl, Cameron, and Kennedy by next Christmas. Wasting her time waiting in this line isn't conducive to her career.

Other than the snide sneers generated by Drake's derogatory lyrics, none of the women in the room make any effort to communicate or even make eye contact. Most are alone, like Ren. Some have friends who showed up to accompany the patients. None of them spoke; a funereal mood like this is a memorial for an old friend even though the affliction inside all of them is too new to be anything to commemorate.

The rain grows heavier, harder, faster.

The news plays on a flat-screen television hung high on one wall. The sound is muted and the closed-captioning scrolls multiple misspelled and improperly autocorrected words across the bottom of the screen as some transcriber tries to keep up with the rapid-fire delivery of an energetic local weatherman. The graphics behind him on the green screen show a big blob of red heading straight for Orlando. It looks like a fucking hurricane. Where the hell did that come from? Ren is damn sure there hadn't been a hurricane for Florida in any forecast.

"Unpressedented" the fumbling fingers of the transcriber typed. "His store a call," "Recordshitting," "Fan nominal." A hurricane that came out of nowhere. No buildup in the Atlantic. No warning signs at all. It appeared off the Space Coast an hour ago and is growing faster than anything anyone has ever seen. They nicknamed it "Hurricane Cheshire" because it had appeared out of nowhere. That doesn't follow any traditional naming patterns of storms, but then this isn't exactly a traditional storm.

Then the Emergency Broadcast System activates, alerting everyone's phone in the waiting room at once. Those who'd brought a friend for Show-and-Tell start whispering in reverential tones like this is a church instead of a clinic. Worry replaces fear and guilt across the faces up and down the rows of chairs. The message on everyone's phones warns them to get home and shelter in place.

A nurse comes out from the back, and Ren hopes to hell she's going to call her name so she can get this over with. The look on the nurse's face is one that maybe hadn't featured a smile since before a Black President was still considered a fantasy. Ren supposes she never comes out to announce any good news.

Instead of calling the next appointment, the nurse issues an apology. "I'm sorry, everyone, but we will have to reschedule all remaining procedures. The weather looks to have become life-threatening, and the doctors have decided to close the clinic for the rest of the day."

More incoherent mumbling between acquaintances, but Ren isn't going to take the news by simply moping about it. She stands up with fists on her hips and glares at the glum nurse. "I've been waiting for forty-five minutes. I made this appointment a week ago. There were forms and referrals and information that I had to sign off on, and I did my fucking due diligence. You get me into one of those white rooms and make this problem go away."

The nurse might not have smiled in years, but she sure as hell knows how to go into Bitch Mode. Her frown turns to growl and she gets all up in Ren's face. Latina temper has nothing on a big black woman's ego. No one tells this nurse what she gotta do.

A finger appears in Ren's face. "Get. Yo ass. Out." In another place and time, Ren might've bent it backward and started a brawl. Ren would've been outweighed and outmatched by the larger woman, but she could've at least made a mark before getting thrown out the front door. But this isn't the place, and now isn't the time.

Ren exhales right in the nurse's face, closes her eyes, and realizes right now isn't her future. Neither is the fetus inside her. The hurricane is the present, and she must think about the weather right now. Because the storm could cause her harm today, while the rest of this shit was far enough off to take care of some other day.

Besides, she must get to the office before they issue a mandatory curfew. She still needs to prepare the Clemente file. Because being promoted to VP *is* her future. Ren turns. Faces the rain. And walks out into the weather.

2"

[Leo]

Leo reviews the data.

Astounding.

The weather is impossible. There's no way a hurricane can form within a few hours, birthing right off the coast of Florida. The winds have achieved a Cat 1 hurricane force within the last few minutes. The rainfall had brewed, become designated a tropical storm, and already matured to hurricane status in a matter of mere hours. The weatherpersons have declared the phenomenon scientifically impossible. Impossible is blowing the hell out of the UCF campus.

Well, it's impossible to explain through meteorological "science." But meteorology is a science like Ringo was a Beatle—it's hard to take as seriously as the rest. There are other sciences, *real* sciences, that might explain what's happening.

Maybe.

Historically, there's never been another occurrence like this. Hurricane Cheshire does not correlate with the meteorological record. Leo has been studying paleotempestology for four years, and he's never researched another instance of a storm brewing from nothing to a Cat 1 in a matter of hours.

And it's going to get worse.

Leo looks at his instruments. There had been all kinds of helium balloon-borne GPS-radiosonde released as soon as the weather formation first occurred. Those devices measure all sorts of things that make the meteorologists melt in their shorts. They worry officials responsible for conducting mass evacs and coordinating emergency support. Leo's area of expertise is in reading history to tell us about today and maybe predict tomorrow. He's less adept at reading live results and anticipating what comes next.

But he knows, based on history, that there's no reason to panic. The chances of injury or death are low if he keeps his cool. Leo always keeps his cool.

The depletion of heavy oxygen isotopes in the atmosphere piques Leo's interest. The data indicates the storm will continue to increase in intensity. Greatly increase. Of course, Leo is used to finding patterns when he already knows the outcome. This time, he isn't studying a storm from centuries ago. This one rages right outside his window.

"Galileo?"

Leo turns. It's Professor Previn, as pale as if she'd seen a ghost. She's the only one at UCF who calls him by his given name. She has taught him everything she knows, and he had surpassed her expertise months before. She had once been a pioneer in paleotempestology, but that was a long time ago. Like the storms of old that left their evidence in beach ridges and tree rings, he has learned everything he needs to know from the elder scientist.

She holds out an electronic tablet face-up. "Did you see this?"

He can't see what's on the screen.

Then the lights flicker, thunder rolls, and they're plunged into darkness. The generator out back of the laboratory should kick in, but for the moment, just the glow of Professor Previn's screen lights the room. Like a bug in the dark, Leo steps toward the glowing source. His shadow jumps and shudders out of the corner of his eye, like something unseen has spooked his silhouette. The pale illumination of the electronic tablet casts the professor's countenance into an inscrutable rictus.

Consternation or curiosity? Revulsion or revelation?

Leo has goosebumps up and down his arms. He feels like a character in a terrible movie right before the general tells him that the missiles are in the air or the comet is on a direct course for Earth. He takes the tablet from Professor Previn and scans the data like a scanner reads a barcode, picking out the parts it needs for processing.

"What does this mean?" Leo inquires, the first question he's had to ask the professor in a year.

"You think you know more than me," Professor Previn reminds Leo. "Prove it."

Leo rechecks the numbers. Instruments on planes flying over the strengthening hurricane are reporting data back to UCF, but the information is inconsistent with any historical record. The depletion of oxygen isotopes reads as uneven. Fifty miles off the coast of Florida sits a quagmire of conflicting readings. Spikes and trenches are resembling the waves off New Smyrna Beach. The pattern ought to follow the rotation of the storm, but instead, the measurements veer in an amorphous and non-circular shape.

Leo opens the settings on the professor's electronic tablet and makes the program color various sets of data differently; then he fades out the other information used to gather the overall shape and scope of the storm's rotation of precipitation. He focuses on the data relating to oxygen isotopes. The rings of chaotic color around the hurricane's eye fade until he is left with one single metric. He could see it in the shadows, reminding him of one of those pictures hidden until he relaxes his eyes and it comes to life. The screen shows an enormous amoebic shape. Fingers resembling tentacles reach out from a black nucleus. On the map, the shape reminds Leo of a giant squid stretching forth with rubbery arms. Yet, the shape displays more appendages than a squid's eight arms. There are hundreds of antennae wriggling out from the massive center.

"This is impossible," Leo whispers.

"Stupid kid," Professor Previn spits. "Just because you learned more than me about paleotempestology, you think you have nothing left to learn. You think you know everything, Galileo. That your studies are like an empty Erlenmeyer and you've filled the beaker up to the brim. But there isn't an end to information. There isn't an *everything*. There's always a something else."

"This?" Leo asks, staring at the image on the screen. The laboratory is still pitch dark. The generator hasn't kicked on. Maybe he shouldn't expect things to work like they're supposed to. The world isn't what he thought it was. "This is something else?"

"Science can't explain whatever it is we're looking at," Professor Previn says. "*This* is the impossible."

The impossible. It's the only thing possible. He can't seem to understand what he's looking at. The data suggest some sort of event that defies any science Leo has ever heard of. He must think beyond books and precedence.

Is it a landmass surfaced off the Atlantic coast? Something like Atlantis returned due to seismic shifts? Or some sort of biological event, like algae gathering en masse? Is it a magnetic fluctuation beyond previous possible gradations? A temporal manifestation that will change the way Leo views fundamental physics?

Is it fucking magic leaking out into the real world?

Leo stares. He can't speak. His mind cannot process. He doesn't know anything for sure except one thing. He stares at the shadow covering many, many, many square miles of ocean. The tentacles of the shadow. They all reach out in one direction. They stretch out toward land. Like it is coming. Coming right for Florida.

2.5"

[Carlos]

Carlos Licha left the coast. His first time more than a mile away from the Atlantic in three and a half decades. It hadn't been an easy decision. But as he'd stood one last time upon the beach and stared out at the storm, he had known he faced something he couldn't ride out. It was like a monster wave coming in, and not even the best surfer who ever lived could master it. In such a case, one needed to get the hell out of the way.

Carlos had never retreated from anything before. He had been attacked by a blacktip shark a few years ago, and he'd punched that fucker right on the snout until it let go. He should've had stitches, but instead, he went home, superglued the wound shut, and he was back out on his board the next day.

But as he'd stood staring east over the ocean that was the one thing he had ever really loved, he realized the ocean didn't love him back. Or rather, something had corrupted the sea. Like the cancer that had killed his brother. The ocean had been a loyal partner to Carlos all these years. She had always been there, giving him pleasure, dependable as the daybreak. Sure, sometimes she threw a tantrum or displayed a dangerous side to her personality (shark-bite dangerous), but what partner didn't have her qualms? But this is something different. Like his partner had gotten a murderous thought that she couldn't shake. The ocean had become dangerous. Looking out, Carlos had seen something terrible gazing back.

Now he sits in the bed of a Toyota pickup that some kid had jacked up on big tires, moving west, leaving his partner behind. He has a small backpack of essentials and his board. He wasn't going to leave his board behind. Maybe after this temper tantrum of supernatural proportions, he could return. Maybe his home would still be there, maybe not. But the sea would remain, and the waves would welcome him back, and all would be forgiven. Whatever is wrong with his partner will subside, and everything will be okay again.

Carlos pats his board as an owner turns to his dog for reassurance. The board offers no such comfort.

The rain pelts him as they move inland along with a parade of other commuters. Carlos barely notices. He's used to being soaked. He's lived his whole life in the water. The only oddity is the bland taste wicking off his tongue. He prefers the taste of brine.

The gray skies mask what's happening offshore. But Carlos could feel the change in the sea. Maybe like a spouse who suspects their loved one of secretly cheating or an innate worry that maybe all isn't right with your kid, Carlos knows something is corrupting the ocean. There's some bad influence on the sea. He pictures a deviant gulf of trouble whispering in the Atlantic's ear, urging the ocean to break bad. Some alien parasite infecting the host and making her do terrible things.

Carlos had fled from the shores and joined up with a long line of other evacuees. This isn't the first rodeo for the long line of motorists. Hurricane evacuations are familiar to Floridians. This one is different in the lack of preparation time. The traffic is heavy, but not as heavy as it normally is. Many coastal inhabitants had been caught off guard by the sudden development of the storm and were still packing their things. Others knew enough to travel light and had gotten the hell out sooner than later. For some, that delay might make it too late.

The ocean is throwing a tantrum, and someone is bound to get hurt.

Carlos stares back at the line of vehicles. The wind and rain obscure distance. Headlights diminish after three or four cars, but he knows the line stretches back to New Smyrna. People marching toward safety. Running away from the danger. He stares into the storm, and he feels it. He's felt it before.

Sometimes, out on the board, floating offshore while he waits for a set of waves, he lets go of the thoughts and worries and cares of man. He feels the depths of the water and the immensity of the sea. It stretches on and on and on, so big the human mind can't wrap its head around it. The waters extend over the whole planet.

Now he feels the same thing, studying the driving rain, staring at the millions of droplets descending from the sky. There is something beyond the veil, deep and large and so big that Carlos can't wrap his mind around it. Like looking into the shallow waters off the beach and realizing it's a glimpse into infinity, Carlos sees the same thing on the surface of the storm. There's something beyond the veil. Something immense and unknowable.

Something that's looking back.

Carlos shudders.

He turns and raps on the back window of the Toyota truck. The young man has a pretty passenger. They both look back. "Can we go any faster?" Carlos shouts over the wind and the drum of rain. They both point out the windshield, wipers working double-time, to a line of red brake lights blinking unto infinity, disappearing into the down-pouring distance. It was a stupid question. But sometimes the one thing that centers the vast unknown is breaking it into small, stupid bites. Of course, they can't. They are at the mercy of every other moron engaged in escape.

Carlos turns back. He ignores the headlights starting to make a line back to where he'd come from. He considers the damage these bastards had done to his ocean. The junk that washes up on shore, the garbage hooking his toe or bobbing by his board, more and more often now than ever. Maybe the world is fighting back? Maybe something ancient and angry has been awakened? Perhaps this is justice being birthed upon the world?

Whatever it is, it's coming. Carlos had thought he could get away, but whatever is beyond the curtain of rain, it's following them. Carlos had originally believed there was something wrong with the ocean itself, but he realizes it's *in* the ocean. And it's not going to stay there.

It's reaching out.

It's coming for them.

They might be running away like roaches scurrying away from the light, but they're being followed. Hunted down. The sole of the world hovers above like a heavy footfall waiting to squash them all.

Carlos turns again. Raps on the window. Makes a motion with his hands to say, "Can we go around?" Of course, nothing can be done. Merely another stupid question. But the one way Carlos knows how to deal with the impossible is by asking stupid questions.

3"

[Marcus]

Marcus Roquefort sits across from the reporter from the *Blahblah-blahg*. It doesn't matter who she is or what she asks; he's going to answer whatever questions he wants to, and she's going to publish it. He needs to establish a record out there, and the young people who read online shit on websites with #stupidnames are the kind of constituents who will put him over the top against old dinosaurs like Magnum Preston Immonen III.

"I mean, Magnum, P.I.," Marcus tells Ms. Ming. "Am I right?"

Ms. Ming stares at him like he accidentally slipped into French and she only knows *Oui* and *Ménage à trois*.

"You jumped into the race kind of late, Representative Roquefort," the reporter presses. Her dress is super-short, and he concentrates on avoiding the allure of her smooth legs and where they might lead. "What are your plans to win the primary challenge against State Senator Immonen?"

"I thought we're talking about free speech and the press?"

Ms. Ming leans forward, the top of her dress cut as low as her hemline was high. He glances down the front and sees enough to know that she's probably had some work done. Proportioned and perky. Whatever it takes to succeed in the industry. Marcus knows that game.

"I thought I was asking the questions."

Marcus shrugs. "Well, my primary opponent is old enough to be a great grandfather, and his policies show it. He scoffs at global warming."

"He supports the Paris Climate Accord."

"I know what he *says*, but I'm talking about what he *does*. I've drafted a state bill that protects Florida from the global warming crisis. In five years, Miami will be in the ocean unless we do something now."

"There isn't a scientist on the planet who has claimed such, and there is no data to support your assertion."

"Scientists aren't always right."

"And you're saying you know more than the people who study climate change?" Ms. Ming challenges, uncrossing her legs and crossing them again. The planet seems like it's getting hotter by the moment. "You're bold, Representative Roquefort."

"I am," he agrees, letting charm and entendre leak from his dazzling white smile.

Ms. Ming stares at him across the space between their chairs. There's no one else in the large executive suite. He had a sense during his press conference that Ms. Ming knows more about one of his potential opponents than he does. Either about Immonen or his eventual nemesis on the November ballot, the incumbent governor of Florida. The suggestion was it's something scandalous. He wonders if she maybe wants to share it with him.

"Are you flirting with me, Representative Roquefort?"

"Please, call me Marcus," he sighs. "And I'm engaged, as you know."

"You're also a politician. I'm pretty sure that being 'engaged' doesn't matter."

"Government servants don't have scruples?" Marcus quizzes, trying to look hurt.

Ms. Ming shrugs off his pouty lips. No one shrugs off Marcus's pouty lips. Does she have some super-powered ability to resist his charms? Or is she a lesbian?

Ms. Ming stands up, and the pink dress hugs her fit body. Narrow hips, tiny ass, breasts sculpted by a talented surgeon, stomach as flat as his fiancée's libido. The cotton material moves with her as she steps toward him, closing the gap between interviewer and interviewee. Her dark hair frames an exotically handsome face. Her brown eyes stare deeply into his. Marcus finds her immensely attractive.

"I get the impression you're very curious to know what's under the hood, Marcus," Ms. Ming taunts. "You like to know what makes people tick?"

"Everyone has something different that fills up the tank, Cassandra," Marcus coos.

"Please, call me Miz Ming," she corrects. "Do you want to know what makes Reginald DeLand tick?"

That's what she'd set up. That is what she'd been hinting at—the governor's *husband*. Ms. Ming has dirt on Governor DeLand's marriage.

"I have to win the primary before I worry about DeLand," Marcus says cautiously. He wants the information, but he'd rather have dirt on Magnum P.I. at this stage of the game. "Senator Immonen might prove to be a difficult candidate. He has a lot of friends."

"It's not as fun when someone just gives you what you want, Marcus," Ms. Ming says coyly, tilting those hips provocatively. "You have to work for it a little. Magnum is all yours. You win the primary, then I'll give you the scoop on DeLand. In the meantime, I want all access to you in the run-up to the primary. Exclusive interviews. Intimate exposés."

"Intimate?"

"Mmm," Ms. Ming agrees.

She is so close, Marcus could breathe her in. He glances up from where he's sitting, and she gazes down into his eyes. "You're going to win this whole goddamn thing. And I'm going to take home a fucking Pulitzer."

Marcus nods. There's a knock on the door, and Ms. Ming steps back, typing in her phone like she's busy with anything other than seduction. Sherri Kambietz, his campaign manager, opens the door without waiting for an invitation.

"I need to speak with you, Marcus."

"Well, what is it?" he barks across the room.

"In private, maybe?" Sherri requests.

Marcus can't get up right now without exposing the terms of the exposé. His erection is raging, barely concealed by the folded hands placed carefully in his lap. "It's fine right here." Sherri raises an eyebrow in a doubtful expression. "Right here, Sherr."

Sherri trudges across the room like a freight car loosed from its coupling. She watches Ms. Ming on her phone with a suspicious glint. Then she focuses back on Marcus. She holds out a fresh press release, the same thing he's read every damn day in the run-up to his announcement. The headline jumps off the page—Governor DeLand has issued a state of emergency for Central Florida.

"She's considering the mandatory evacuation of Orlando," Sherri announces.

"What?" Marcus asks, his hard-on deflating.

"It's true," Ms. Ming confirms, looking up from her phone, worry written where there had so recently been seduction. "The National Hurricane Center is tracking Cheshire. They're worried the motherfucker is going to head straight inland."

3.5"

[Edd]

Edd regrets ever leaving his leaking house.

The streets of Orlando are flooding in the downpour. The old Toyota his mother used for grocery runs threatens to stall every time he plows through a puddle. A *lake*. Now he's too far from home to go back. The routes to return are all submerged.

He must see if Mom's all right. He had tried her phone, but she's always leaving it behind, and sure as shit, the terrible Tony Bennett ringtone had warbled from the end table beside her favorite chair when Edd had called. Her Toyota had still been in the garage, so someone had picked her up. The one who would come out in a storm to fetch her is Old Tom Tillerman. He's been creeping around Mom for months now like a stray tomcat, trying to woo her with his federal pension and his faded Marine tattoos. Edd isn't going to let some old alpha bastard use a meteorological emergency as an excuse to steal his mom's heart.

Traffic's a bitch. The idiot fucking governor had declared mandatory evacuations before she realized the roadways were already shit and reversed her decision, issuing a mandatory curfew instead. Half the city had started making their way out of town before the roadblocks went up, and now they're all trying to get their asses back home to shelter in place. The radio warns people caught out after curfew would face ticketing. But Edd still has a while before curfew. He dreads being stuck at Old Tom's apartment with Mom and her elderly lothario.

Traffic stops, right there in the middle of the throughway. Cars fill the lanes side to side, and water fills the street and deepens, pouring down dangerously. Why the hell would these fucks stop in the middle of the street in the face of a fucking oncoming hurricane? He remembers something Brownstarro69 (half starfish, half exotic man) had said once on a campaign to free furkind from Fuzztown a few weeks ago—"All it takes is one asshole." Brownstarro69 was referring to scoring some virtual anal in a bunny-brothel after they liberated Fuzztown, but Edd had taken it as an insightful commentary on society in general and now Orlando traffic in particular.

All it takes is one asshole.

Had someone t-boned someone else? Did someone stall in an intersection? Had a tractor-trailer turned left when everyone else was turning right? Or had some swarm of northerners, all scared shitless by the rain, come collectively to a screeching halt? Regardless, forward momentum is arrested, and some-fuckin'-body should be put in jail for it.

Time ticks. A minute. Minutes. Half hour. Horns honk in a cacophony starting every few moments, but nothing changes. Edd swears and smacks the steering wheel. The rain washes out the world, everything except the brake lights right in front of him. He reaches for the door handle a half dozen times, ready to get out and see what the shit is going on. The rain will drench him in seconds and he'll have to sit in a traffic jam soaked to the bone. An hour passes. His engine coughs, and Edd beats the dash, swears, honks, reaches for the handle yet again, then hesitates once more. The engine sputters and dies. He cranks the key but the starter refuses to help save his ass. Then water starts leaking *through* the door, a trickle that announces the engine isn't going to work anymore—this vehicle isn't submersible.

Edd grabs the handle one last time. When he opens the door, the water rushes in, all the way up to his seat. Instantly, he feels like he wet himself. Where's one of Ma's adult diapers when he needs one?

He curses his mother as he steps out into the rain. It's like standing under a waterfall. The flood's up to his knees. He wades forward from his car to the next.

He's on a quest, like Jessiqua trying to find her way across Humana. Instead of lookin' fine in a wet t-shirt, he's an overweight guy without a goddamn umbrella. Lightning flashes frequently, lighting his way. Thunder rumbles in a constant discord. He passes between the cars in front of him and almost gets kneecapped by a passenger-side door. It's a kid, maybe twenty, who might be the bastard offspring of a rat mated with some fugly bitch. He's as much furkind as Jawzz or Miss Turrid.

"Sorry," Ratboy hisses. He has tried and failed to grow a mustache, making thin whiskers to enhance his already vermin-like appearance. "You gonna walk, too?"

"Engine stalled," Edd says. "I ain't waiting around to drown."

"Whattaya think's goin' on up there?" Ratboy shouts over the drum of heavy rain as they move forward, wading through water as high as Edd's knees.

Edd shrugs. "All it takes is one asshole."

Ratboy nods like a parishioner in a pew. Preach, Reverend Brownstarro69.

The rain is undulant, unending, an unnerving nuisance that seems intent on drowning them by fully saturating the air itself. What space isn't filled with water is affected by wind, a brisk bluster making the water slap him as hard as Mom had ever smacked him whenever Edd tried to lip off and he was within her reach. And the woman had some *serious* reach.

Edd is extremely worried about her, a pang warning him that he might never get a chance to be slapped ever again.

More people start exiting their cars when they see Edd and Ratboy pass, or as they realize the water's rising and the vehicles around them are dying. Already, any cars behind them are stuck for the foreseeable future. The water is going to get higher before it starts to recede. Come storm's end, there will be the biggest goddamn traffic jam Orlando has ever seen.

Ratboy points off to the side of the street. Bright lights manage to penetrate the tidal waves of rain, like a beacon of a lighthouse shining through the fog. Edd nods. Ratboy leads, and he follows. They manage to make their way across the lanes toward the curb. The water keeps getting deeper.

The sidewalk is a different situation than the roadway. The jammed traffic manages to impede the rush of water down the street, making the water deep but weakening the current's force. Nothing slows the pace of the water flowing along the sidewalks. Between the bright lights of the storefront facades in front of them and the street filled with stalled cars shining stubborn headlights directly behind them and lightning bolts making everything shine in intermittent flashes, Edd sees raging rapids as intimidating as fording a river in the old west.

"Fuckin' flume," Ratboy says.

Edd glances back. Lightning cracks overhead and illuminates at least a dozen people following them through the storm. Maybe more concealed beyond the veil of the rainfall. Edd recalls how the caravan of westward travelers on those old westerns would tie the horses together and cross the river.

"Link arms," Edd shouts. That's what Jessiqua would do. "We cross together."

Ratboy links up to Edd's left. Someone links up on his right. More and more, until there's a whole crowd shuffling as one like they're some flashmob replicating a *Golden Girls* skit. They wade across the flooded sidewalk, the current pushing them, flushing them, wanting to sweep them away like stubborn turds stuck to the side of the porcelain bowl.

"Oof," gasps Ratboy, losing his footing. He trips and slides, his grip wet and slippery, in danger of being swept away by the current. He grabs ahold, trying to anchor himself to Edd and threatening to topple them both. Jessiqua would grab tight, pull Ratboy back, save her fellow furkind. But this isn't a game. This is the real world. Edd holds onto the strong young man on his right, and Ratboy slips away on his left, yelping once, then is submerged. Gone. Flushed.

Edd continues to cross with the crowd. He had nearly been pulled into the floodwaters by Ratboy. Fuck. That had been too damn close. Edd had almost *died*. Ratboy could've killed him because the skinny bastard couldn't keep his footing. He could've doomed them both.

All it takes is one asshole.

4"

[Amaris]

Amaris had nearly made it out of town before they closed the city and erected roadblocks. "Mandatory evacuations" became "shelter in place." Now it's too late to run. Amaris sits in her car under an overhang at a gas station, facing west and peering into the distance as it is erased beyond the steel canopy, staring toward a future that has become blurred and unformed.

She is two hours away from getting back home if she turns around now, but the mandatory curfew begins soon. Amaris won't have enough time to get back to Mom and Dad before then. She doesn't have a phone to call them to come get her or tell them where she's at. She'd left it with Ryan so Ry could text, impersonating her during Amaris's escape. She has no way to get ahold of anyone.

Amaris doesn't feel confident about getting home even if she could navigate the route, avoid the authorities, and arrive after curfew. The rain makes swamps of every street. She imagines getting stuck in a flooded intersection or being carried away crossing a washed-out road. Even if she manages to avoid new lakes and rivers, she worries the police will capture her and she'll have to explain to her parents why she was found on the opposite side of Orlando. Mom would chain her up in the basement if she found out Amaris had been trying to run away.

The other option is to wait out the storm and still make her way to California after the hurricane is over. Amaris could still let Ryan cover for her as long as she can (maybe the ruse will last longer due to the excuse of an unexpected weather event), then allow whatever happens to happen. No one would know she hadn't made it out of Florida when she'd originally planned. Ryan will believe she'd escaped in time. She'll tell Mom and Dad Amaris is already halfway to the Pacific. They don't need to know she's not as far as she wanted to be.

But where's Amaris supposed to shelter until the hurricane blows over? She's never been past Winter Garden, and now she's stuck in Apopka. She knows the hotels around the Attractions, but she's far from Disney, and there's no turning back. No phone for GPS. She'd planned to follow the electronic compass on her car to take routes north until she hit the panhandle, then westward ho, baby. Now, she doesn't know where to go.

She gets out and goes into the gas station. The handwritten sign hanging on the glass entrance door announces that the station is already out of fuel and water. Emergency lights dimly illuminate the interior. The shelves are nearly bare. Foragers still plunder the last of the candy bars and other non-perishables. There's a long line at the register. Amaris grabs a bag of open M&Ms and a warm soda that had rolled under a set of crooked shelves and waits in line. The beleaguered clerk finally rings her up and asks for eight bucks (for candy and a soda!). Amaris hands over a ten and asks, "Where's the nearest hotel?"

"You can stay with me, baby," says the guy behind her, dread-locks to his shoulders and smelling of weed. Old enough to be her dad. "We can ride out the storm. Together."

The clerk rolls her eyes and leans in so that the creep behind Amaris doesn't hear. "Across the street. Probably loaded up but tell 'em Linda sent ya."

Amaris thanks her and takes her stash. The clerk takes extra-long ringing up the pedo behind Amaris so she can make a clean getaway back to her car before he's able to follow her. She cautiously drives across the waterlogged road and pulls into the parking lot of a place called the Lullaby Lodge.

The lobby is concealed by shadows. The essential appliances are running off a generator Amaris can hear chugging out back over the howl of the wind. Candles flicker here and there, barely illuminating a vacant vestibule. Linda warned her that the hotel was probably full, but there's no evidence of it by the lobby.

The woman at the front desk is about as old as anyone Amaris has ever seen, as dark as her family's oil-rubbed bronze chandelier, and lines across her face tell a sorrowful story. Amaris can't help but wonder if this woman had missed her opportunity to escape to California when she was a teenager, or had she taken the chance and eventually crawled back a wrecked woman? Dreams missed or dreams dashed?

"Linda sent me," Amaris says.

"What's a little slip of a thing like you doin' out in a storm like this, girl?"

"Too far from home to go back."

The old woman nods. She seems to know about being far from home.

"Well, we're full up, but I'll be mannin' this desk all night. That leaves the innkeeper's quarters vacant tonight, so you can take my bed."

"Oh, ma'am, I couldn't..."

"The name's Edith. And only a fool says 'no' in an emergency. Otherwise, you be sleepin' in your damn car, girl. The rooms are full up and down the neighborhood, and I know you ain't got no death wish to go drivin' in this storm. The bed'll be empty unless you take it."

Amaris fights back the tears. She's been gone for a few hours and has already screwed it all up. If not for the kindness of strangers, she might be falling prey to the creep who'd been standing behind her at the quick mart. Amaris nods, and Edith waves her around the counter. She points a crooked finger to some narrow steps that lead upstairs and hands Amaris a flashlight.

"Some food in the fridge," Edith offers. "Might as well eat a bit. It'll spoil before this hurricane blows out."

"Thank you," Amaris whispers, tears of gratitude leaking down her face.

"Keep it tidy, all I ask."

Amaris nods and ascends the stairs. The apartment is the only room at the top, the door to the right marked "innkeeper's quarters" and the door to the left an emergency exit. Amaris can hear the wind howling outside the exterior door, rattling the secure exit in its frame. The storm is growing stronger.

Amaris enters. Her flashlight illuminates a small bed against a wall and a little kitchenette opposite the sleeping area. A little table and chair face a television. Beside the bed is a nightstand. A small emergency radio surrounded by extra batteries sit on the tabletop. Edith has prepared for the duration. How long is this hurricane going to last?

Amaris opens the fridge, and the air inside has already turned tepid. She selects a bunch of grapes and sits on the bed, snacking. She turns on the radio, curious about how long the weather will last. Static on her regular station. She turns the dial. *Static static static.* She flips the switch from FM to AM, and there's finally a voice at the edge of the bandwidth. An announcer sounds dire yet wired, like a television anchor warning of doomsday but watching his rating tick to record levels. The hurricane is about as far out of season as Florida has ever seen, he says. The storm lingers off the coast and is still strengthening, he titters. Prepare to be inundated for the long haul, he sighs breathlessly. He continues with a soliloquy worthy of Macbeth or Romeo—"I'll be here with you throughout as we survive Hurricane Cheshire. Togeth—"

Then his voice breaks up and turns to static, too. Then there's nothing across all the frequencies. Just white noise. White white white.

Together, she finishes for the silenced announcer. As the wind roars and the rain gets impossibly *heavier*, Amaris sit by herself on the small single bed. She has never felt so alone.

4.5"

[Rabe]

Rain spatters against the windows, running in rivulets down the pane, fat droplets that make the whole world a blur. Carla's little red dress is hanging across a flat-screen television that couldn't be used anyway. The electricity is out. Rabe hadn't needed lights for the things they'd been doing for the last few hours. He'd been teasing Carla over the last few months about all the carnal craziness he had planned for this evening, and he had made good on over half his list so far. And it's only Friday. He has two more days to check off everything else.

"I'm hungry, baby," Carla coos.

"You gonna have to gimme a li'l bit, sweetness. I may be *Super*man, but that means I'm still a man."

She reaches under the covers and grabs a handful of him, squeezing him hard but not too hard. He manages to stir at her touch. Already. He hasn't performed like this in so many years. Carla is driving him crazy.

"I was talkin' about some snacks, stud," Carla sighs. "I can wait a bit for dessert."

Rabe reaches for the phone on the cradle by the bed. He lifts the receiver, and all he hears is the angry buzz of a busy signal. The circuits are fried in this storm. Rabe opens the screen on his cellphone. Two text messages he doesn't want to read. He has his notifications silenced. He thumbs them away. He tries to dial the front desk, but the same warning sounds come out of the cell.

"Sorry, baby. Room service is outta commission."

"This body needs some refuelin' if I'm supposed to keep movin', my king," Carla pouts, her hand still holding his royal jewels. "And you want me to keep movin', don't you?"

"Movin'," Rabe agrees, his mind swirling as her fingers play. "Yeah."

"I saw a snack machine at the end of the hall," Carla begs. "Chocolate. Anything chocolate."

"Ain't you had enough chocolate, baby?"

"I got room for a *lot* more, my king."

That gets him moving.

Rabe pulls on his pants, no underwear. Pulls on a button-up shirt and clasps the two middle buttons. He shoves his bare feet into his Jordans. Rabe glances at his phone and considers the text messages he cleared without reading. He knows who they're from. He shoves the phone in his pocket and exits the room.

The hall is dark and empty. The dull red of emergency lights leads the way down the corridor to an alcove at the end. The stairway is on Rabe's right and a pair of vending machines are to the left. The Coke dispenser is dark and dead. The glass window that is supposed to showcase candy and snacks only reflects the red light, the selection within concealed by impenetrable shadows. It runs on power and would give up no secrets in this storm.

The Rivington is a fancy hotel. Maybe not five-star, but certainly more than two. They should be giving out free shit at the desk in the lobby. It's farther away than Rabe wants to venture in thin pants and a mostly unbuttoned shirt, but if he comes back without food, it might cost him points with Carla.

That won't do.

Rabe takes the stairs and descends to the lobby. The room is cast in an eerie red glow from emergency lights spaced evenly along the walls.

Upon entering the posh main floor of the hotel, Rabe notes that the restaurant where they ate earlier is now closed and dark. The spouting fountain where water danced is now a calm pond. The fancy glass chandeliers hang dark and useless above his head.

The plate-glass windows across the front of the hotel showcase a hell of a storm. Wind drives precipitation fully sideways like the whole world has tipped perpendicular, and the rain is falling past him in torrents. Wind wails and thunder rumbles in a constant bass. Palm trees fronds fly, spinning in the wind like pinwheels in a gale. The world flickers beyond the wall of rain from the frequent lightning flashes. Rabe can't see the world beyond a few feet outside the glass.

"Is that going to hold up to this storm?" Rabe asks the clerk behind the desk, nodding toward the glass doors.

The clerk is young and skinny and white as cotton. He shrugs like he couldn't give a shit less. "There wasn't time to put up plywood."

"Doesn't sound reassuring."

"And I'm the one standing over here," the desk clerk agrees.

"Look," Rabe starts, "I've got a super-hot babe up in my room and she's got the munchies, if you know what I mean. The vending machines are all powered down. So, you have a secret stash behind that desk? Like Twinkies or some shit?"

The clerk examines Rabe top to bottom. "You look like somebody. You famous? Baseball player?"

"Nah," Rabe dismisses the question. "I ain't nobody. Just a playa lookin' for some snacks."

"Player. Sure," the clerk says, a wink-wink in his voice like he's playing coy. Like the secret of Rabe's fame will remain safe and sound with him. White boys are never anywhere near as cool as they think. The clerk digs around under the desk and surfaces with a Mounds bar. "Chocolate?"

"You got anything besides coconut shit? Who eats that—"

The front plate glass window explodes inward, and Rabe thinks his prediction of hurricane winds smashing glass was accurate until he sees it's an Acura. The car comes crashing through the entrance, tires sliding on the water flooding in and crossing the floor like a surge of surf. Rabe dives behind the desk next to the clerk as the vehicle glides sideways and comes to a stop inches from where Rabe had been standing seconds before.

"Jesus Christ," Rabe swears, staring at the car in the lobby and the wind and rain blowing in through the smashed opening.

The car has steam running out from under the hood, the radiator busted. Some whining sound comes from the motor like it's an injured animal. The windshield is shattered and sagging, and the side window is gone. The driver stumbles out, wearing an expression of terror and confusion. He points back through the hole in the hotel's entrance, hand wavering with shock and adrenaline.

"Th-th-there," he stutters. "I think I hit something."

The desk clerk shakes his head, picking up his cell and trying to call 9-1-1. *Good luck, dumbass*, Rabe thinks. Rabe stares into the storm, everything erased by the driving rain beyond the sidewalk in front of the hotel. There could be anything out there or nothing at all. The rumble of thunder could be the destruction of everything beyond the curtain of rain. He doesn't want to see what's behind the veil of the downpour.

I think I hit something. Or some*one*. There could be a person hurt out there.

What had Rabe done up there in the hotel room with Carla? He'd been trying not to think about the sin, but it's *all* he thinks about. He had done some bad things tonight. Some terrible, terrible things that he'd have to live with for the rest of his life. So maybe he ought to do one damn good thing to make up for some of it.

The clerk somehow manages to get through the busy circuits to 9-1-1 (maybe white people have special clearance to get through jammed-up circuits) and gives emergency services an account of the Acura crashing into the lobby. Someone could be out there lying in the street, and the one thing between life and death is for one person to do the right thing. Neither of these two other assholes made a move to head out into a goddamn hurricane. *Fuck*, Rabe thought. Then he runs out into the raging rain.

5"

[Renata]

Renata had been driving back from the clinic, still pregnant, the problem not solved. Traffic was a bitch, so she tried going around the main throughways back to her office. The radio had warned about mandatory evacuation, but the authorities could kiss her *redonda* ass, and she flipped the radio switch off. Leaving Orlando wasn't an option—she still had several hours to put in at the office.

She called Cybill. It took ten tries through the tangled airwaves. "I'm sorry, Miz Sanchez. They evacuated the office building. I tried to stay, but security escorted me out. The whole downtown area is on lockdown, and there were blockades as I left."

"Are you evacuating?" Renata asked.

It sounded like she was concerned about Cybill's safety, but she wanted to know if her assistant would be available immediately after this storm blew over or if Cybill was escaping her responsibilities for an extended furlough.

"They changed it," Cybill answered. "The hurricane's too terrible. Streets are flooding faster than expected. The storm's offshore and still strengthening. Now the governor issued a mandatory curfew. Everyone's supposed to shelter in place. I barely made it home."

Renata then found herself diverted by detours due to the deluge, drowned avenues impassable as the rain washed out roadways everywhere. She turned and turned and turned and kept getting farther from the office instead of nearer. She couldn't see signs and suddenly didn't know where she was. Renata was lost and unable to see six feet in front of the bumper.

Then the Acura came out of nowhere. It was an intersection and Renata had the red light, but she didn't even see the other car until Renata's Mercedes was at a forty-five-degree angle and she was staring up at the streetlight. The Acura pinwheeled in one direction as Renata spun out in the other. Her head bounced off the seatback, and the airbag came up and punched her right in the face, causing her to see stars before everything went black.

Now, she blinks. Conscious again. A handsome black man is wearing what looks like pajamas, standing in the soaking rain, shouting something through her rain-splattered side window. Renata watches his lips move through the bleary tempered glass, trying to understand what he's trying to tell her. She's been in an accident. A real-life car crash.

Lightning flashes so close that the bright white blinds Renata for a few moments, the crash of thunder deafening her even further. The hair on her arms stands on end, and she could smell the acrid scent of ozone in the air. The strike must have happened a few feet from where she sits. Her eyesight returning, she sees the fear upon the man's face. The man who's checking on her condition.

Her condition. Renata's hand goes to her belly, wondering if things had taken care of themselves in the crash.

"Get in," she mouths to the good Samaritan.

He scrambles around the shambles of her Mercedes. He yanks at the damaged passenger door several times before it finally squeals open with the sound of grinding metal and tinkling glass. He slams it shut behind him as another bolt strikes nearby, behind the nearest buildings, illuminating in silhouette the structures across the street and briefly illustrating where the Acura that broadsided her ended up—inside the lobby of some posh lodge called the Rivington.

"Wait out the fuckin' lightning strikes so we don't die on our way," the stranger says, "but then we'll run for it."

Renata nods.

"You staying at that ritzy place?" she asks, surveying her would-be rescuer. His white clothes were soaking wet and have become transparent. He has a sculptured chest and an impressive package. The man looks fine, all flushed and dripping.

"Yeah. Getaway weekend."

Renata smirks and nods knowingly. Getaway. Right. This guy is as married as her grandma and gramps. But it isn't his damn wife in the Rivington. Ren's knight in shining armor is just some sad playa. Damn.

"You're hurt," the suave dude tells her, like a doctor making a terminal diagnosis.

Not the doctor's services she needed today.

Ren looks down at her left leg. Blood has stained her tan pants red from her waistband to the bend of her knee. She leans away from the smashed door and checks her thigh. A piece of metal the size of a pencil had punctured through her door and into her thigh. She doesn't even feel it. But it must have been bleeding for the last five minutes.

"Shit," she says and clamps her hand over the wound, wrapped around the shard of shrapnel perforating her leg.

They can't sit here in the car. She needs medical attention. Her day is continuing in the same vein as it had started—she needs a doctor to get rid of something she doesn't want to be stuck inside her anymore.

Ren peers through the spiderwebbed windshield as another light show erupts across the sky. The cracked glass lights up, the blades of lightning making her vision shatter into a million shards.

The thunder makes the car shudder.

The thunder continues, growing and growing and growing, getting impossibly loud. Louder than any storm could produce. For a moment, Renata fears a bolt of electricity has struck the car itself, making the vehicle explode around her, intent on deafening her before she dies. But the flash fades even as the sound grows.

It isn't thunder.

She stares out the driver's side window as the event continues to unfold in the concealing darkness. The crazy deluge of rain washes over the view, making everything seem like she's looking for a shark lurking below her in the depths of the sea. Shadows try to make everything ominous, and the sound promises something terrible is occurring. The noise drowns out everything else.

The curtain of precipitation is alive, water so thick it's like the dark of night. Like when Ren was a kid and she'd wake up after a nightmare. The shadows were alive, and her imagination could produce all sorts of malevolence. Now, the water is her amorphous medium of fear, and it's manifesting in eerie shapes and disturbing suggestions. Like something is watching her from beyond the curtain of precipitation. Something massive. Something evil.

Then the rain lets up enough to expose what's happening to the hotel. Renata has been in enough hurricanes to know the ebb and flow of the storms. The downpour lasts for impossible moments before it lets up, a brief reprieve that lets everyone breathe for a minute. This time, Renata's breath is taken away as she stares at the impossible.

"What the everlovin' fuck?" Renata swears, but she hears no sound issue from her lips over the cacophony occurring in front of her. Her window still works. She opens it, needing to see it with her own eyes, without the rivulets of rainwater distorting the view. It doesn't help her to understand what she's looking at.

The Rivington disassembles like someone running a slow-motion construction project in reverse. The roof is already gone when the image is revealed by the lull in the weather. The street-facing wall is gone, too, so the hotel resembles Renata's Barbie dreamhouse she played with when she was a kid. A wave of water splashes in her face like someone threw a bucket of water at her head, and when she finishes sputtering and spitting, she sees the second floor of the hotel is simply gone. Removed. Erased.

She tracks something moving inside the shadows, concealed by enough rainwater to be indiscernible. The storm blows another round of torrential rains and thunder rolls in a long baritone.

It is big, bigger than the Acura that had been right there a moment ago and was gone the next. Bigger than the minibus that had said "Rivington" on the side, that disappeared as quickly as a white bunny into a magician's top hat. As big as the hotel rooms that disappeared one by one, like Legos being taken apart and taken away.

The sound finally fades and the rain subsides long enough to see across the street. To see that the Rivington is completely gone, all the way down to the foundation.

5.5"

[Amaris]

Amaris Azmi reclines on the small single bed, staring up at a stained ceiling, pouting about rerouted plans for escape because of this stupid storm. She should've been well on her way to California already. She might've been headed in the direction of superstardom, every mile getting her closer to being besties with one of the Jenner girls. Either Kylie or Kendall—doesn't matter.

She has only thought of her parents once since she settled down in the innkeeper's quarters, and even then, only as a matter of happenstance. The old woman who normally occupies this apartment has an aloe vera plant on the top of her bureau, and Amaris briefly remembered when she scraped her knee learning to ride a bike. Mom had put some salve from the plant on the road rash. Yet her heart offered no tinge and her brain suffered no guilt, Amaris's thoughts moving on to moving on after a moment's remembrance.

California doesn't have any damn hurricanes.

Amaris sips from the soda she pilfered from the fridge. It's already warm, the lingering chill from the insulated fridge counteracted by the mugginess of the room. Lacking A/C, the humidity and warm front have made for an effect akin to a sauna, the steamy interior making Amaris restless and ready to run. Yet, outside, the wind howls and rain makes for a constant hum, like television static intermittently interrupting a spooky horror movie where the actors are constantly screaming.

Amaris will be in one of those horror movies someday. Maybe chased by some terrifying creature of disgusting deformity or stalked by a deranged serial killer who preys exclusively on pretty, young women. Or perhaps she'll star as the badass protagonist popular in recent years, the heroine who picks up a weapon and fights back. Regardless, this weather is the perfect setting for such a scare. Maybe she'll write a screenplay, then star in the movie herself...

Thunder builds beyond the thin wall of the hotel, a rising crescendo that swells into impossible noise, then gets even louder. The rumble suggests the world might be ending beyond the drawn drapes of the small room. Amaris stares at the curtains, wondering if a runaway train is about to plow through the wall. She hesitates, then gets up and crosses the room. The floor shakes like the world itself is quaking. What kind of hurricane...?

Driving rain whipped by wild winds obscures the view outside the window. Amaris presses her nose against the pane, staring through the downpour. She glimpses the scene across the street in a brief lull in the heavy rain—there had been a tall hotel with some fancy name standing there. The high-rise had been right next to the gas station where Linda works, the woman who'd sent her to shelter here. The whole structure is now gone. Disappeared.

"What the hell?" Amaris curses.

Hurricanes don't suck away entire *hotels*, do they? Businesses in central Florida are constructed with cinderblocks and follow strict building codes, certainly able to withstand the wind outside Amaris's window. She thinks of the old nursery rhyme with the three pigs—the wolf blew down the house made of straw; he huffed and puffed the house made of sticks until it collapsed, but the house made of brick protected the preyed-upon pigs. Amaris stares as she calculates the size of the wolf necessary to huff and puff and blow down a building as big as the one missing across the street.

Missing *building*. Impossible! But it's gone.

Will the lodge she's in right now be the next to fall?

Amaris runs to the door and practically leaps down the narrow flight of stairs to the front desk in the small lobby. She searches for the old woman who let her stay in her apartment. Edith had told Amaris she'd have to man the desk all night, but the lobby is empty. Edith's gone. Maybe she saw what happened across the street and ran for it, saving her old buns and to heck with everyone else. To heck with even Amaris sleeping upstairs.

Amaris peers outside, through the front glass doors in the lobby showing the wild maelstrom mucking about outside. Beyond the watery view, shifting and changing every second, something starts to resolve, like a picture in a darkroom becoming clearer as it soaks in the special chemical bath. Two figures come staggering toward the glass doors, fighting from being knocked over by the wind—a black man supporting an injured Latina.

They hit the glass front entrance and bounce back, the man falling on his backside and knocking over the woman he's supposed to be helping. Edith must have locked the doors behind her before she abandoned her post. The man, dripping wet and staggering against every gust of powerful wind, grabs the exterior handle and shouts something that's carried away by the din of the storm. He points at the lock, and Amaris finally shakes off the shock. She runs forward and unlatches the deadbolt.

The door sucks outward, saved from being torn away by the massive commercial arm that usually acts as a closure. Now it serves as an anchor. The tinkling bell once announcing a new customer is ripped away and carried skyward, gone forever. Like ten-story hotels.

The man drags the woman inside and struggles to pull the door closed. He finally latches the deadbolt, but the door shakes in its frame, barely able to resist the storm.

"Shit, girl, you leave drowning people to their death?"

"I'm sorry," Amaris warbles. Her voice is high and unrecognizable. "I saw what happened. What happened to the hotel across the street?"

She isn't sure if she's asking a question or rambling.

"Help me with her," he says. "She's hurt."

"Let's first get a little farther away from the thin glass pane separating us from the fucking hurricane," the injured woman suggests.

Amaris gets on the other side, and they help the woman limp across the lobby. The woman's pants are ripped, and blood stains the material. She has one arm slung over the man's shoulder, and the other cradles her belly like she has an upset stomach.

They manage to get the woman up the stairs to Edith's small apartment. Amaris checks the tiny bathroom and finds a first aid kit. Amaris and the man appear to know absolutely nothing about taking care of an injury or dressing a wound, so the injured woman rudely rips the first aid kit out of Amaris's hands. She pulls out a roll of gauze, antiseptic spray, and some scissors before shooing them away.

"Turn around," she barks.

The man turns his back as the woman cuts her pants from the waistband to the impalement. With a cacophony of curse words, she wriggles out of her pants. Amaris turns and stares out the window into the rain as the injured lady tends to her wounds.

"I'm Amaris," she says. "And I'm freaking terrified."

"Name's Rab— It's Robert. And kid, I'm scared shitless. Whatever happened out there—whatever I saw. It was fucking impossible. Like goddamn aliens are attacking. Like the world turned crazy."

"What was it?" Amaris whispers, unsure if she even wants an answer.

"I don't know," Robert sighs. "And I don't want to find out."

6"

[Cass]

Politicians. Fuck 'em all.

Cassandra Ming is stranded because of the bitch calling the shots on mandatory evacuations. Marcus Roquefort had offered to get her the hell out of Orlando. He had a private car waiting to escort them out of the city, but it ended up that it wouldn't have even mattered if he was Jesus Christ himself—traffic was a bitch for everyone. By the time they'd forded the unmitigated clusterfuck called I-4, the highways heading north were all washed out, and the governor was telling everyone to turn around and get back home. Shelter in place. Mandatory curfews. Even state representatives weren't exempt.

"How close is your house?" Marcus asks as the driver takes an entire city block to make a U-turn.

"The hell out in Mount Dora," Cass says.

"Oh," he sighs. "That isn't going to work."

"And what does that mean? You're going to leave me on the side of the road?"

A look crosses Marcus's eyes, and she sees that he's thinking about it. If Cass didn't have incriminating evidence on his future foe, he would pull aside and kick her to the curb right now. But she knows things that he wants to know. Cass could help him in ways Marcus needs to be helped.

"No," he finally decides. "No, of course not. You'll have to come home with me."

It takes an hour to get home through the weather. "Home" is a helluva small word for the sprawling estate where Marcus Roquefort resides. Cass couldn't see where they were through the incessant rain until they're up close. The trees act as enough of a canopy to stave off the downpour and reveal the entire front facade of Castle Roquefort.

"Are you shitting me?" Cass asks, incredulous. "Do you know how many homeless people are struggling to survive across Orange County, and you live in a house worth millions?"

"There won't be so many homeless after this surprise hurricane drowns them like rats in the gutters," Marcus quips before the driver opens the back door of the car and holds out an umbrella. "That comment is off-the-record, of course."

"How do you sleep at night, Roquefort?"

"Between Egyptian cotton sheet that cost a thousand dollars," he answers. "And don't give me your bullshit sanctimonious claptrap, Miz Ming. You're not here to make sure the dredges of society get a voice. You made a choice that'll move you closer to having your own castle."

Cass follows Roquefort inside, the steady winds threatening to knock her sideways. The marble steps up to double glass doors are slick with rain and seem to move and shift as they feature a dozen elongated waterfalls. The driver's umbrella folds backward, then he loses his grip and it sails away like Mary Poppins's sans the nanny. Cass is drenched instantly. Her pink dress clings to her like a swimsuit, hugging her body more like a tattoo than couture.

Her hair is straight (her hair is always straight, her Asian physiology resistant to all styling and sprays), but now it shines like she applied hot wax. Cass's makeup runs down her cheeks and chin. There isn't a mirror in the vestibule, and she deigns to imagine the horror movie mess of her face.

A goddess emerges from the back of the house like a queen making an entrance, a roll of thunder like the tympani of drums in her honor. She looks like a life-size Barbie, her dimensions proportionally accurate to the plastic doll's, her blonde hair is flawlessly styled, and her face seems entirely manufactured.

"Marc, what in the world were you doing out in a *hurricane?*"

The Barbie exudes cattiness. Cass dislikes her instantly. Cass had flirted with Roquefort to advance her position in his political ascent, knowing full well he is engaged to some celebutante who's angling for a reality show, but Cass had expected more ditz than bitch. This woman looks ready to eat up and spit out. Cass isn't intimidated by anyone, but she is cautious around crazies that she deems dangerous. This vindictive brat is waiting for a reason to slap Cass around and toss her out into the storm.

"Would you rather I stayed at a hotel, Allie?" Roquefort questions.

Allie redirects her gaze from Marcus to Cass, eyeing the dripping young woman up and down, trying to assess what exactly Marcus was suggesting. She appears ready to rip Cass to shreds. *Bring it on*, Cass thinks. She's been a woman for six years now, and she's ready for her first catfight. Cass's mother had insisted she enroll in self-defense classes when Cass had still been Carter and everyone in school was bullying him. Cass is confident she still retains a few moves and enough attitude to land Allie on her ass.

"No," Allie says. "No, of course not. I didn't want you to risk being out on the roads. They say it's dangerous out there."

Roquefort gives his fiancée the waggle of eyebrows that somehow makes him look both juvenile and sexy at the same time. Allie doesn't smile, but the edge of her extreme antagonism dulls a bit. She still shoots daggers Cass's way, as if she knows any woman in a pink dress so tight it might be molded to her body has ulterior motives. Cass wishes it wasn't so cold in the mansion that her nipples are practically cutting through the thin material.

"Who is she?" Allie asks as if Cass is too inconsequential to address directly.

"I'm a reporter for the *Blahblahblahg*," Cass answers for herself. "I was doing an interview when the evacuation order came through. Representative Roquefort was kind enough to offer me an escort out of Orlando. When we were rerouted, he graciously offered me a place to ride out the storm."

"Ride out?" Allie counters. "You're not waiting for a Lyft?"

"I'm afraid there are no Lyft drivers out and about during Armageddon, sweetheart," Roquefort says. "Miz Ming can stay in the guest quarters for the night. We'll revisit the situation with the storm in the morning."

Allie appears ultimately peeved. Roquefort seems to relish in the jealousy. Maybe he figures he'll get laid by the Barbie tonight if she thinks it'll keep him from sneaking out to the guest quarters after she's asleep.

"Thank you for your hospitality," Cass says. She doesn't know what would've happened if she'd been stranded somewhere in the city. Probably on a cot at some shelter, unable to sleep for fear of being groped by a random pervert.

"I'll show you to your room," Roquefort offers.

"No," Allie overrides. "Follow *me*."

Cass sighs and wanders after the woman-who-might've-modeled. She wants to sleep with Roquefort to spite this evil wench. There's a terrible storm outside, but there's no less strife on the inside. As Allie leads through the winding halls, the storm grows louder and louder and louder, as if it's transforming into something else…

6.5"

[Carlos]

Carlos is trapped inland.

He resorts to his instincts. Like being caught in a rip current when he swims parallel to the shoreline until the powerful forces pulling him in the wrong direction subsides. The sea had been trying to draw him outward where he knew he belonged. "Come home," the sea had seemed to call in those moments. "Swim out and keep on swimming."

But surfing is, at the end of the experience, turning your back on the ocean, facing toward shore, and being pushed back toward land. The ocean gives back what isn't meant to be. Like the scatter of trash along the shore, or the old shoe washed up at high tide, the waters expel what isn't sea-worthy. At the end of every day, Carlos had always gone back to his home on the beach.

Dry land.

Now he is metaphorically swimming parallel to the rip current. He's stuck in Orlando, between something that wants to pull him (and everything) back in and the higher ground that seems to be getting less high as the night wears on. What does he say about sharks and nature? "Leave 'em alone, and they'll leave you be." But there's something in the ocean, and it isn't leaving him alone.

Does that mean it isn't something natural?

What's the alternative?

He's stuck indoors with a bunch of human beings, the last place on this earth he would have guessed he'd be spending his night if anyone had asked yesterday. But the world has been turned upside down since then, expelling him from home and sea, driving him inland as his greatest love turned into a raging homicidal maniac. He thought about a zombie movie he'd watched once when he was younger. The Atlantic had become an evil monster.

Maybe it's fortuitous he finds himself in a church.

Carlos has never been the religious type. His mother had forced him to go to the Catholic Cathedral in Puerto Rico when he was growing up, taking catechism and making confessions. He hadn't set foot on the hallowed ground since he'd come to America. Carlos worshiped at the altar of Mother Nature. But that was before Mother Nature had given birth to whatever bastard is trying to reach out to him, even all this way from the ocean...

He surveys the room of frightened faces illuminated by the glow of dozens of electronic screens. How strange in a place of an archaic cult that modern amenities light the room rather than religious fervor. The *pings* and *whoots* of ringtones and alerts drown out the whispers of prayer. The altar has been abandoned for access to information. Everyone is trying to find out what the hell is going on. Carlos had never really listened during the homilies. But surely this has something to do with the devil.

"You hear any new news on what's going on?" asks a young woman who has her hair bunched in knots and a tattoo of a dolphin under her left eye. Carlos doesn't know what to make of her. He's not good at personal interactions.

"I don't know," he says. "I don't have a phone."

The woman looks at him like he has told her he didn't have a heart and she couldn't figure out how he's still alive. "Well, my phone's dead."

She stares at Carlos like he's supposed to charge it himself. He knows there's a generator out back feeding a trickle of electricity into the church. The congregation at the house of worship is near the narthex, so he assumes that's where the juice is flowing. Carlos shrugs.

"You weren't looking at a phone, so I figured yours was dead, too," she snaps. "I assumed you were waiting in line to use a charger."

Carlos doesn't know what she expects him to say about that. He says nothing. He's good at that.

"Jesus," she swears and stalks away.

Jesus isn't going to help us, Carlos thinks.

He stares at the stained-glass window. He's been watching it glow intermittently since he settled down here in the church. The young couple in the Toyota was headed to her folks' home in Winter Springs and Carlos hadn't been invited. He'd jumped out at an intersection when they stopped for a passing big rig, and they surely never gave him a second thought when they'd noticed he was gone.

His board is leaning against the fourth station of the cross along the east wall.

Carlos gets up and goes to the window. The stained glass illustrates a scene of Jesus carrying the cross. The crown of thorns drips blood that goes from ugly brown to deep red whenever the lightning strikes somewhere outside. Jesus looks tired and beat, but he trudges onward. Toward certain doom. Carlos glances at his surfboard. Is that his cross to bear?

He peers out a small, clear section of the stained glass in the corner of the window. The window is under an awning, so the water doesn't directly obstruct his view. However, the thick downpour acts as a curtain blocking anything beyond mere inches, even when the lightning tries to illuminate more. Like God is attempting to give Carlos a glimpse, but the darkness knows better than to give up its secrets.

"Anything out there?"

The voice tickles his ear as the speaker is so nearby, and Carlos tries not to cringe. He doesn't like to be in close proximity to other people, and this guy seriously encroaches on his personal space. Leaning over his shoulder, Carlos could smell the fetid stench of coffee on his breath and the under-smell of body odor triggered by nervousness. A feverish heat radiates off the other person.

The other man is his age—white hair, wrinkles like rivers across a ravaged face, liver-spots like freckles across his exposed skin, and a white collar under his black lapel. They had both lived an equal amount of life and had taken different roads along the journey, but here they are. Same place at the same time. The priest had dedicated his whole life to having faith in the unknowable.

"What do you think it is, Padre?"

"I believe it is a reckoning," the priest says. "Our sins have come to haunt us."

Carlos turns and stares at the holy man. "'The end is nigh kinda shit?"

"The end has been here for a long while," the pastor proclaims. "This is the end of the end."

It was the opposite of any message of hope or salvation. The Man of God hadn't suggested they were witnessing the rapture or the second coming. The priest thinks God is all out of second chances. The message was the doom and gloom of Revelations. It was the plagues of the Old Testament. It was some Noah and the Ark Armageddon shit out there. God damn the rest of the book.

Carlos had felt something in the sea. Something dark and powerful. Dangerous. Maybe it had been some abhorrent evil come to smite all humanity. Maybe this *is* the end.

"You think it's the devil out there, Padre?" Carlos asks.

"I think it's something even worse than Satan. I don't think it cares about sin or lies or souls. I think it wants to destroy it all. It isn't the devil. It's the opposite of the Creator Himself. It is our undoing."

Carlos stares at the priest. The clergyman tries to peer out through the small, transparent corner of the stained-glass window. Jesus weeps upon the caricature in the glass, but the priest isn't looking at Jesus. He's peering past. Beyond. At something that can't be stopped by mere prayer.

Carlos grabs his board and leaves the church, heading out into the rain and wind and dark. He'd rather chance the unknown than be stuck with a bunch of trapped mice waiting to die.

7"

[Leo]

Dexter Johnson is the one person in the science wing Leo could find to help him with his endeavor. Everyone calls him DJ. DJ seems to think it's the pinnacle of coolness, suggesting someone like a disc jockey spinning records on the radio or the sassy sitcom character played by Candace Cameron. DJ is as big a dork as anyone else in the science wing because... well, *science wing*.

The combination of the late hour and a mandatory curfew has given most college students an excuse for an impromptu party. Usually, there would be the overachieving grad student burning the midnight oil in a lab here and there, but even the nerdiest of nerds is somewhere else tonight, getting drunk or getting laid.

Leo found DJ in the Lens Lab. That's what the real science majors call the room dedicated to Optics and Photonics. That's an actual major—the study of prisms and binoculars and monocles and shit. Before the Department of Optics and Photonics, the meteorology department used to be the butt of all jokes, so Leo appreciates their existence. Never more so than tonight, when he finds DJ still working on the development of a new periscope aperture.

Dexter is even dorkier than Leo. Leo might've never seen a woman naked IRL, but DJ doesn't even bother to check out premium online porn. The dude is entirely asexual and antisocial. He lives within his interior world, and everyone avoids him, even the professors in the O&P department. But tonight, Leo is more grateful for DJ than if he was scalping the last ticket at the *Lord of the Rings* anniversary rerelease.

"DJ," Leo cries as he finds the tall, thin, crooked kid bent in two over a table. DJ doesn't startle. He's always preternaturally calm, as if he'd been born without nerves. "I need your help. With science."

"Please tell me you're not referring to paleotempestology as a legitimate science again," DJ drolls. "At least refer to your studies as climatology. Or meteorology. Something that is recognized as an actual word rather than babble."

"Paleotempestology is recognized as a serious study of meteorology by the entire scientific community," Leo argues.

"False. The *Journal of American Science* debunked the entire branch of study as bogus."

"That's the same journal that ridiculed the field of optics and photonics."

"Touché."

"Don't talk about my tushie," Leo quips.

DJ rolls his eyes as if puns are beneath someone of his scientific caliber. "What do you want? Don't you know there's a hurricane coming?"

"Yeah. And you know what study might come in handy in this fucking storm? Pretty sure it doesn't have anything to do with bifocals."

"Does that mean you're going out in the maelstrom?"

"What kind of a scientist sits in the classroom while the event is occurring right outside?" Leo challenges. "Does Doctor Henry Jones read about old shit in a book, or does he fucking run through the goddamn Temple of Doom?"

"Indiana Jones would raid the shit out of this hurricane."

"Well, saddle up, Junior," Leo says in his best Sean Connery voice, which is a terrible Sean Connery voice. "Let's crusade this storm before we need a damn ark."

They commandeer the UCF science division van filled with a full complement of research equipment and drive out of the garage into conditions a hell of a lot worse than Leo had expected. The weather off the coast features sustained winds unheard of in the annals of December Atlantic storms. It already looks like the end of the whole fucking world out there.

The van is more tank than Grand Caravan, built specifically to navigate storm conditions. Special tires divert water on the roads, minimizing the possibility of hydroplaning. The undercarriage is as much a motorboat as an automobile, traversing a washed-out intersection with mechanical hydropropulsion. Sensors indicate debris in the pathways, and special weights make the vehicle bottom-heavy and resistant to tipping from the wind. Hurricane glass and a reinforced body make the van as durable as a classic Sherman tank. The shell is insulated against electricity due to downed power lines. The worst danger would come from toppling trees and flying debris.

"This is nuts," DJ says.

"Don't talk about my nuts," Leo zings.

DJ ignores the comment. "The university would suspend us indefinitely if they knew we were out in this shit." DJ doesn't look like he necessarily regrets disregarding regulation.

"Yeah. Professor Previn specifically grounded the beast. She said it's too dangerous to be out here. But what's science without a little danger?"

"Optics and photonics, as a rule, specifically *avoid* danger."

So he says, but DJ has a devious grin. Leo knows damn well he's imagining himself in an Indiana Jones fedora. Racist asshole's probably picturing Leo as Short Round.

"I can't see through this downpour," DJ complains.

"The beast has assisted navigation," Leo explains. "It uses radar and cameras to help steer her. You should appreciate the use of optics in saving our asses."

The rain washes over them in waves. Sometimes, they couldn't see any more than a few inches in front of their faces, the wash running over the windshield blinding them. Other times, the rain abates for a moment and the lightning lights the night, showing trees bent precariously or already toppled—roofs ripping at the edges, waving like shingled hands in the wild wind—the occasional human appears here and there, outside, surveying the damage to their property or somehow trying to get from here to there—stranded motorists left as castaways along the metropolitan street, stuck right in the middle of millions of residents yet unable to safely traverse even the short distance to take shelter from the storm. DJ doesn't stop to help anyone, and Leo doesn't suggest any different.

There are no emergency vehicles out on the streets. All emergency services have been suspended as the storm, against all precedent, ramps up in intensity. There may be a mandatory curfew, but no one bothers to enforce it.

"What the hell are we looking for, Galileo?"

DJ never calls him by his full name. Was it a sign of respect for coming out in this badass storm?

Leo fiddles with the instruments in the back. Sensors measure air pressure, the concentration of heavy oxygen isotopes, as well as connectivity to the NHC aircraft in conjunction with a fleet of independent drones also assessing the storm. Leo stares at a computer model of Hurricane Cheshire. The thing is nearly as big as the entire Florida peninsula. The eye sits several miles off the Space Coast, staring west. Looking at the frightened prey, millions of frail victims waiting inland. Leo studies the whirling patterns in reds and greens, moving counterclockwise in an intimidating hypnotic glare.

"This is something else," Leo mumbles. "This isn't like anything. Ever."

"Fucking global warming."

The aberrations resembling tentacles on the instruments in his labs are still there. But they aren't stationary shadows that stay offshore near the eye. They keep moving. Stretching. Like vines creeping out across Florida, snakes slithering closer and closer to Orlando. Some thinner strands have even already infiltrated the city, like the shoots of strawberry runners pioneering outward from the main patch. Leo stares at the nearest tentacle and plots a course—he needs to see one up close.

7.5"

[Edd]

Two dozen are crammed inside the small shop called Lighthouse Coffee. The aroma of the French roast permeates the interior, reminding Edd of his mother. She drinks three cups a day, two creams, no sugar, in her favorite mug that reads "I already have two sugars," with faded pictures of Eddale and his sister Claudelle from when they were preteens. His mother still uses it and washes it every day.

The people surrounding him are all wet and smell like soggy socks, a stale, putrid stink of old people's locker rooms. Maybe Ratboy had gotten out of this situation luckier than Edd had, sucked away by Mother Nature and sucking at the teat of the hereafter.

Edd goes to the front door and stands beside the one other person in the store with whom he cares to exchange any words. She's pretty enough, at least, and dry. She's dressed in a cute, little barista outfit with a coffee-brown apron. Her hair is pulled back into a sanitary bun, and she wears a co-ed UCF shirt from the college. Glasses make her look smart, but let's face it... She's working in a coffee shop, so...

"There's something out there," the barista says. "In the rain."

"Yeah, the wind's blowing all kinds of shit around. Maybe we should step back from the glass windows."

"I'm not talking about the wind. There's something else out there."

"Anyone foolish enough to navigate this nightmare deserves whatever's coming for him."

"Not someone," the barista insists. "Some *thing*."

The light from the coffee shop's sign shines feebly but remains the brightest beacon along the block. The barista told the crowd the owner had insisted on installing the big generator out back after the last hurricane—"We're going to be the last ones closed in the next storm and the first ones open. Folks need coffee in a time like this." Now the Lighthouse emits the only remaining light left up or down the boulevard.

"Maybe you should douse the exterior lights," Edd suggests.

"Would you rather see or not see?" the barista asks, and it seems like a question more existential than explicit.

Edd shrugs.

He stares out the window, everything beyond blurred by the constant precipitation. The Lighthouse Coffee sign barely illuminates beyond the boulevard. When the rainfall abates a bit, he can see the flooded street and the junkyard of abandoned cars half-submerged in the rising waters. Edd spots trees toppled by gale-force winds. Then something moves. Not some*one*. A thing.

Edd flinches and takes a step back. "What was that?"

"I don't know," the barista whispers as the downpour resumes. "It was there and gone so fast. Now it's hidden behind the rain."

"It seemed like it...slithered."

The barista shrugs. She seems frightened enough that if Edd took her hand to hold it, she might let him. The thrill of touching this pretty woman sends shivers up his spine, already tingling with the trepidation of whatever is out in the precipitation. The circumstances remind Edd of the Quest of the Elderbears, where Jessiqua found romance with an unlikely and unattractive brute named Armadillon, who had saved her from the Cave of Curses. Intense situations sometimes make for strange bedfellows.

Edd ponders the possibility of a backroom stock area, where there may be enough burlap sacks to form a makeshift bed and perhaps a candle or two to set the mood.

"My girlfriend says that pythons have infested the Everglades," the barista reveals.

Edd pumps the brakes on fantasies of doomsday seduction.

"Girlfriend?" As if that's the most important part of the convo.

The barista looks up at him with a scrunched face and squinted eyes. Her glasses magnify her indignation. This generation is offended by everything. Edd feels like he gets the stink eye for farting in public because it contributes to the methane emissions causing global warming rather than anything to do with bad etiquette. Does she release gas in some new, hipper form of flatulence?

"Please tell me you're woke?" she quips with attitude.

"That might be a goddamn nightmare out there, but I sure as hell ain't sleepin'," Edd defends. "I was checkin' if the emphasis was on 'girl' or 'friend'."

"Girl."

"Okay."

"Anyway, she says the pythons are moving farther and farther north. Into Central Florida. Maybe that thing creeping out there in the hurricane is a big-ass snake."

Edd peers again into the blurry bluster of the storm. Shadows suggest fifty-foot monsters, then a cloaked Dracula, then a dancing dinosaur, then a marching army of aliens. Then the slinking snakelike shape slithers by again. The shadows hide the true nature of whatever it is, and suddenly Edd doesn't want to know.

Then a tank arrives. A motherfucking *tank*.

It parks on the sidewalk right in front of Lighthouse Coffee. A college kid in a UCF parka steps out from the passenger side, the quick flash of his face revealing someone nerdy and nervous. Then the driver's side opens, revealing that the badass tank was being driven by a gangling white boy with the dorkiest fucking glasses Edd has ever seen, as poorly paired with the vehicle as if Edd was driving an old Ford F150 4x4.

The two try to run the short distance between the illegal parking space and the coffee shop's front door. For a moment, a gust of wind slows the heavier boy in the parka, and he's moving like he's been put into a slow-motion effect in a movie, Keanu dodging bullets in *The Matrix*. It looks cool as shit. But the other boy, taller and so thin, stops in his tracks, straining against the wind, full-stop against the gale even though he leans 45 degrees forward. It's a delicate dance between manpower, physics, gravity, and the weather. The gangly kid looks caught in suspended animation. Edd wonders if maybe he'll blow away, gone as surely as Ratboy.

Then the wind abates and the movie starts moving forward, both boys finishing the short distance between tank and coffee. The front door opens against the wind, and the two struggle mightily to close the door again before a large tattooed man steps forward to help them, using arms as big around as pythons (is that what Edd had seen out in the shadows? Snakes? Or...?). The two nerds collapse inside in a wet heap on the floor, huffing and puffing like they'd run the Walt Disney World Marathon.

"What in hell were you guys doing out there?" the barista asks the boys.

"Looking for answers," the thin geek manages to wheeze.

"And what did you find?" Edd asks, thinking about the slithering shadows at the edge of his perception.

"Something that shouldn't be here."

8"

[Marcus]

It's 3:00 a.m. Marcus is on his back in his king-sized bed, watching shadows flicker across the ceiling. Allie is beside him, on her side, facing away. She doesn't snore, as if beautiful women never sleep deeply enough to allow even the slightest ugly sound to emanate, although she does make a cute little whistle every once in a while that he isn't sure is a soft exhale through space in her perfect teeth or the most musical gas ever to be passed.

Three candles flicker atop the bureau across the room, ivory sticks with sturdy wicks, driving the darkness back into the farthest corners. Allie had marched Cass right to the guest room farthest away along the endless hallway of the second floor. Now Marcus can't help but think about the sexy Asian a dozen yards away, maybe sleeping naked (she surely hadn't had a pair of PJs packed—and that little pink dress had been soaked through and through), maybe waiting awake for Marcus to sneak down to her room.

The wind moans outside the windows, the rain spattering the glass like fingernails tap-tap-tapping endlessly. This house was built like a fortress. Hurricanes in Central Florida aren't unheard of, so Marcus had specified the most rigorous standards against a storm when they'd built this mansion. The contractor had boasted, "A Cat-6 could come through and the shingles would still stand up like it was a summer's breeze." He doesn't have to worry about the roof blowing off or the walls coming down. The house could withstand even a tornado.

The reason he hadn't immediately retreated here after the press conference instead of following the evacuation notice had been two-fold. Firstly, an elected official defying the governor's order wouldn't sit well with some voters. Especially those who had honored the evacuation notice because they'd had to, while richie-rich Representative Roquefort sat in his fancy, weatherproof, multi-million-dollar bunker. The other reason had been Cassandra Ming. He had liked the idea of spending the night with her at some hotel outside Orlando.

That body…

Marcus eases out of bed, moving in increments to regularly monitor if Allie would awaken. Eventually, he's standing beside their bed, watching his shadow, created by the flickering candles, dance over his fiancée. She remains as still as a plastic doll. She might have been a sculptor's idea of perfection rather than a real woman. Marcus creeps across the room, plush carpet conspiring to mask his escape in this midnight escapade. The door opens silently, oiled hinges as culpable in this caper as the carpet. He slips out of their bedroom successfully, adept as any goddamn cat burglar.

He moves down the hall and away from any light source, the shadows deeper and able to conceal darker deeds. Marcus listens to the storm beyond the walls, a constant thrum, like the mansion is a secret super-villain's lair located behind a waterfall. Certainly, there are eviler souls in the world than Marcus Roquefort, but someone with stronger scruples might wonder if the constant bass is the soundtrack to his impending moral doom. Instead, Marcus is focused on impending fornication.

He reaches the guest bedroom located at the end of the hall. Marcus turns the knob. As he's touching the brass fixture, he starts to feel a vibration through the palm of his hand. At first, he wonders if it's his electric yearning for sex with some stranger, but then he realizes it's the house shuddering under the assault of the hurricane. Built to withstand extreme inclement weather, it instead feels like the death shudder of something frail finally on the verge of expiration.

Marcus dismisses his concern. They built his bunker to withstand worse than this weather. He opens the door and sneaks into the room, closing it quietly behind him. He is rigid and ready. The bed in the guest room is a dozen feet away. The only light comes from a single candle flickering at Cass's bedside. He wonders again if Cass is wearing anything. He steps forward, eager to find out.

He sees the little dress hanging over the arm of a chair to dry. He spies a pair of skimpy underwear and a little pink bra in a pile on the floor. She *must* be naked. Marcus stands beside her bed, reaching for her covers, when the sound of Armageddon shakes the mansion to its very foundation, a crash that sounds like all the thunder in the world coming down upon their heads.

Cass sits bolt upright, automatically pulling the blankets up to her chin to cover herself. Her gaze registers brief confusion, roused from sleep in a strange place, then everything overridden by impending danger. Her eyes meet Marcus's, and what exists in her gaze is fear.

"What in the fuck was that?"

Then the house shakes as if shoved; the whole complex is knocked off its foundation. What sort of wind could *move* a strong structure like this? It's as if the hurricane is a storm of impossibility.

Cass leaps out of bed, dragging the blanket with her and wrapping it around herself like a sarong. It ends up displaying her smooth legs up to her inner thigh. Shorter than a miniskirt. Almost short enough for a peek. The world might be ending outside these walls, but Marcus is still a man. He takes a moment to appreciate the brief glimpse of what might've been. Her skin is an even olive tone that shows no tan lines or a single blemish. He would've relished exploring her exotic body.

"Less leering, more evacuating, Roquefort," Cass snaps.

She turns to face away from him and bends over to grab some baggy sweatpants that must've been Allie's from when it was cold last week, two sizes too big to fit the shorter woman. She lets the blanket fall and displays a perfect ass. She pulls on the pants. They hang loosely on boyish hips, whereas Allie would've filled them with curves. Cass adds a sweatshirt hanging from the bedpost. Marcus doesn't even get a glimpse of a side-boob. The sweatshirt features Allie's alma mater from the University of Florida, the mascot alligator smiling from under the school's logo. Cass steps into her sensible flats.

"Your hurricane-proof shelter is proving faulty," Cass says, heading toward the door.

Marcus follows, in pajama pants still tenting out and a t-shirt featuring the Orlando Magic. "I'm not sure that was the storm."

"Did you schedule a bulldozing? It sounded like half your house was ripped aw—"

When Cass opens the bedroom door, a blast of wind and rain soaks them both instantly. The hallway is now a balcony. Marcus blinks, wondering briefly if he's still in bed beside Allie, an erotic dream of coupling with Cass turning into an impossible nightmare. But the bedroom he'd shared with his fiancée is gone. Everything on the west side of where he stands has been demolished.

"My— Uh— Wha—," he stammers. His head can't make sense of what his eyes are seeing. "Allie!"

"Shit," Cass exhales. "Oh, shit."

Marcus stands there. He almost takes a step forward, like he's going to find Allie, even though there's nothing left of that part of the house for her to be in. It's all gone. Half his home was erased, like those pictures one sees of tornadoes that took away this house and left the next. Marcus's house is ripped right down the middle. And every stick and scrap of debris from the missing section is gone like some giant vacuum cleaner had sucked away everything that had been here a moment ago.

"Allie," he whispers, a soft, short eulogy.

Then Cass has her hand over his. Pulling him along. Toward the stairs to their right. Through the driving rain coming down *inside* the house. Against the gale-force winds blowing along the hallway. Each step splashes in water pooled on the travertine tile steps. Then they get to the garage, still intact, and Cass picks out the brand-new Cadillac

Escalade. She jumps into the driver's seat.

Marcus stands there for a moment. He stares at the door between the house and the garage. He should go back to see if Allie somehow survived. He should at least check on the woman he'd intended to marry. If there's a chance she survived... Marcus checks where Cass is on the scale of feeling like a rescuer, and she puts the Escalade in low as she glares at him.

"Get in or step back," she says.

Marcus gets in.

8.5"

[Renata]

Renata's leg aches, her mind reels, and something turns inside her belly. It might be nerves as she considers what's out there. Or it might be something *in* here, right under her belly button. She isn't sure what's worse. Ren wishes with all her soul she'd scheduled the goddamn procedure for earlier in the morning. She could maybe deal with being impaled in the leg and the mystery of disappearing buildings if she didn't have to think about still being pregnant. The near future is frightening and full of pain, and the far future isn't any fucking better.

She has dreams of being a powerful badass executive, but how do those dreams fit into this nightmare?

How can the future even remotely resemble what she thought it was going to be?

They're hiding out in some little hotel called the Lullaby Lodge. They've huddled in a small apartment the girl called the innkeeper's quarters. She said her name is Amaris. Robert and Amaris stare out a window into the storm. They're talking back and forth, but Renata has more important things to think about. She had been at a clinic earlier to get something cut away and they'd canceled on her. Now she's been cut anyway, and she still needs a doctor to sew her back up. She doesn't need a medical degree to know if she doesn't get this taken care of soon, it'll get infected and she'll have a problem worse than what she had when she woke up this morning.

Robert arrives at her side. "We decided we need to keep moving."

"*You* decided? You think I'm going to leave my fate in the hands of some cheating prick and a clueless teenager?"

"We didn't decide for you," Robert snaps. "Your ass can stay and stare down the fucking storm. If you think you're gonna be safe here, you have shelter and food and a bunch of other tenants. Stay if you wanna stay."

"You'd leave me behind?"

"I don't know you. I don't owe you a damn thing."

"Just like you didn't owe that other woman you ditched back in that hotel. The building that *disappeared*?"

Robert's eyes narrow. He isn't the dangerous black man he wants to portray. He's another neutered brother. Renata wishes she could say the same about that son of bitch she'd spent the weekend with down in the Keys.

Robert looks at the teenage girl staring out the window. She is tense and intense, like she's standing watch, prepared to spy something dangerous inside the storm. Robert glances at his phone. Renata can see there's no signal. Robert meets Renata's eyes one last time. She sees fear.

"Stay or go, I don't care. But whatever took that hotel and everyone in it? I'm not waiting for it to come back."

"It was the storm," Renata states. "A twister or a gust of hurricane wind or something."

"There was something else inside the storm," Robert says, sounding sure.

"Let's go," Amaris says. "Please."

Renata exhales loudly and struggles to get to her feet. She's wearing a pair of baggy beach pants the caretaker had left behind when she fled the place, the only thing in the drawers that would fit Ren without rubbing against her wound. "How are we getting out of here? Stealing a car?"

"I have an Outback parked in the lot," Amaris says. "If it isn't underwater."

Robert contemplates and nods. "It might sit high enough off the road so we won't get waterlogged if we drive carefully and avoid washed-out intersections."

Robert and the teenager help Ren get back downstairs. They stand in front of the glass door entrance to the Lullaby Lodge. Amaris points in the general direction of the Outback as Robert props up Renata. They wait for a break in the storm, like racehorses in their blocks ready for the signal. Outside, the city resembles the inside of a washing machine, water swirling and swishing, blasting and blinding. The wind whips across the world against the backdrop of wet. Then, a lull. And they go.

Robert gets into the driver's seat, and Amaris helps Renata to the front passenger door. Amaris gets in behind her. The wind rocks the vehicle back and forth, and Renata feels like she is being jostled by the crowd at a Beyoncé concert. The wind wails around them, certainly no song, the sound ominous and haunting instead of beautiful and inspiring.

"This was a bad idea."

"Staying put was a good alternative?" Robert asks. "Didn't you see that an entire hotel disappeared?"

"I don't know what happened to that building," Ren says, "but I can sure as hell see what's going to happen to this little Outback."

"Hold on," Robert said. "We're getting out of here."

The Outback fords a deep gulf of stormwater as it exits the hotel parking lot, avoiding a stalled Honda abandoned in the middle of the road and dodging a toppled elm tree blocking two-thirds of the avenue. Robert leans forward so his nose is inches from the windshield, wipers working overtime to assist in his ability to navigate. The headlamps penetrate a few feet in front of them—Renata watches his feet paddle the brakes and gas back and forth, two-footed driving for maximum reaction. This is stupid.

"We should've stayed," Renata says.

Then they pass a fire engine standing on end, like a toddler balancing on his head with legs pointed up. Emergency lights paint the darkness and rainfall like some abstract renaissance painting full of bright reds and blues. The truck's hood looks like an accordion, and the engine has been shoved into the front seat; anyone who'd been driving is now a person-pancake. Steam or smoke issued from the crumpled remains of the front end. The wheels still turned, evidence of the recentness of the wreckage. There are no signs of survivors as Robert rolls by.

"What the absolute fuck?" Renata asks.

The flashing lights catch something large and dark flying overhead through the night, like a pterodactyl arrived from the prehistoric past diving down to snag some prey. Renata reacts, flinching away from the flying form. Then the shadow hits a pylon Renata hadn't even seen until the object explodes against the concrete column. It was a car, and it had sailed right over the Outback like a daredevil doing a stunt.

"What's going on?" Amaris cries.

"There's an overpass," Robert says as they roll between the pylons. "Above us. But the bridge is out."

They pass another smashed vehicle, this time a police car embedded in an embankment; it had landed on its roof, crushed, most of the lights smashed except for one blue strobe weakly penetrating the darkness and precipitation. If anyone had survived, they're trapped behind doors that aren't going to open ever again.

"There could be survivors," Amaris says through tears that hadn't stopped since they'd gotten into the car.

"If we stop here, we could have the next vehicle that tumbles off the overpass land right on us," Robert warns.

"Keep moving," Renata says. She isn't ready to die to be some fool hero.

They drive on, into the storm, forging ahead and leaving the carnage in the rearview mirror. Renata can't help wondering—what took out the bridge? There had been no concrete debris or rubble from a demolished overpass, only falling cars spilling over the edge. Behind them, Renata hears an explosion, another car falling off the precipice of the overpass, and is relieved they didn't stop and become the next victims.

There are two kinds of folks in a situation like this, the heroes and the survivors. Renata plans on surviving.

9"

[Rabe]

"What?" sobs the teenage girl in the backseat. "What hap—hap—happened to the bridge?"

"This is a hurricane, kid," Renata answers. "Shit gets ruined."

Renata doesn't sound like she believes her own tough-bitch b.s. Her voice wavered a bit. Because what the hell *had* happened to that bridge? Robert has never seen anything like that. And he has seen the aftermath of his fair share of tornadoes working for the insurance company up in Nebraska, a white-collar job in no way resembling a rapper on the verge of superstardom. But Carla would never have slept with a buttoned-up State Farm rep from Omaha. Now Carla isn't going to sleep with anyone else ever again.

Where was the debris? The overpass was gone—the remnants of concrete pillars and asphalt surface should have been littered all over the area, potential obstacles strewn across the roadway. Like the Rivington (where he'd expected to spend all weekend naked with Carla), it had simply disappeared. There hadn't been sections of the hotel's roof scattered in the street or a resilient wall still standing here or there—the structure had been gone all the way down to the foundation. Like an invisible demolition crew had moved in and torn it apart brick by brick at superspeed.

What the fuck is going on?

This is a hurricane, kid. Shit gets ruined.

True. But this was more like shit getting *removed*.

Robert feels real terror, a stark fear beyond the natural apprehension of facing a fierce storm. This is something more than a hurricane.

"Check my phone service," Robert tells Renata.

"You want to call nine-one-one? You think someone's going to save our asses?"

He exhales a hiss. He wants to make one phone call. To hear her voice one last time. Tell her how he feels about her. That he's so sorry for being gone. She thinks he's on a business trip, and now he's going to die before he tells her the truth of it. But Robert wants the chance to tell his wife and kids he loves them.

"You wanna check for service or you wanna drive?" he snaps.

Renata sighs and checks his phone on the console between them. She shakes her head as if confirming what absolutely anyone would already know. She doesn't appear apprehensive in the least. Renata seems sure of where they are headed. Robert doesn't have the first fucking clue.

"Try the radio," Robert says. "See if there's any news about this crazy weather."

Weather. There's more than that going on, but the teenager in the backseat is already losing her mind. Robert's daughter is ten, and he feels he owes it to his baby-girl to treat Amaris with the same protective Daditude as he would his own child.

Renata turns through the stations, the digital scanner stopping at static, then static, then more static. Finally, something on the airwaves on the AM dial.

"—gory 3 by morning. Sustained winds of 80 miles per hour are being reported off the coast of Titusville. Bands of wind and rain continue to batter Central Florida. The hurricane's effects extend across the entirety of the peninsula. Take shelter immediately as catastrophic conditions will impact more the five million Floridians over the next few hours. This is the biggest thing you may ever see, folks, so get to safety bef—"

Robert reaches over and turns it off before the announcer terrifies Amaris any more. Outside, the wind howls, gusts rocking the Outback to and fro like a cradle. Debris, oftentimes dangerous, flies by, appearing out of the veil of a downpour without warning and illuminated briefly in the headlights, then disappearing back into the darkness—big break-aways of billboards, pinwheeling pieces of a porch, spinning sections of signs sailing by like flying saucers, rocketing remnants of rigid rail and flying fence posts. What they could see might be worse than anything they could hear.

"What the hell was that?" Renata yelps as something moves in Robert's peripheral vision.

She grips the dash like they're in a roller coaster car reaching the apex of the first drop. Renata's eyes are as big and round as golf balls, her expression as animated as if she'd seen something impossible, like a zombie stomping around at the edges of the blinding downpour and depthless darkness.

"What what?" Robert demands.

"What did you see?" Amaris asks from the backseat, voice cracking like she's about to start bawling again.

"I don't know," Renata mumbles. "Something…slithering."

"Fucking Florida gators," Robert says. He glances in the rearview mirror at the teenager who isn't much older than his own daughter. "Excuse the language."

"Sometimes a good fuck is all you got," Renata says.

A good fuck was all Robert had gotten out of this trip. He'd come to Orlando to cheat on his wife. To spend a weekend with Carla. He'd acted all Rabe and Li'l Angeni. But he's just an insurance salesman from Nebraska. With a wife of fifteen years and two kids. He hadn't rapped anything but his knuckles going door-to-door, selling policies to people who needed a safety net. Where's Robert's safety net? He feels like he's in free-fall without anything to catch him.

"There's something out in the storm," Renata hisses. "I caught a glimpse. Like big tree roots wriggling and growing longer. Or albino tentacles straight out of Lovecraft."

"Love-who?"

"Don't a brother ever read a goddamn book?"

"That shit puts ideas in your head, lady. Like being afraid of a home invasion after watching a scary movie. You're seeing what someone suggested once upon a time, made up out of darkness and raindrops."

"I saw what I saw."

Robert tries to look and drive at the same time, avoiding obstacles and searching out aberrations. Something had disassembled the Rivington and erased all evidence of his evening with Carla. Maybe the storm wanted to give Robert a clean slate? Erase the sins he had committed in Orlando and let him start anew? Perhaps his family never needs to know what happened here in the hurricane.

Something slithers in the street, a white strand mostly obscured by the water covering the road. Robert glimpses it briefly, passing right where his high beam is pointed, like the monster in the muck inside the giant garbage compactor from the oldest *Star Wars* movie. He saw *something*, imagining a telescoping alien neck popping up with an eye at the end, blinking. Then the Outback runs over it, thick enough to throw Robert against the seatbelt and cause him to lose his grip on the steering wheel. The vehicle turns, slides, and hits the submerged curb while slipping sideways. The Outback tips precariously at forty-five degrees, teeters back and forth on two wheels, deciding whether it will settle back on all four tires or continue over onto its side. Then a gust of hurricane wind decides it, pushing the Outback over onto the passenger side door.

"Oof," Renata exclaims, holding herself steady against the roof as the side window explodes in shards of safety glass.

Water rushes in a foot deep, even along the sidewalk. Amaris panics, hollering, unbuckling, and climbing out of the backseat door, up and out of the vehicle. Robert is cinched in the seat sideways, pulling at the belt and trying to pop the latch. He finally releases the restraint and helps Renata get loose. She's sputtering and spitting in the rising floodwater. He boosts her out of the Outback and climbs up, both instantly soaked to the bone by the downpour.

Robert can't help thinking about the thing he had seen slithering through the water. What had Renata called it? Something out of Lovecap?

"Amaris?" he calls out against the wild wind, standing beside Renata on the sidewalk and steadying himself against the tipped vehicle. "Kid?"

He searches around, seeing nothing but darkness and whipping rain and Renata and the roof of the Outback in any direction. He dreads glimpsing the white tentacles. Instead, it's storm everywhere. Amaris is gone.

9.5"

[Cass]

The Escalade powers north through the storm, constantly rerouting to circumvent the numerous roadways becoming entirely impassable around the greater Orlando area. Cass cannot see signs along the road (green glimpses obscured through the rainfall and darkness), so she doesn't exactly know where she is. The routes out of this hellish nightmare twist and turn as she encounters flooded intersections and entire underwater avenues. She recognizes some of the markers leading her into APK, and the occasional lull in the weather affords her a glimpse of storefronts. She can confirm her location as somewhere in Apopka. Looks more like Atlantis. She's close to home, but she isn't stopping for anything. Not even her things. She's driving until this hurricane is in the rearview mirror. Time to leave this damn life behind before she doesn't have a life to leave.

Florida has been nothing but a nightmare since Cass had moved here for college and stayed to start her *Blahblahblahg*. The heat and humidity and hurricanes, sprinkled with never knowing when you might cross an alligator. The place is a damn swamp. She's moving back north. Immediately.

Then there's this asshole. Marcus Roquefort is supposed to be the next United States Senator. Cass had been planning to help him and move to D.C. to cover him exclusively, like Lois Lane and Superman. Then this storm hit. Now, Marcus is curled up in the passenger seat, crying like a little bitch because Hurricane Cheshire wrecked his house and killed his fiancée. Leaders don't waffle in the face of great strife— they rise and take a stand. Marcus is a punk.

Cass fears the vehicle may tip over. Marcus had assured her the Escalade was reinforced with protective plating to armor against a political attack and is therefore as heavy as a tank. Cass creeps along at five miles an hour. They approach the on-ramp to Route 441 out of Apopka. The highway leads north and away, up past Okefenokee Swamp into Georgia. Once she's out of Florida, Cass will take a hard left turn and aim for the Midwest. No fucking hurricanes in Iowa.

Marcus can come with her or stay behind, she doesn't care. He's along because he got into the Escalade before she could escape. Otherwise, Cass would've left his ass behind. If he tells her he wants out, she'll pull aside and let him go. But the Escalade is going to stay in her possession until she gets away from Hurricane Cheshire. It isn't stealing so much as *commandeering*.

Water covers the on-ramp to Route 441, and no physical markers denote how deep the puddle is. Cass could go around, finding another route north. Or the Escalade could handle the small lake between her and a straight shot out of here.

Cass drives forward, too eager for escape. The highway is too damn close to turn around. The Escalade *has* to be good enough to get her through. She needs to get out of here. She needs to get away.

The engine stutters as the water rises over the wheels. Deeper. Deeper. Too damn deep. The engine chokes, struggles, and ultimately dies. Drowned.

"Aww, damn," Cass swears.

"Are you fucking kidding me?" Marcus cries. "Why the hell didn't you go around?"

"Why the hell didn't you grow a pair of balls and drive yourself if you want to criticize my driving, you big pussy," Cass snaps. "You'd either still be curled up in a ball on the floor of your guest bedroom or ripped to shreds by the hurricane if it wasn't for me. I saved your ass, Marcus."

"We're stuck on the road with the biggest mother of all hurricanes coming, and we're probably going to die. Excuse me if I don't give thanks."

"I'll settle for giving me a break. We either ride it out or we see what's the closest building that doesn't look ready to blow down."

"If it ripped apart my mansion, then there isn't anywhere that's safe."

"Well, 'safe' sure as shit isn't sitting in this Escalade," Cass says. "I'm not the type to wait for a shining knight to show up on a white stallion, Princess."

She opens the door and the driven rain drenches her immediately. Water deeper than the bottom of the door rushes in and soaks her half-way up her calves. Marcus lifts his feet like a schoolmarm hiking her skirts to avoid being splashed by a puddle. Fucking *princess*. She stares in-to the stormy night and there is nothing—depthless, indefinite, dangerous.

She glances back at Marcus. "Coming or staying?"

"You'd leave me here?"

"Like you left Allie."

Cass sees the sting of the words. She'll go alone if she doesn't have another choice, but she doesn't want to. She's afraid of being out there by herself. There seems to be something behind the veil of wind and rain, something watching, something *waiting*. If the one option ends up that she faces it alone, then she will, but she'd rather have something she could throw in the way if she encounters something hunting her in the darkness.

"You're such a bitch."

"That's right," Cass agreed. "Now, come on, Princess."

Marcus crawls across the front seats of the Escalade and exits behind her through the driver's side door. The headlights barely pierce the storm. Cass squints against the driving rain, like peering through a waterfall and trying to see what's behind. The deluge remains relentless, unable to be wiped away or shielded effectively. It's as if the whole world is trying to become underwater, graduating by degrees into fully water-logged. Cass wonders how much more saturated the air can become before she'll need gills rather than a mouth.

Marcus whines behind her in a constant spew, his words and meaning drowned out by the drum of rain and wail of the wind. Still, the tone tells her he's complaining about being stranded and wet pants and what in the world is behind the impenetrable precipitation. Gills might be okay. At least Marcus couldn't make noise through gills.

He grabs her hand and holds it tightly. A few hours ago, he'd wanted Cass to fuck him. Now, he wants Cass to save him. Men. They always want something.

The Escalade's engine might have flooded, but the battery still worked. As Cass and Marcus wade away from the stalled vehicle, the taillights paint the dark and the deluge a scarlet red, a weary warning signal for striking out from the limited safety of the SUV. The world grows darker with each step away from the Escalade. With the unrelenting rainfall obscuring distance and definition and the susurrus sound of water drowning out all other ambient noise, it's like descending into the ocean in a submersible, leaving behind all traces of the surface world.

Intermittent lightning flashes often enough to give Cass a glimpse of the world and prevent her from walking into a wall or stumbling over a downed tree. A gust of wind drives her back every third or fourth step like she's doing some strange hurricane version of the Hokey Pokey. Marcus yanks on her hand as insistently and incessantly as a toddler who must find a bathroom. If he needs to pee, then the drenched fool needs to piss his pants. Nobody would know the difference.

Lightning momentarily illuminates Marcus and he is pointing into the darkness. Cass pauses, stares. His mouth gets within an inch of her ear and she can finally hear him shouting over the wail of wind and sound of rain. "I saw something," he hollers.

Cass stares, trying to sort the waves of rainfall and the distorted shadows of the world beyond, revealed in great flashes of lightning during the occasional lull in the otherwise unrelenting precipitation. The world is in constant motion, probably no different from standing underneath Niagara Falls, inundated with water and water and water. The wind howls like a kaiju wolf. The whole of reality has become the storm.

And Marcus saw something in the storm.

Cass stares and tries to separate downpour and darkness from something else. A large object looms nearby. She can *feel* it. Maybe a building? Maybe construction equipment? Maybe a small cluster of stalled tractor-trailers?

Then it moves. *Slithers.* Like the tail of an alligator that would have to be as big as a Home Depot or a length of a snake the size of a subway train. Impossible. Cass pisses herself because who will know the difference? Who the hell knows what she saw?

10"

[Carlos]

Carlos finds himself waist-deep along a side street in an Orlando satellite city called Apopka. This metropolis and their goddamn cutesy local names—places like Mount Dora and Dr. Phillips, and even a town called Christmas. He longs for the beach and familiar places like Bethune and Smyrna and Daytona. Instead, he's wading through filth and sludge and floating flotsam in the pouring rain because he doesn't want to seek the shelter and the company of other pathetic survivors.

He'd rather chance the maelstrom of the supernatural hurricane.

Even miles and miles inland, Carlos feels the presence of something else in the water. The floodwaters extend from here to the coast. The whole peninsula is drowning. High ground in Florida is rare indeed, and the low ground has already filled up. The hurricane raging off the Space Coast is camouflaging the real threat out at sea.

Carlos could sense there's something *else* is out there, like someone may notice a lump in their neck or an anomaly in their skin tone— there's cancer in the storm.

Lightning flashes in the night and the rain abates long enough for him to see across one side of the narrow street to the other. He is in a residential area, affluent homes on either side. Newer vehicles sit in driveways slightly elevated from the street, yet floodwater already creeps higher than the tires. Spanish moss gives the shaking silhouette of the trees lining the submerged road the shape of hoary guardians standing sentry along the avenue. Dark streetlamps illuminate nothing. The neighborhood appears abandoned by human residents, but something else looks poised to move into the vacancies.

Carlos counts a dozen gators swimming along the street, like reptilian traffic following the prescribed route through suburbia.

Shitshitshit.

Carlos has communed with manta rays, survived the stings from jellyfish and Portuguese man o' wars, and come face to face with a dozen different sharks in all his years, but he's always been a saltwater kind of guy. He doesn't know alligators. He's never even seen one up close. Now, he's swimming with a whole congregation of the reptiles. He's surrounded by them.

They're all moving westward, away from the ocean. As if they know as well as Carlos that something is coming. Something is wrong with the world. Nature has been broken. But one rule busted may lead to others. Carlos always believed if you left nature alone, nature would do the same. But perhaps now these gators would take a greater interest in a human. Maybe they want a snack for the road. Carlos might be a tasty drive-thru meal for deadly predators. Or a *swim*-thru. He's invading their world.

What's invading the whole world? Carlos believes there's something in the hurricane. Big. Bad.

Carlos remains calm. Panic is always the quickest way to calamity. No one ever got out of a jam by flailing around hopelessly and crying like a baby. No one waits nearby to swoop in for a rescue. His best solution is to keep steady and move forward. Be one with the gators. An eclectic group of evacuees with a common goal—survival.

He ponders climbing on his surfboard and getting his ass out of the water. Carlos pictures one animal with a wide mouth coming right for his backside, taking off one cheek with the snap of jaws. He resists jumping out of the water. That might seem unnatural. Gators don't ride boards. They're one with the water. Carlos knows how to be one with the water.

The lightning flashes again, and now there are even more beasts. One glides by not three feet from where Carlos moves forward. The cold and dangerous eyes are focused on something other than easy prey. Then the world plunges back into darkness, the ambient light of night one step away from absolute black. Carlos cannot see the gators. They might be right next to him or surrounding him or one might, at this very moment, have its mouth wide open, ready to take a bite.

He keeps going, his feet finding purchase on the pavement three feet under the surface of the floodwaters.

Carlos still has a hunting knife strapped to his ankle in case of salt-water attacks. He was always ready for sharks. He may need to use the weapon against a rogue gator.

If one attacks, the rest will follow.

Feeding frenzy.

He doesn't reach for the knife. Gators don't have knives (except for a mouthful of sharp edges). He continues to be one with the congregation of alligators.

It's better than going back to being a part of the congregation of fellow humans in the church with the faithless priest. People will eat you alive as soon as any alligator.

Carlos does gradually steer slightly diagonal. His board scrapes roughly off the hide of what he can assume is a gator's back. A tail whips him in the hip once, a thick slap that almost sends him under the water. Something rubs against his right hand, and it comes up with skinned knuckles—he keeps it above the surface and hopes the rainwater doesn't run the leaking blood too much into his surroundings. He doesn't know if gators sense blood in the water like sharks, but he prefers to avoid a zoological lesson here along the flooded freshwater streets of suburban hell.

His foot kicks a curb, and Carlos steps up onto the boulevard. He ascends a steady incline away from the street, away from the river of floodwater. When lightning lights up the world once more, he's standing in front of a porch already poached by an eight-foot-long reptile. The gator stares at Carlos as the blades of light dance from cloud to cloud to cloud above. After several long seconds of a staring contest where neither opponent budges one iota, the two are plunged again into darkness. Carlos half-excepts a whiff of gator breath right before it chomps off his face.

Instead, he retreats away from the porch and makes his way blindly to the house next door. Some landscape lights powered by solar batteries are about ready to die after a long night. The lights act as a feeble landing strip to Carlos and his board, and Carlos collapses into a hammock hanging from two porch posts under the eaves. The wind blows raindrops even under the overhang, but it also rocks Carlos back and forth, and he finally succumbs to the exhaustion of this day.

As he opens his eyes one last time against the tide of slumber, the world crackles with brightness from the electrical storm raging above. Gators fill the streets for rush hour, all filtering down into this one neighborhood in Orlando, all trying to get away from whatever is behind the veil of the storm. Except for Carlos and his neighbor gator. They're done running. They understand there's no escaping. Like any disaster, survival will be random and determined not by resistance, but only by happenstance.

Carlos takes his stance.

Naptime.

At least he found a hammock.

Then he sleeps, and his sleep is plagued by gators and sharks and hurricanes and disasters. On any other night, that would have been the nightmare. But tonight, it's a pleasant escape from what's *really* out in the storm.

10.5"

[Amaris]

How in the heck can I get lost in the space of one single second? Amaris wonders.

Amaris had climbed out of her Outback after the wind tipped it over. She'd had to pull herself up out of the rear driver's side window and drop down along the Outback's roof. She took a right turn as soon as she'd stepped onto the pavement. It should've been easy to wade around the vehicle, putting the Outback between her and the wind, a right turn, and she'd be there. But the damage to the vehicle had shorted out the headlights, and the meager ambient light of the urban world did little to light her way. Wild lightning hindered her sense of direction and made the world dreamlike and stuttering. Amaris turned the corner of the tipped vehicle and the wind knocked her backward, feet going out from under her as she twisted to keep from cracking her tailbone. She landed on hands and knees in water so deep she dunked her face in the turbid puddle. Amaris managed to get to her feet, spitting and sputtering, to fight the wind back to the Outback. She must've gotten turned around because she waded ten feet forward without finding anything but wind and rain and floodwater.

Amaris tried to backtrack and ended up even more off course.

Wherever Robert and Renata had remained, Amaris felt like she was getting farther and farther away. But the hurricane winds wouldn't allow her to stand in one place until someone found her. Amaris had to keep moving. She might've been standing in the middle of a road where the occasional crazy escapee still drove around trying to evacuate Orlando, or in a floodplain that could turn into a raging waterway at any given moment. Amaris had to push onward.

So now Amaris finds herself alone in the dark, in the storm, the wind like rough hands shoving her to and fro in a mosh pit. She stumbles repeatedly, each time worrying the storm surge will wash her away. The pelting rain numbs her flesh. Somewhere ahead, a light source must be running off a generator, creating enough brightness to stave off the blinding rain and suffocating night. Like a thirsty man lost in the desert to a lush oasis, Amaris wades in the direction of the source of salvation. Her other option is to stand defenseless in darkness.

Her toe finds a curb and she sighs in relief. She steps up off the street. Safe. Or, at least, safer. Until...

Something moves beyond the curtain of driving rain. Amaris recalls what Renata had said she saw in the Outback— *I caught a glimpse. Like big tree roots wriggling and growing longer. Or albino tentacles.*

Amaris stands perfectly still. She stares, trying to see, not wanting to see.

She imagines a python, an alligator. Could a shark have swum all the way inland in overland flooding? Maybe dropped from the sky like a sharkicane? Or a hyper-evolved swamp monster like this mutated storm, something unnatural and impossible. Amaris should never have watched so many freaking horror movies. She blames her parents for her terror. She blames them for being out here alone and in danger. Everything's their fault!

She decides waiting to get smashed by a toppled tree or sucked away by a sentient tornado isn't going to solve her problem. There's a glow in one direction that might be the moon or a headlamp or an alien ship. It's something other than the dark. Amaris wades forward toward the source of the light. When nature wreaks havoc and shows its awesome power, all the intellect and advancement of human history is reduced to the instinct equal to a moth to a flame.

The marquee seems to float in the sky like an advertisement for Heaven, and Amaris wonders for a moment if she has died and even the hereafter is franchised. Maybe it'll be her name up in lights, star of the show, Best Actress in the Afterlife awards. As she moves closer, the glow resolves into a sign, the beckoning beacon indicating a coffee shop called Lighthouse Coffee. She's close enough to see faces peering out from behind the front plate-glass window. She's nearly close enough to grab the front entrance handle when the rushing water sweeps her feet right out from under her. She falls into the flood again.

Amaris stutters and splashes in the floodwaters, unable to get her legs under her, a strong current sweeping her down the sidewalk and away from the Lighthouse Coffee sign like this was a flume at Blizzard Beach. She kicks and flails, forgetting everything she ever knew about swimming and surviving. How many times had she swum out around a rip current? So many hours spent swimming off the coast of New Smyrna forgotten as she finds herself in danger of drowning along an urban boulevard.

Amaris grabs the metal post of a sign. She can't manage to get her footing. Finally, her tennis shoes grip some concrete and she gets some leverage against the raging tide, standing with the signpost still firmly gripped in her fists. Spitting like a drowning rat, she stands up and holds firm against the strong flush of floodwater.

Amaris feels blind; nearly everything in every direction has been erased by the night and the storm. Wind whips waves of rainwater, sweeping them horizontally, as if the rain is coming from every direction instead of only from above. If she ever wondered what a saucer felt like in a dishwasher, she has proof positive at this moment.

Lightning flashes in the distance, lighting the world for one instant before plunging it again into black the next. Thunder rolls. Lightning flashes again, illuminating the unending water before leaving her blind once more. Over and over. The rain abates in the space of a few dark seconds, as if someone has popped a giant umbrella directly overhead.

As the lightning turns the night into day again—a series of bright fingers across the sky—Amaris sees half a block in every direction. A McDonald's is right next to her, nearby, a bank, and then a barbershop. Jackknifed in the flooded street beside her is an eighteen-wheeler, the trailer advertising for a Publix grocery store. Not six feet away stands a mailbox, squat and blue along the waterlogged sidewalk. The world seems suddenly regular. Then darkness again.

Long seconds tick and tick.

Renata's words come back in the pitch—*albino tentacles*. Amaris starts to shiver from cold and fear. She shakes violently, so hard she can barely hold on against the strong current trying to pry her free from the anchor of the sign.

Another series of lightning strikes in quick succession, like the flickering flash of a camera snapping a half-dozen pictures. The world stutters in quick blinks. But Amaris realizes the mailbox is gone, swallowed by the raging river of the floodwaters. Gone in the blink of an eye.

Or swallowed by something else.

Then night blankets her. Long moments of darkness. Amaris swears she can feel something in the water, a slithering thing close enough to touch. She holds her breath, trying to stay still, sensing something sinister nearby. Then the lightning flashes on, a bright single strike that gives her three seconds of perfect clarity.

The eighteen-wheeler is gone.

Just—friggin'—disappeared.

Then blackness swallows her like a giant fish surfaced in the floodwater and gulped her down whole, just as the whale had gotten Jonah. She can't see anything at all, as blind as she was at Ryan's last birthday party when she played Pin the Tail on the Furry. Isn't there something in the dark? Something dangerous? Something...*supernatural?*

Thunder rolls, but no lightning precedes it. Impossible.

The world becomes light again—and the bank is gone. Between McD's and the barbershop is a vacant space. Nothing. The whole building disappeared in mere seconds. The greatest heist in history. No. She shakes her head like she can make it go away. Just *no*. It wasn't demolished or blown down or eroded by rain and flood. It's entirely *missing*.

Then Amaris Azmi screams.

11"

[Leo]

Leo had watched the teenage girl lose her footing and get swept away in the current. She had been so close. If she'd been more determined, more careful, more eager to survive. But she'd let nature win, and Hurricane Cheshire had swallowed her up like she was the last donut in the box after a grad-school all-nighter.

"That kid," the slob beside Leo cried out. The grown man had the look of a slovenly adult who still lived in his parents' basement and probably didn't have a steady job. Or any job at all. His skin was the white of a subterranean shut-in, patchy brown facial hair revealing an innate unwillingness to embrace adulthood, a stained shirt advertising anime comics stretched over a wide waistline. Online blogger? At-home transcriptionist? Full-time gamer?

"She wasn't being careful," Leo said. "I think Bambi was steadier as a newborn fawn."

"We need to see if we can do something," the slob suggested. Would he have volunteered if the victim hadn't been young and female? Surely the slug would've let Leo die without batting an eye. Leo refused to be motivated by the relative youth of the victim. He believes they should treat the helpless the same whether they're old and ugly or fresh and new—Leo thinks everyone ought to find their fate.

The slobby bastard then donned a bright yellow raincoat someone had left hanging on a hook by the exit and stepped into knee-high galoshes. He pulled up a rubber hood over his round face, and he looked like a human-sized rubber ducky. A barista seemed impressed with the poor bastard's effort (although she didn't volunteer to accompany him) and passed him over a waterproof flashlight. He exited out into the storm, the first gust almost sending him reeling right into the rush of rainwater that had carried away the timid teen. Then the yellow duck-man disappeared into the veil of heavy rain.

Now Leo turns away from the glass front. He had waited a few minutes for the duck-man to return, surely without the girl. The hurricane is fascinating to watch but dangerous to observe. He isn't going to be able to publish a major scientific paper on the meteorological impossibility he's currently witnessing if a tree comes through the display window and kills him or he's crushed by a hydroplaning Grand Caravan driven by someone who dared to be out in this mess. Besides, he needs to check his readings and record some data.

He finds DJ in the back at a small bistro table where college kids would usually be studying for tests, working on a thesis, or updating a blog. DJ had set up a series of cords interconnecting a laptop to auxiliary hardware, external memory, and enhanced performance. "I've got this thing mainlined to the max," DJ says. "I was able to piggyback on a Fed satellite link and connect to every device they have out there measuring this storm. Although Hurricane Cheshire is eating up recon drones, weather balloons, and data buoys like they're catnip. This storm's a bitch."

Leo studies the screens. The hurricane is still gaining strength off the Atlantic coast. If it moves inland, the devastation to Central Florida will be unprecedented. It'll make Irma and Charlie pale in comparison. Cheshire looks apt to out-fuck any previous destruction. This was going to be *bad*.

"What about the data we collected in the Beast?"

"Uploading and correlating with existing evidence from the other sources," DJ says. "Almost done."

Then the screens update and compensate for additional information. Leo stares at the charts and interactive maps. He points at the shadows stretching across Orlando, extending east from the Space Coast. The same kind of shapes he'd noticed back at the laboratory, now with even more details. A shadow with endless arms. The individual tendrils reaching through the metro area are more defined, fine filaments that might have a thousand separate strands. As Leo watches, he can see them wriggle and reach.

"Two things. What the fuck are those, and how the fuck did this storm come out of nowhere?" Leo asks.

DJ shrugs. "I'm your tech guy. I can optic the hell out of this storm and even pull up sonar data, but I have no idea what I'm looking at. It's like naming countries on a blank map of the Middle East—I ain't your man."

Leo *is* the man. This is what he's always wanted—observation to lead to revelation. Putting together the clues from the past to predict the future. Because you should always be able to see where the road is leading if you know where you've already been. The future isn't random or unknowable but simply inevitable.

"I can rationalize the origins of the storm itself within the confines of science," Leo says, maybe to himself more than DJ. "A perfect conglomeration of conditions to create a meteorological supercell out of nothing. Maybe a manmade effect of rogue experimentation? Has cloud seeding gone nuclear? Climatological evolution mutating in a single cataclysmic event?"

DJ shrugs. Doesn't know and doesn't care to consider.

"But what the hell are these?" Leo asks, tracing the dark tentacles reaching in from the Atlantic.

"Some things you can't measure by instruments other than the peepers God gave you," DJ says.

"God," Leo dismisses. "The only God is information. And you might be right about that part. I've got to get my eyes on whatever these instruments are indicating."

"Live recon?" DJ asks, eyes lighting up like this is a real-life version of one of his video games.

Leo nods. Pulls on his slicker, waterproof boots, and gloves, then grabs his weather-resistant camera. DJ wears some strange shit that almost resembles a wetsuit for SCUBA diving with goggles better suited for skiing and a rubber skullcap Leo's grandmother might use to keep water from poofing her perm. He looks flamboyant and ridiculous. Like the perfect decoy if they happen to run into any renegade predators taking advantage of the floodwaters.

They exit into the hurricane, Cheshire smacking into Leo like a blast of jet exhaust. He stumbles sideways and forward, trying to regain his balance, nearly toppling into the same gutter where he'd watched the girl get swept away a few minutes ago. No rescuers would come rushing out to save a forgettable Asian millennial.

DJ has a fistful of Leo's raincoat, stopping him from a short dive into a shallow stream. Leo gets his balance and nods his thanks. DJ shrugs. Leo points east. They start walking, making their way through the rushing river around their feet. The wind roars around them, the spatter of constant rain like the rush of Niagara Falls in the springtime.

There's no point in talking. The wind and rain are sonically all-consuming, subsuming every other noise. The hurricane has become everything, a behemoth grown to a size that seems to contain its own gravitational force, like a black hole sucking everything into it—sound, light, structures, trees, and vehicles, everything and anything, even people.

Leo pictures those shadowy tentacles showing up on his instruments. What are they? What strange particles in the storm register as unreadable renderings so invasive and ominous? Paleotempestology studies heavy oxygen isotopes—perhaps this is a concentrated manifestation of isotopes resulting from the inexplicable creation of a major hurricane right off the coast of Central Florida? It should be impossible, but impossible is for greater fools than Galileo Enomoto. Impossible is only the most current occurrence science hasn't explained yet.

Four blocks from the coffee shop, DJ holds up a hand like a crossing-guard directing a gaggle of school kids. He taps his ear. He's getting a reading on sonar. Their visual equipment is worthless in the downpour as buckets of rain wash out the electronic screens, but DJ can *hear* the strange things showing up on the sophisticated instruments through his waterproof headphones.

DJ keeps his hand up, palm out, but the hand starts wavering. With his other arm, he points ahead, finger extended, indicating something to Leo. Leo can't see what's through the veil of rain. He can't see what DJ is pointing at in the storm. But Leo can see DJ's expression—and DJ is terrified.

DJ has never shown much emotion before. DJ had never had an expression beyond passivity or looking pissy.

Something beneath the water slithers past Leo's calf. DJ's eyes grow wide. His mouth opens to scream, but DJ is underwater before he makes a sound. Like the swimmer in *Jaws* yanked beneath the surface of the sea by the great white. But DJ doesn't resurface. He's gone. In the blink of an eye. Taken by the storm.

11.5"

[Edd]

The girl had been swept down the street by the raging floodwater. Edd sloshes through water as deep as his knees. What's he doing? He isn't a hero. He isn't a warrior like Jessiqua, who puts herself in harm's way for the greater good. Edd is content to stay in his basement and live life vicariously through an avatar. So why in the hell is he out in a hurricane, risking his ass to save some stupid girl?

Thank God the barista had given him a flashlight with a strap that wears like a headband. Edd needs his hands free to grip the edges and handholds of the storefronts and businesses along the sidewalk. Otherwise, he'd be on his ass and washed away like a turd. Edd turns his head to shine the flashlight left and right. Rain and rain and rain. The powerful beam picks up the occasional reflective sign.

He knows what his mother would say if she knew what he is doing and why he is doing it—she'd call him a pervo and suggest maybe he ought to be on some sort of database for deviants. But he doesn't want to date the girl in danger, even if it turns out she's over eighteen. He doesn't even want a kiss. He wants to be the prince who saves the damsel in distress. Edd wants her to give him the same goo-goo eyes Snow White gave Prince Charming.

What's wrong with wanting to be the hero?

What's wrong is that it's miserable and dangerous and ultimately futile. Online, unfavorable conditions can be overcome by persistence and thumb dexterity, re-spawning and playing hours and hours to make progress. In real life, there's water in Edd's boots, soaking him to the bone, and the wind threatens with every gust to knock him into the street and sweep him to the Everglades.

This might be the stupidest thing he's ever done. He should've stayed put. He's spent the last twenty years in that goddamn basement, and that's where he ought to have planted his big ass through this whole storm. Mom had decided to go out on her own; he ought to have let her live (or die) with her own choices. She's probably sipping tea with Old Tom Tillerman before Mother Nature destroys all of Orlando while Edd wades through a flood, undoubtedly containing wastewater that rises nearly up to his waist.

"Fuck being a hero."

But then the flashlight on his head shines on something moving. For a moment, he imagines some terrible horror. But it's only something terrified. Against all odds (although, to be honest, the water did all run in one direction), he has discovered the lost princess. She doesn't need rescuing, though. She's sitting on the top step of a stoop outside a shuttered law firm. The eaves overhead protect her from the rainwater running in rivers off the roof but does little to restrict the winds blowing rain sideways, more horizontal than vertical.

Edd continues to make his way along the facade of the commercial buildings, grabbing at any handhold as he makes his way along. He finally arrives at the law firm. Edd manages to grab ahold of the handrail and climb the three steps to get himself out of the raging river running along what had once been a sidewalk but is now a flume. She's trying to use a plastic bag from a Publix to shield herself, and she peers out from behind the rippling sack. She squints her eyes against the shine of the flashlight, and Edd takes it off his head, shines it at their feet. The girl appears at once weary and relieved. Certainly, it isn't the unbound joy of being rescued. Because Edd could only offer companionship, not salvation. Of course, he couldn't make a hurricane disappear.

She needs a wizard instead of Prince Charming.

"Do you need help?" Edd shouts over the storm.

She looks up at him like she doesn't understand. Maybe she hadn't heard him over the wail of wind and roar of the rain. But then he realizes she had. And that he hadn't made any sense. There is no help in this situation.

"I saw you get swept away by the water," Edd hollers. "I came to find you."

The girl appears to be unimpressed, maybe even bristling with a little trepidation. She wore the expression of someone pretty and alone who's been cornered by someone who looks like Edd. She might agree with Edd's mom about the deviant database idea.

Edd points back the way he had come. "There are others. Back there."

The girl shakes her head, the wind making the plastic bag try to smother her. "Too dangerous."

"Maybe not for both of us. Together. We can watch out for each other."

He watches as she calculates the danger of some stranger against the horrors of the storm. Finally, the girl nods. She's so young. Edd feels sick about wanting to be her Prince Charming. She needs her Dad, not some douchebag. Maybe a big brother…

"My name's Edd," he says.

"Amaris," she replies, almost inaudible above the wail of wind and grumbles of thunder.

He puts the flashlight back on his head. Edd takes her hand, and she's shaking, scared of the storm and strangers but mostly of being alone.

He takes her back the way he'd come, the rain somehow getting even worse. Edd marks the reflective signs he'd passed coming from the other direction. He recognizes a Dunkin' on the corner, empty and chained up, Edd pawing along the frontage to orient himself along the street.

Then he's attacked. Something barrels out of the storm, and Edd pictures an alligator or zombie or even a Sasquatch. He manages to shove Amaris backward, out of the path of the impending assault. Edd takes the full brunt of the fast predator, bristling against sharp teeth or piercing claws or superhuman strength. He feels his bladder let go, but he's so wet already that the piss doesn't make an ounce of difference. Then he's down, underwater, the attacker atop him.

This is it, he thinks. *The end.* No re-spawn in the real world. Jessiqua would never have been terminated so easily. It's a coward's death. Edd screams like a girl, but the sound is drowned and choked with sludge. The dirty, knee-deep water floods his mouth and tastes like crap. Certainly, there's shit among the flood. He gags, sure he'll either drown in the flood or choke on his vomit.

Then he's up, sputtering, a mix of sewage and maybe his bile. Edd coughs and tries to inhale, getting a face full of rain from above, making him choke all over again. The teenage girl steadies him as he wheezes like an old man—Amaris is the one who fished him out of the drink. Instead of being Prince Charming, Edd has become the princess in need of rescuing.

He feels around for lost limbs or amputated appendages; everything seems accounted for—arms, legs, penis, head. Other than Edd's pissed pants and wounded pride, he seems to have suffered no injury. Then what the hell had attacked him? It had seemed like a swamp monster specifically adapted to the hurricane.

It's a nerd.

The dude who had knocked Edd flat stands on the other side of Amaris. Her shoulder is under his armpit, holding him above the flood. He's in full geek gear. Edd recognizes the Asian as the little creep from the coffee shop who'd seen Amaris get swept away by the flood and had dismissed her certain death as something inevitable.

Well, the geek's inevitable death had been thwarted by the same girl the asshole hadn't bothered to save.

12"

[Renata]

Robert had lost his shit. When Amaris disappeared, he'd started hooting and hollering like a damn fool. *AmarisAmarisAmaris!HeyHeyHey!* The girl wasn't some fucking dog that had thrown its leash; she's a scared human being who would've come back if she'd been able to. Renata worries the white tentacles slithering through the water might have snagged the teen. Is Ren next?

This whole situation is supremely unfair. Ren always has proper plans for everything. Even when the unexpected occurs (her hand balls into a fist and settles right over her belly button), she's ready with a solution. But this storm hadn't been announced. No forewarning. It had struck out of nowhere. The hurricane had spawned spontaneously off the Atlantic coast, and the outer bands have spun out across Central Florida. She hadn't had a chance to properly hunker down or consider evacuation. Ren is stuck in the middle of a hurricane with a completely incompetent jackass.

"Follow the current," Ren shouts over the wind and rain. The water is up to her thighs, the puncture throbbing hotly against the cold temperature of the flood.

"Low rent?"

She's in the company of someone stupid enough to get them both killed, no matter how proficient she tries to be.

Dawn arrives somewhere beyond the rain and cloud cover. The world has turned from black to deep gray. Like looking through thick static. Trying to find a shape as someone shakes to erase an Etch-a-Sketch.

They've been walking for a while. The intermittent lightning had illuminated their way through the end of night, and now morning gave the world some definition. Mostly, rain and rain and more rain. At every intersection, Ren continues downstream. If the teen is wandering directionless, the natural flow of the world would be steering her nascent compass. The wind and water both flow in the same direction, so Ren moves with nature, nudged forward as if destiny is wrapped up together with the hurricane, both forces leading her to the same destination.

The sidewalk is swamped; the water is knee-deep and moving like the lazy river inside the resort hotel where she'd vacationed last summer. The memory seems as distant as a desert right now as she wades through a raging storm and is subject to any number of possible deaths in her near future. It's as if she's been transported to some alien world or unearthly dimension. This is as far from her regular life as she can imagine.

There must be buildings alongside them, lurking near yet indiscernible from the downpour, erased by nature, modernity rendered moot by ancient forces. Ren feels entirely unmoored, as if she's been tethered to the present by a thin lifeline and that cord has separated. She has been expelled into a wet, harsh reality where no one cared enough to pay attention to whether she survived or died. This fucking world.

Renata wades away from the deeper river moving down the middle of the street between whatever structures line the avenue. She senses Robert right on her ass and ignores him. Like the rest of the world around her, Ren doesn't give a shit whether Robert lives or dies. He's a liability, something in her way, and she'll rid herself of him the moment he threatens to drag her down with him.

Salvation resolves by degrees from the downpour, the shape of bricks and the font of familiarity becoming clear as she wades forward.

The boulevard slopes upward until the edges of the storefronts rise higher than the water level in the street behind her. The world suddenly makes sense again. The nearest business is a bank, the blue and red logo of a familiar national chain marked on the front wall with a sign that remains dark. The hours marked on the door say it would normally be open, but Ren isn't optimistic. Every business is probably closed in the cataclysm. She pulls on the handle of the glass front door. It opens outward, unlocked.

"What the hell?" she says.

Inside, it rains as hard as outside. She steps across the threshold between the sidewalk and the bank interior, and there's no difference. The marble floor is slick and puddled. The *entire* bank beside the front door and the surrounding wall is gone. Ren moves farther inside and sees—no counter, no tellers, no vault, no other structure besides the front façade and the marble floor. No roof, no debris, nothing.

Just—gone.

"What?" Ren shouts over the screaming wind and hysterical sky.

Robert stares wide-eyed at the missing bank, too. It wasn't blown down like the Big Bad Wolf had huffed and puffed. It didn't just collapse under the brunt of the storm. No tornado Ren had ever seen could disassemble and then clean up so completely, removing debris as thoroughly as the most efficient demolition crew. This was something other than the storm.

And Ren couldn't think of one plausible explanation for what that might be.

"We need to find shelter," Ren hollers.

Robert, of course, acquiesces.

They move on, following the flow. If Amaris had been swept away, maybe they'd find her downstream. Ren is sure that if the girl turns up, she'll be floating face down in floodwater. She feels a duty to try and a dread about succeeding.

The weather isn't natural but rather *super*natural. The rain seems to fill the sky. This isn't Ren's first hurricane, but she's never experienced anything like this. The atmosphere seems more water than air, like

God has decided fish have been doing a better job as caretakers of His world and deserved a chance to save the land. But there's no God. She puts her hand over her belly as she slogs through the floodwaters. God, Ren hopes there isn't.

Robert taps her on the shoulder, and Ren jumps. She briefly imagined a pale white tentacle rising behind her and touching her on the shoulder with its tip. She glares at Robert—if looks could kill. He shrugs, then points to their left. His mouth opens like a fish trying to suck air, moving and making no sound. At least, no sound Ren could hear over the roar of wind and rainfall and frequent thunder.

He jabs his finger at a dark alley. Ren looks down at her legs, water up over her thighs again. The flow is feeding into the alleyway, the current taking a turn into darkness. After five feet, the rest of the alley is swallowed by shadow and the blur of the downpour. Ren imagines all sorts of danger—desperate muggers, dead teenage girls, monsters with pale white feelers trying to slither up her wide-legged beach pants like albino snakes.

"Oh, hell no," she mouths, and while Robert might not be able to hear one word, he understands completely.

He examines the dark, and for a moment, she worries he might go in alone, that he might leave her and disappear. And the one thing worse than going into that alleyway is staying out here by herself. Amaris might be inside the alleyway, alone and scared, trapped and in danger, or dead and forgotten. Ren and Robert might be her only damn hope.

Then the girl's fucked.

Ren moves on, with or without Robert. She needs to put some distance between herself and that darkness. There are too many possibilities, too many "maybe this thing is gonna kill your ass." Ren wades forward, against the flow now, the whole hurricane trying to push her into the alley, into the darkness, to swallow her up and erase her. But Ren isn't finished being alive. Not yet. The world may want her dead, but she isn't done surviving.

12.5"

[Marcus]

This is a goddamned situation.

Marcus stands in the middle of a road up to his ass in floodwater, the heavy rain drowning out the world all around him. He feels like he's been submerged in one of those sensory deprivation tanks Allie had always sworn by whenever she got too stressed out. He wants to be dry and safe and breathing something other than all this fucking wet.

Cass finally seems scared. The bitch is made of ice. She'd kept pushing him forward, relentless and fearless, but then she'd seen something she didn't like, and now she wants someone to save them. She doesn't think Marcus is going to be her hero. Neither does Marcus. He's already proven he's less than brave. He doesn't give a shit what Cass thinks of him. He's all for a cop or a soldier or even a gun-toting Republican swooping in to save the day. Marcus is fresh out of pride.

A buzzing sound slithers through the sibilance of the rainfall, and for a moment, Marcus worries maybe it's electricity from a downed power line and he's about to get electrocuted in water that slops up to his crotch. He doesn't want to get shocked in his dick. He stands on his tiptoes as if getting his cock above the surf would somehow save him.

Then he wonders about something worse than getting his dick

electrocuted. What had they seen slithering in the surging surf? Something pale and unnatural and unexplained. Like snakes that didn't have an end. Reptiles that went on and on and on and on. Like the albino tentacles of a giant squid right here on the outskirts of Orlando. Something *impossible*.

The buzzing grows louder.

Then the source appears, making Marcus's fears of shorted-out scrotums and otherworldly aquatic monsters moot. A small aluminum boat comes out of the veil of rain, moving too fast for safety, revving past the place in the road where Marcus and Cass stand frozen in fear. Two young men stare as they pass. They both wear smug grins, and one flashes Marcus the bird. The other takes a second look at Cass and decides against slowing down to offer the lady a ride.

Survival trumps the allure of sex.

Assholes. What the hell are they doing out in this maelstrom if they aren't helping people stranded in the hurricane? There's a pile of supplies between the two young men, stolen merchandise (televisions, portable electronics, power tools) peeking out from beneath a blue tarp whipping in the wind. Marcus had heard of such scavengers during past storms. They're looters. Funny how some folks are too lazy to get a job yet become innovative enough when it comes to risking life and limb for stolen goods.

Marcus hopes they both get their dicks electrocuted.

Then the motor on the boat revs in the distance, loud enough to hear over the symphony of the storm. The wind and rain play hell with acoustics, but Marcus swears the sound is coming from above, where there are power lines and cell towers. Then a flash of light, bright enough to penetrate the curtain of precipitation, like the morning sun momentarily flares in the sky or someone has shot an emergency flare. But that wasn't it.

It was the boat.

It was the looters.

It had exploded. In the sky.

Was it the sickly white tentacles that slither and swim in the dark-

ness? Do the appendages belong to a Kraken? A giant squid-like creature from some late-night B-movie monster flick? An alien invasion?
Something else?

Cass turns to Marcus. *What happened?* she mouths. He shrugs. Her
eyes are wide and white, terrified. Marcus needs an anchor, something
to prevent him from feeling unmoored and adrift in a world that wasn't
making much sense, but Cass isn't the stability he needs. She's as scared
as he is.

Remember your training, Marcus tells himself. *You're a fucking community
service leader!*

Politics is a dirty damn business. People can be worse than any kind
of monster one can imagine. Marcus has seen elected officials rip apart
political opponents like a creature from the blackest lagoon or chop
someone's reputation into ragged little chunks as effectively as a
maniacal slasher in any B-movie. Maybe some creature plucking boats
off of the surface of the flood and squeezing it into an explosion in
the sky isn't so different from City Councilman Allen Lewis using sextor-
tion pics of Judge Meredith McEntire to ensure a favorable outcome
in his emoluments corruption trial.

"Marcus got this," he says, although no one can hear over the storm.

He steps sideways, pressing forward into the undulant sheets of rain.
He grabs Cass's hand without asking. He's done playing the quivering
bitch, and he's taking charge of this shit-show. If he's going to be a United
States Senator from Florida after all of this is over (and maybe President
of the United States sometime in the more distant future), it's time to
start acting less like Kevin Kline in *Dave* and more like Bill Pullman in
Independence Day or Harrison Ford in *Air Force One*. Marcus didn't want
to be a goddamn Dave.

He takes a left when he sees a street sign indicating they've come
to an intersection with Seminole Street and leads them away from the
location of the explosion in the sky. Maybe he'd momentarily wished
the looters' dicks got fried, but he hadn't seriously wished them to be
baked in a flash of a fireball. They might've been assholes, but they
were also Marcus's target demographic. There are plenty of assholes

he needs to be left alive.

The eaves overhang the sidewalk on this stretch of street and protect Marcus and Cass enough from the rain to be a little less soaked and suffer a little less storm. He's able to see Cass a little better as the canopy blocks some of the downpour, and he notes that the UF shirt she swiped from Allie is soaked through. His eyes follow the swell of her chest.

Fear is a powerful aphrodisiac. They might die right here and now. Marcus wants a moment of human touch before the end, and he gazes at Cass with hungry eyes. A sheer waterfall cascades down off the eaves, making a private little world for them right here. Like an open-air bedroom in a tropical locale cordoned off by silk curtains. He leans in.

Cass leans back.

"Are you fucking kidding me? Right here? Right *now*?"

The overhang mostly muffles the drum of rain, and they're sort of sheltered from the constant wail of wind on this side of the street. After long minutes of reading her lips and interpreting hand gestures, he can finally hear her again.

"This might be our last chance."

"I'm not dying with my pants around my ankles," Cass says. "If we ever get down, Representative Roquefort, it's going to be a mind-blowing celebratory fuck in the poshest downtown penthouse. I'm not resigned enough to our imminent death for some desperate fornication against a goddamn Ferragamo storefront."

"Live first, love later," Marcus summarizes.

Cass points down the street, a patch of yellow light reflecting off the stream of water running down the sidewalk and the sheets of precipitation shedding from the sky. "Go toward the light, Marcus. Someplace looks open. Let's get inside before we both end up dead out here."

They move forward. The last business on the street is still open, powered by a generator that lights the last beacon in the neighborhood. Marcus has never been so happy to see a coffee shop in his whole life.

13"

[Leo]

They're back at the damn coffee shop.

Leo detests coffee shops. He's got nothing against the coffee it-self—he drinks five cups a morning. But the shops... They've been taken over by self-important millennials who think sipping from biodegradable cups and sucking from those shitty recyclable straws is the same as do-ing something about global warming.

Leo smacks a stack of repurposed lids off the countertop. "This kind of half-assed effort to be green isn't going to fix shit."

"It's referred to as 'climate change,' but the climate's *always* been changing," says the slobby bastard who's been giving him the stink eye ever since the teenage girl had saved them both. He rolls his eyes.

"You're an idiot," Leo says.

"You college kids think the government can solve every problem. Well, they ain't solving shit out in that storm, are there?"

"The term 'climate change' is a Republican construct to deflect from the real problem. The world's weather is fucking wonky. Look out the window." Leo normally doesn't engage with these conservative pricks, but he's had enough for today. "Only a fool would think humans didn't have something to do with that."

"Only a pussy would let a girl get washed away and leave her to die. Then she ends up saving your ass."

"Yeah, she's a regular goddamn hero," Leo says. "She's saving one guy at a time. While I'm trying to figure out what's wrong with the whole fucking world."

"You're what's wrong with the world, you little shit."

Leo stands up on wobbling legs and points a finger in the guy's face. He's older than Leo, but acne still smatters his sagging cheeks and broad forehead. "Listen, douchebag, I lost someone out there. He got taken by the freaking flood. There's something strange going on here, and I mean to find out what it is. I've got more important things to deal with than your attitude and whether or not I should pause and save the next klutzy motherfucker who gets swamped by the storm."

The slob storms off, plopping into the seat across a small table from the teenage girl who'd saved them both. She might be having second thoughts about being such a selfless hero.

Leo is left to his thoughts. What had happened out there? Something had snagged DJ and pulled him under. One moment he was pointing and scared; the next, he was *gone*. And hadn't Leo felt something under the water? A snake? Gator? Something else?

Leo pulls up the data again and studies the dark shapes outlined by multiple instruments. They all reveal a shaded form vaguely resembling the many tentacles of a great Kraken. Leo had initially thought the instruments might be picking up radiation or ambient energy waves or a thermal event, but now he wonders if maybe it's reading a physical presence. It would have to be something as big as half the state of Florida. The center mass of the shadow spot on his map is right off the coast of Daytona, aligned with the eye of the hurricane, but thin fingers from the dark spot extend north and south and east into the Atlantic for a hundred miles each way. The phalanges stretch even farther west, reaching inland with myriad wormlike appendages toward Orlando.

Leo lines up a chronological series of data maps over the last few hours. The results take his breath away. He blinks and rubs his eyes. Over the last several hours, the offshore mass has grown substantially, and the reaching tentacles have multiplied a hundredfold. As he scrolls through the time-lapse data, Leo can see the wriggling movement as they creep inland. Like a monster the size of South Carolina extends thousands of thin fingers toward Orlando.

Leo surveys the room for someone to share his incredible discovery with and sees he's surrounded by the same shallow mono-thinkers who typically occupy such establishments. The slob and the hero teen appear passably unstupid, but Leo knows better than to share with either one of those two. He's on the outs with little beauty and her beast.

The front door opens, and a couple burst in. The guy isn't dressed for being out in a hurricane, a preppy bastard probably too privileged to be caught stranded in a storm. Beside him, a young woman who appears as if she'd rather be anywhere than stuck here with him. Fortunately, they look more intelligent than anyone else already using this place for shelter.

Leo scurries over to the newcomers and grabs the male by the arm, trying to turn him around. The guy swings around with his fist balled, and if he had better aim, he would've knocked Leo on his ass rather than the glancing blow to the shoulder. On second thought, the punch wouldn't have even yielded a faint bruise—this guy is a pussy

"Hey, asshole," Leo snaps, "I'm trying to explain the situation here. Not a good idea to piss off the one guy in the room who might be able to get us out of this mess."

The boujee dude is wet and scared and half-crazy. But underneath the veneer of terror, there's someone of moderate success. At *least* moderate. He's well-groomed, wearing an expensive necklace, and has the air of someone used to being the center of attention. Leo thinks he looks familiar. Where's he seen this guy before?

"You know how to stop a fucking hurricane?" the pretentious prick asks.

"You know it's more than just a hurricane."

The woman steps up. Her demeanor isn't so skittish, working to center herself in a world that's gone nuts. She has more balls than the guy she's with—probably has a better arm on her, too. She's Asian, but not Leo Asian. Maybe Chinese? Taiwanese? Did it matter one fuck?

"What's out there?" she asks.

Leo smiles. He scurries back to his station in the corner of the coffee house, excited for an audience who wouldn't look dumbfounded or disinterested. He believes there's something out there in the storm, something that isn't on any science website. This is some Sasquatch kind of shit. Mythical beasts. Loch Ness monster. In Orlando.

He taps the screen, outlining the shadows stretching fifty miles inland from the Atlantic shore. "I thought these were misreadings due to the storm. Indication of radiation. Maybe heavy oxygen interfering with our instruments. But now I know better. It's registering mass. Those are physical manifestations."

"All of it?" the guy asks.

"No, just the one little tentacle over on OBT. All the rest is a fucking glitch," Leo sneers. "Of course, I mean all of it. It's all or nothing."

"I saw something out there," the woman says with a haunted voice.

"You definitely didn't see nothing," Leo agrees.

"And who the hell are you? You tell us, 'Sure, so it's a big monster. Attacking Florida,' and we're supposed to say, 'Yessir, sir!'"

Leo offers his hand. "Galileo Enomoto. I study weather at UCF. Everyone calls me Leo."

"My name is Cassandra Ming. I'm a reporter. For the *Blahblahblahg.* Call me Cass or Cassie, but don't you dare call me crazy."

"I'm Marcus Roquefort. State Representative Roquefort."

"You're a civil servant?" Leo quails. "Then maybe *you* can do something about this!"

Marcus raises an eyebrow and starts to stutter. "Well, now, I wouldn't use the word *servant.* And I don't know what agency is going to be responsible for...that."

"*That?*" Leo repeats, looking at his screen. "That's more than *that.* Call them all, Representative. Every number you have, call everyone. Police, firefighters, angry Republicans, gamers eager to start shooting with *real* guns, the National Guard. *That* is going to take the entire United States military. *That* is going to take everything we've fucking got."

13.5"

[Rabe]

Renata doesn't let him stop.

Robert had wanted to wait it out inside any number of abandoned storefronts they'd passed. The overcast sky cuts off much of the light, making the world twilight all day long. Driving rain fills the air. Ren says she refuses to huddle indoors—easy targets for the next time something terrible dismantles another building and they disappear as completely as the bank had.

The illumination of the morning serves to be even more depressing than the pitch of the night. At least darkness had concealed their dire situation, whereas the daylight casts a dolorous focus on the new normal. The hurricane hadn't been some nightmare that had evaporated after the dawn. The sun on the other side of all this shit isn't enough to diminish the drear of the ominous meteorological anomaly.

Even by the light of a new day, they are still royally and irrevocably fucked.

Then there's something brighter than the dull gray glow around them. Something artificially upbeat in this glut of natural negativity. An LED sign shines as an SOS signal breaking through the thick precipitation, like a flare flashing the way for all those who are lost.

Robert *is* lost. Even if he finds shelter and gets out of this god-damn storm, he's still *lost*. There hadn't been a signal on his phone all night. He hasn't been able to check for a message from his wife. He can't call and tell her he loves her. Robert can't hear his kids' voices to give him a little hope in this horrendous situation. He's never felt so alone.

He wishes he had never left.

He'd wanted one weekend without the responsibilities of being husband and father. He had wished for two days of living life as someone else. Cinderella had gotten her wish; why couldn't Robert? This is the twenty-first fucking century with all the equal gender shit going on—why can't a cool, confident black man have the mother-fucking Disney Princess experience?

He'd wanted to get bippity-boppity-boned.

Now he's only concerned about living long enough to see another sundown.

It's a coffee shop. Renata gives him a nod as rain runs in rivulets down her solemn face. If Amaris had come this way, they'd finally found a place where Ren thought the girl might've stopped for shelter. From what Robert has seen, this is the only way anyone could've gone. The flood had been deeper and more dangerous in every other intersection they'd passed since losing the teenager. The current flowed against them so powerfully in any other direction that going upstream seemed hercu-lean and suicidal. Robert wonders if they're being driven in a prede-termined direction by forces unknown, corralled like lowing cattle.

Like a trap.

He considers the disappeared bank back behind them and shudders.

The wind slams him as he reaches the storefront, inches from grab-bing the front entrance handle. Renata is on his left, out of reach. How-ever, she's close enough to grab hold of a streetlamp before the unex-pected gust can knock her over. She reaches for Robert, but the wind pulls them apart rather than blowing them together. Robert leans in, head toward the sustained blast until he's leaning forty-five degrees, face nearly in the surface of the choppy floodwaters. It looks so comical;

he half-expects the wind to cut off and he'll end up face-first in the water. Somewhere, God's booming laughter would roll like thunder across the heavens.

But the wind doesn't subside. It blows like a big exhale from a creature the size of a southern state. He can't move—his legs are stiff as stilts, and his fit body is ramrod straight against the weather that wants to topple him into floodwaters eager to sweep him away.

There's a figure moving beyond the glass door of the storefront. A hand sweeps away the clouded condensation on the interior, and Robert glimpses a pair of dark eyes peering from inside the coffee shop. Then the eyes disappear, and Robert understands. This is every man for himself. This is the end of times, and the selfish few will survive.

Instead, the door opens and Amaris is right there. She has arms linked with another coffee shop patron—a big man with a red rain slicker as bright as a ripe cherry. Then there's another person, then another, a human chain stepping forth and wading toward Robert. Amaris leans into the wind the same as Robert, and he expects the wisp of a girl to take flight like a kite and become airborne, linked to the ground by a dangling chain of humans. Instead, the wind subsides enough—as if the effort of the last long seconds has been entirely expelled. Robert imagines the massive creature inhaling now, taking a breath and getting ready to blow even harder. Like the big bad wolf taking care of all the little pigs. *I'll huff, and I'll puff, and I'll blow the whole fucking world down.*

Amaris snags him as the wind eases enough to put him off balance. He would've dunked in the drink if the teen hadn't had her small fist wrapped in his shirt collar. He manages to regain his footing and wades forward a couple of feet, taking Renata's hand. Then Amaris reels them both in like she's pulling up a shark eating a barracuda, the best catch in her fledgling fishing career.

As soon as they're inside, Renata grabs Amaris in a hug like they'd known each other for eons instead of hours. "You're okay!"

"I got lost," Amaris says, hugging back.

"I found you." It seems like Renata needed to find the teenager more than Amaris needed to be found.

Robert helps the big man in the red raincoat from the human chain as he tries to pull the door closed, fighting the floodwater dammed around the entrance by stacks of coffee beans. The sacks form a short retaining wall in a half-circle around the vestibule area. The water itself seems to push back as they try to shutter the shop.

"Why isn't the door closing?" Robert asks.

The rescuer in the raincoat reaches down between the door and the frame, feeling for obstruction. "Something's wedged in there. It feels—" His eyes grow big and his mouth makes the shape of an "O" before the guy disappears, so quickly it's like a magic trick.

The door handle is ripped out of Robert's hand as the other man is pulled under. Wide-open again, Robert steps into the doorway, searching the choppy floodwaters along the sidewalk in front of the coffee shop. The wind starts wailing again, returning to its previous gale force. The rain obscures everything beyond a couple of feet. The only evidence of the other man's existence is a quick glimpse of a discarded red slicker as the current takes it away. The man had been ripped right out of his raincoat.

A hand appears on Robert's shoulder, stopping him from taking another step outside.

"Close the damn door," Renata says.

"But—"

"He's gone."

"What the hell was that?" Robert asks as, with Renata's help, he pulls the door closed against the sucking wind, this time without any obstruction between door and frame. He twists the deadbolt latch closed.

"Gator? Python? I don't know," Renata says as she turns around and grabs hold of Amaris again. "And I don't want to know."

14"

[Carlos]

Carlos had been napping in the hammock for a couple of hours, and when he woke, the storm was worse than ever. Daylight turned the world gray instead of black. He'd checked on his next-door neighbor, but the gator on the porch was gone. He had waded cautiously out into the street, but the congregation of alligators had moved on. Away from the sea. As if they, too, were running from something more dangerous than a mouth full of sharp teeth.

Now, Carlos wades through a business district where light after light has been extinguished. Has the world been abandoned? He had thought all these years it would be a blessing if everyone else disappeared and left him alone, but now that it has happened, he finds it eerie. Maybe if the spirit of nature hadn't gone topsy turvy at the same time... Maybe if the sea hadn't betrayed him.

The water is deep along the street. Cars are submerged to their side window mirrors here and there. The current is strong, pushing him along to get him to move faster, faster, faster. The waves are whitecapped in the wild wind, splashing him in the face as regularly as any afternoon out surfing. Water drenches him from below, to the side, and down from above.

Lightning jumps from cloud to cloud in the shape of a halo directly overhead, accompanied simultaneously by a crack of thunder so loud it vibrates in Carlos's very bones. The entire world lights up for a moment. He sees a swell of floodwater rolling in, completely covering the tops of vehicles and washing up the boulevard to the storefronts along this section of the city. He rides the crest up, feet leaving the asphalt of the street, then down again into the trough before it settles back to even.

Water splashes into his face, down from the sky and the sea spray from the wind.

Sea spray?

Carlos smacks his lips. Brackish. He tastes some salt water. How in the hell is he tasting salt water?

Sea water?

He has lived all his years by the motto that ignorance is bliss. And he's lived a rather blissful life. He has avoided the entanglements of personal relationships and even managed to mostly mitigate interaction with the public. He doesn't watch the news or pay attention to social media. Carlos doesn't even own a television or a phone. He doesn't read books.

When his brother died, the lawyers had needed to track him down to tell him in person. He hadn't known about the September 11th attack on the World Trade Center until October 6th, although he had suspected something odd when the beaches were empty and the skies were quiet for a few days. He couldn't name more than one or two of the last six presidents. Carlos couldn't say whether there had lately been a World War III (surely Russians hadn't stormed the beaches of Florida). When he heard music playing from speakers along the shore now and again, he thought music didn't sound very musical anymore. Hadn't for a long time now.

He had lived and breathed and communed with the sea—until the sea turned on him.

Now the sea is following him.

For the first time in his entire life, he needs to know what's going on. Current events have finally caught up to his present. Whatever is happening in the world is now affecting him. He needs to know if this is going to pass and whether he'll be able to go back home. He had thought this unnatural tantrum would follow the pattern of any other storm, and it would eventually pass. Maybe not...

One storefront still had a light on. A coffee shop with water a foot up the exterior door. With the winds still increasing and debris flying dangerously about, Carlos doubts the redoubt of the glass frontage. Still, a light in the storm indicates there are probably those inside seeking shelter. And as much as he detests the situation, he must find someone who can tell him what the hell is going on.

Someone lets Carlos in after he pounds a moment on the front entrance. Water pours in when they open the door, and it takes three guys to shut it again against the gushing floodwater. About fifty people huddle inside. Several of them work at reinforcing the glass storefront using tabletops and torn-up countertops as planks to shutter the windows. Maybe these people aren't quite as stupid as he'd thought they were.

Carlos scans the crowd and finds what he needs. He can always spot the one person in any group—he'd see them in a beach chair with a textbook or strolling the shores with some scientific instrument or the guy trying to surf by using facts and analysis rather than getting up on the goddamn board.

The smartest one in the room.

He's young and stationed at a makeshift command center, electronics hooked up to precious power and screens lighting his face with a sickly glow. He must be important if everyone would rather listen to him than stare at their stupid phones. The kid was probably born with a computer keyboard in his hand.

Carlos approaches as the young Asian nerd speaks to a group of six others surrounding him in a half-circle. "—tensifying even as we speak. The eye is centered off the coast of New Smyrna, but the thing is still gaining speed and intensity. It's going to get worse."

"Great, kid," Carlos says. "That's the 'what.' I want to know the 'why.' A hurricane doesn't appear out of nowhere."

"It isn't just a hurricane," a woman with a slight Latino accent says. "There's more to it. There's something out there in the water."

"I've already seen more gators today than I ever cared to see," Carlos grumbles. "And there's the flotsam and jetsam of every storm. Is this your first hurricane, *chica*?"

The woman scowls at him. She appears on the edge of hitting someone. Carlos would rather it be the nerd.

"I'm not talking about the Florida wildlife, *viejo*." She glances toward the front windows, and Carlos wonders if they're trying to keep out the rising waters, or something else? "We've lost some people. And it wasn't a gator. Or a snake."

"Then what?"

"I don't fucking know. That's the problem."

"It's not just our problem," the nerd interjects. He's staring at his computer screen with a deep frown. "There are reports from the upper Midwest. They're experiencing a freak blizzard."

"What does a snowstorm have to do with a hurricane?" a sharply dressed asshole asks.

"It's what's *in* the snowstorm that's interesting," the kid says as his eyes scroll across the screen. "There's something in the storm. It was hunting some people up at a ski resort. Something terrible. Something huge. Like fucking Godzilla huge."

"You think that's what's going on here?" Carlos asks.

He remembers the way the gators were fleeing from the east. And he can still taste the salt water on his lips. Something *is* coming. Something big.

Carlos hadn't watched a movie in decades, but he had seen *Godzilla* films as a kid. Those old Japanese films had looked so fake, and yet he'd still found them so fascinating. Hadn't there always been another monster besides Godzilla in those movies? Like Mothra or some such shit? If Godzilla is in a blizzard up north, then what the hell's out there in the sea?

14.5"

[Cass]

While Leo fields questions and poses suggestions to the group, Marcus tries to retain leadership status among the eight people gathered around Leo's temporary command center. Yet it's immediately apparent to anyone paying attention that Representative Roquefort has no idea what's going on. Leo is the one with enough resources to propose realistic goals. No one else can even get their phones to work anymore, but Leo has a command center. Satellite is the last communication resource. Cass has always known geniuses and not politicians would save the world. Of course, it could've been a mad scientist who's brought this nightmare into the world in the first place.

Cass is sitting beside Leo, opposite the rest of the few coffee shop patrons who had expressed interest in this conversation. Most of the other people barricaded in the shop appear resigned to wait out the storm and shelter in place. This isn't the first hurricane for most of them. But many don't realize—or don't want to acknowledge—that this is a different kind of phenomenon than anything that's come before. Leo gives the handful of interested listeners scientific formulas and mathematical probabilities and gobbledygook incomprehensible to the average person. But what he's *saying* is he thinks they're all totally fucked.

While Leo continues to geeksplain, Cass reads through the reports on the situation in the upper Midwest in Montana. The news is half-assed journalism at best. Second-hand accounts and no reporter with the balls to go into the heart of the situation. Cass considers the war reporters on the front lines of major combat, taking heavy artillery to get to the truth of the conflict and report back the horrors of battle. Those pussies up in Montana wouldn't even put on a parka and wade into a snowstorm to find out what's going on.

She lets Leo and the others hammer out the particulars, but she intends to join them out in the storm as soon as they put together the plan to get the fuck out of this coffee shop. This is the story of the century. Cass wants her shot at a Pulitzer.

As far as she can piece together from the shoddy reporting, something big is stomping around a ski resort in the Rockies. Big and impossible. It sounds like a blurb for a big-budget movie. Conspiracy theories suggest coronal discrepancies and space-time rips to account for the presence of the accompanying meteorological manifestations, but the real bizarre component is the monsters. What do they call them in those anime movies? Kaiju? Thus far, the government has been officially mum on the situation. But the Montana governor has already quietly called in the National Guard, and the President purportedly has the Air Force on standby.

Cass departs the major news feeds and skips down the rabbit hole of social media. Conspiracy theories like land mines threaten to derail her from finding even the scant scat of truth. She feels like a kid again, tiptoeing through her Aunt Annie's backyard where her pet Labradoodle had left puppy biscuits in a scattershot across the neglected lawn, where every step could be a load of shit. After years of investigative journalism, Cass knows the stink of crazy well enough.

And she also knows a nugget of truth when she sees it.

Someone had posted "the truth" on a site frequented by whistle-blowers, who were usually ex-intelligence officers. Deepnet kind of information. Highly anonymous. Some super top-secret shit ended up here. Someone posted intel ostensibly from a reliable source. If it's true, then Cass realizes she wasn't far off—the mad scientists *had* done this.

"Listen up," she interrupts as Leo gives his plan to escape the coffee shop. "I think I found out what happened. Or sort of what happened."

"You believe what the internet has to tell you?" Renata scoffs.

"I know the difference between nutty and maybe, lady. I call out people's b.s. for a living."

"Let's hear it," Marcus says, trying to wrest some sort of control over the situation. He's in over his head, but he's trying to stand on someone's—*anyone's*—shoulders to regain status as top dog.

"Some scientists were trying to crack the problem of global warming," Cass summarizes. "They thought they were helping the world. Trying to stop us from ruining the planet. But it looks like they accidentally opened the space/time continuum. They punched a hole into the future and tomorrow has even worse problems with the weather than the present does. Maybe the scientists inadvertently proved they were right to be worried—if that's tomorrow out there, it sure as hell needs saving."

"Maybe," Leo concedes. "That theory addresses the inexplicable hurricane suddenly off the Florida coast. But what about the...other thing?"

"According to the reports from Montana, there's a monster stomping around a snowstorm at a ski resort," Cass says. "Crazy-big creatures came along with the insane weather."

"The mass Leo's showing us on the equipment is...alive?" Amaris asks.

Robert glares at Leo's screen like he wants to fight the computer. "Something as big as motherfucking *Cuba*?"

"Local weather watchers in California are posting about unnatural quakes in Death Valley, also," Cass says. "Maybe something's stomping around the desert, too."

"Kaiju from the future?"

Cass shrugs. It sounds nuts when one says it out loud, but they've all seen something crazy out in the storm. There's some *thing* out there.

"That's impossible," Leo argues. "It goes against a dozen biological and physical constraints."

"You follow the clues, dude. And I'll be right behind you," Cass says. "But sometimes the truth isn't science and reason. Sometimes the truth is the story, more like fiction than fact. Because the world doesn't always make sense."

Leo stares into her eyes for a long time, as if looking for the truth. Plenty of people have tried to find the truth of Cassandra Ming before, and Leo isn't going to be the one to find anything in there. Because Cass's story isn't what it appears to be either. Maybe that's why she can accept the impossible a little more easily than a person ruled by what they see and shackled by the way things are *supposed* to be.

Sometimes things aren't really what they're supposed to be.

Cass puts her hand on Leo's shoulder. "Science is always telling you to look at the evidence. Check the facts. Observe and report. You're taught to check what fits in test tubes and can be cooked over Bunsen burners. But what happens when what you see isn't what you think you see? When the evidence is *wrong*?" Cass taps her chest where her heart is. "When the inside doesn't match what's on the outside?"

And Leo *really* examines. He's a scientist. He knows how to make an observation. He checks the quantifiable variables and notes the subtleties of Cass's features. Realization dawns on his face as he notices Cass is trans. She doesn't know if Leo is woke or a joke, but he nods as if maybe he understands what she's trying to say.

"You're telling me I should keep an open mind?"

"Wise words to live by," Cass agrees. "Even science proves itself wrong on occasion."

"Science proves itself wrong *all the time*." Leo points at his computer screen. "Let's say you're right. That means this thing in the Atlantic off the Space Coast is from the future. Some abomination scientists brought into the present when they opened a portal to tomorrow while trying to mitigate the effects of climate change on today."

"Either on purpose or by accident, they made things worse."

"A future with hurricanes and raging snowstorms and maybe earthquakes out west," Leo summarizes.

"How can something so massive even survive?" Amaris asks.

"By eating," Leo says.

"Eating what?" Edd wonders aloud, even though everyone would probably rather not know the answer.

Leo replies anyway. "Everything," he says.

15"

[Amaris]

Amaris isn't sure how the line between the cliques had been established, but there are two distinct groups inside the coffee shop—the majority who seem resigned to wait out the hurricane as they had done with so many previous calamities and the ragtag renegades who refuse to accept this is only another passing storm.

Amaris thinks of her parents. They've been in denial for the last few years, believing Amaris would eventually conform to the way they wanted to see her. They've thought she might settle down and study, get scholarships to the best schools in Florida, become a doctor or a businesswoman or enter politics. Something "important." Her dreams of Hollywood would surely fade as she grew up and matured beyond childish wishes. They've always wanted the world to be shaped by the way they preferred it to be.

The *other* clique inside the coffee shop shared her parents' way of wishful thinking about what was going on outside. Leo had tried to convince them of the internet reports of massive monsters in Montana and supernatural seismology in California, but the other patrons had dismissed the data as "fake news" and called Leo a "climate-change conspiracist" and a "Chicken Little." It isn't so much the sky is falling—it's that the sea is coming for them.

"It's more than a hurricane," Robert had added, pleading with an unconvinced crowd. "I saw an entire building disappear. Something sucked it up like a vacuum catching a misplaced earring."

The crowd had stared at Leo and Robert like they were the CNN crowd watching two FOX News anchors. They weren't going to believe a thing either of the men said. No matter how sound the logic or how convincing they sounded or how bad it appeared outside, no minds were changed. Being persuadable is so passé.

Amaris could've supported Robert's observations. She had seen a bank get gobbled up, entirely erased as if it had been an architectural sketch rather than a brick-and-mortar building. She'd witnessed a semi-trailer disappear like a magic trick. But Amaris noted not even Marcus Roquefort, an ambitious politician with oodles of charisma, bothered to try to make a passionate speech to attempt to change a few minds. Minds could no longer be changed.

The others don't understand. It's no safer here in the coffee shop than out there in the storm. Whatever massive monster Leo's instruments are indicating, it's coming for them. It had already started stealing some of the local buildings. Amaris has no reason to believe this shop couldn't be next. It isn't safe here. She knows that. So do Robert, Renata, Leo, Cass, Carlos, Edd, Marcus, and the barista who'd decided to join along. Everyone else had decided to stay.

Of the thirty people in the room, about a third plan on escaping rather than sheltering in place.

Amaris looks around at the ragtag group she's aligned herself with. She'd always been a part of the "in" crowd in high school, glamorous and underachieving, exuding diversity-distinct coolness. Now she finds herself joining up with the science nerd, a guy who lives in his mom's basement, an elderly surfer who looks like he might've been homeless even before the hurricane, and a black man posing as a thuggish bad boy and is certainly neither bad nor a thug.

Not her normal kind of crowd.

After this is all over, her kind of people will be famous and flashy and fabulous. This experience is fodder for her future fame. A story to tell on a talk show after she becomes *legendary*.

"What's the plan, kid?" Cass asks.

"Cell towers are down, and satcom is all we have left," Leo says. "My computer could be the thing that saves our asses today. I've juiced up every battery pack I can and sealed them all in plastic bags. I need everyone to help—tuck them somewhere to avoid prolonged submersion in floodwaters. These batteries might be the difference between life and death."

"That means keep them high and dry, folks," Marcus clarifies unnecessarily. He wants to be the leader, but no one is turning to him for guidance.

"I've got rain jackets for everyone," Renata says, giving one to Carlos and another to the barista. Monica? Allie? Maybe she hasn't even heard the young woman's name... Amaris thinks the coffee shop gal decided to come along because of Amaris. The barista has been sneaking glances at her ever since she'd arrived. She'd brought Amaris three drinks over the last few hours.

Edd stares out between two sheets of plywood covering the front window. "The world's never going back to the way it was."

"This isn't the end of times, guys," Marcus disagrees. "We retreat. Regroup. Reassess. Eventually, the military is going to come in and bomb that thing back to whatever hell it came from. Then we rebuild. This is America, dammit."

"If the military was going to swoop in and save the day, Roquefort, it probably would've happened already," Cass says. "The beach bum says he tasted salt water out there. That means the whole fucking coast is already underwater."

"Alright, alright," Leo interjects. "Doesn't matter what anyone else is planning or what tomorrow is going to bring. What matters is surviving the present. And how we're going to go about it."

"Right," Renata agrees. Water leaks through the front along the jamb, raising the water level higher and higher. The wind and rain seem, impossibly, to be getting worse. "Let's get the hell out of here."

The lights in the coffee shop flicker and die. The chugging of the generator out back falls silent. The water must have finally flooded the machine and rendered the last bastion of electricity along this block as dark as the rest of the neighborhood.

A couple of phone flashlights flicker on. Someone lights a candle. A few regular flashlights appear. Some are from the folks who want to stay back. Leo has one. Renata has another. The group who'd decided to stay behind has refused to let anyone open the front door. The entrance/exit had been permanently barricaded against the rising waters after they'd let Carlos in. The offered escape route is through a back window in the storeroom.

It's time for the renegade group to escape. The barista has piled boxes of coffee beans in a makeshift stairway up to the exit point—a small window six feet off the floor and protected from the fiercest winds by the narrow alley out back.

Amaris is second from the back of the line. The barista is right in front of her, and Robert brings up the rear. He isn't going to let her out of his sight again. Amaris hasn't asked him his whole story, but she knows enough by the way he's looking after her. He's a dad. A dad worried about his kid, who is somewhere else. He can't do anything about that, but he can do something about Amaris.

Amaris is terrified. She notes the feeling, taking a moment to absorb the emotion. She'll need this in the future to draw upon as she stars in some horror movie about this whole crazy week. When things get back to normal and Hollywood makes her a star. When Amaris Azmi becomes the lead in a big-budget production of the summer blockbuster called *Horroricane*.

The barista wriggles through the open window, flashing Amaris a quick grin that gives the teenager a little buzz. Then the barista drops down into the rushing river flowing through the alleyway. Amaris is next. As she pushes halfway through the window opening, the whole world begins to roar, like whatever monster had been so many miles away in the sea has come to this place in the world and let out its otherworldly howl.

15.5"

[Renata]

Ren shoves Leo forward. She's second in line and has no intention of being one of the first to die. The noise behind her sounds like the end of the fucking world. She doesn't pause for even a glance over her shoulder as she uses Leo as a stout shield and practically hydroplanes him on the water in front of her. Her injured leg nags with each flex of her thigh, but she pushes forth, ignoring the pain. Ren tangles her hands into his bulky backpack and keeps pushing, making him continue forward, giving him the choice to either keep his feet moving or stumble and go under the water.

If Ren pauses to give him a choice, Leo might turn back. But there's no turning back. Whatever is happening behind them isn't going to be changed by two insignificant motes of dust against an eruption of volcanic proportions. Renata is gonna save her own ass.

Leo has the stupid flashlight somehow attached to his rain cap, and the beam bounces all over the goddamn place. He can't seem to keep his head steady. He's bobbing as badly as a buoy being battered about on this stormy sea. She needs him to aim straight so she doesn't ram him into a wall. She feels like a captain sailing her vessel through a white squall.

A hand grabs her shoulder, and she puts an elbow in an asshole's face. Reflex. She fears it's someone who wants her to stop and go back, maybe Robert turning her around to save the teenage girl. Amaris can save herself. She's proven it already.

But dammit, it's the old surfer. Carlos. Trying to help her, not halt her. He shakes off the blow to his cheekbone and points to her left. She twists Leo around so his flashlight bounces off the cinderblock valley of an alleyway and illuminates a perpendicular route leading out into the street. She can't hear the old man's voice over the roar of thunder, a sound she knows isn't coming from the sky but rather from the coffee shop that is... That *used* to be behind her. She doesn't need to hear exactly what he's saying. She knows she wants to live and that he's showing her the way out of Armageddon.

Carlos dives under the water, disappearing. She expects to never see him again. He has been aloof and a loner ever since he'd reluctantly introduced himself to the group, then mostly hovered nearby to gain intel from Leo. She had expected him to disappear at his first opportunity. Renata certainly can understand looking out for number one. Ren and Carlos were both like roaches—they'd survive this thing because they accept they're just the vermin. Ren would rather live to have regrets than die nobly sputtering in shit or munched up as monster mash.

Renata shoves Leo down the side-route, pushing against a current working to push them backward. The pain in her thigh is intense, but she can't show weakness or they might leave her behind. She must keep pushing forward. The roar of destruction behind them is still deafening, unending, a constant rumble like the longest roll of thunder that has ever sounded. Renata doesn't look back. Whatever is happening, it would be worse to see than to imagine.

Carlos is waiting for them at the mouth of the alleyway, and she's surprised. He seems more into self-preservation than even Ren. He plucks the flashlight off Leo's helmet as the ungainly nerd coughs and sputters from eating wake for the last five minutes. Renata worries the surfer will disappear with their single source of light. But maybe Carlos needs Leo as much as Ren does. The kid knows what they're up against more than anyone else in this dysfunctional little group.

The rumbling behind them finally starts to subside.

"What the fucking fuck?" comes a voice from right behind Ren, hollering to be heard over wind and rainfall and sloshing floodwater.

Speaking of roaches, Marcus has managed to follow them down the perpendicular exit from the alleyway.

"What happened back there?" Leo hollers hoarsely after he finishes a particularly wicked coughing spell.

"The coffee shop," Marcus can only say. "The coffee shop."

"No shit," Ren snaps. "The coffee shop is fucking gone."

"We need to keep moving," Carlos says. He points the beam of light into the wall of wind and rain, in the exact opposite direction of the place they'd escaped from.

"Not that way." Leo's voice is gravelly and barely audible over the sound of the hurricane. He points a shaky finger in another direction. "North to high ground. Like we planned. Then we make our way west."

Carlos considers. The best route might be directly opposite of whatever the hell happened behind them. Instead, he nods. If the thing wants them, it's going to get them. And it might be smarter to get out of waist-deep water. Is it better to see what's coming or let it get you from beneath the waves? Ren didn't want to be gotten either way.

Carlos starts wading forth, Marcus next, Leo after, then Ren in the rear. It doesn't matter the sequence. The monster that had vacuumed up the coffee shop could pluck any of them out of the line if it wanted to. If tentacles slither hidden beneath the waves, the wriggling appendages could snag anyone at any time and drag them away before they could even scream.

"It sounded like a demolition team imploding an old building," Marcus hollers over his shoulder.

"It was more than one building. That had to be every structure along that whole block. The entire strip mall must've been destroyed," Leo shouts back. "What do you think happened to the others?"

"Maybe they made it out," Ren offers. She doesn't know, but she can't have Leo losing all hope. She needs him to survive. She needs him to think they can all make it out of here. Smart little nerds like Leo can fall down the rabbit hole of worry and self-doubt too easily. They think of every possible fate, and most people's fate is shitty. She must help him hold out hope. Ren doesn't want him thinking he needs to do anything stupid. Like—

"We should wait up. For the others," Leo suggests. He doesn't sound sure. He's saying it because he thinks he's supposed to suggest it. The kid thinks too damn much. "Marcus, did you see anyone behind you?"

"I was right behind Ren, and I never looked back," Marcus says. "If they were following me, they'd be right here, kid. We need to press on. Get away from the nightmare."

Ren senses Leo hesitating. He doesn't strike her as the hero type. But waiting here for a minute or two isn't a hero moment. It's a foolish gesture. He knows it. Leo wants someone to talk him out of it. He knows they must keep going. They need to get farther away. Ren puts her face up to Leo's so he can hear her over the rain and wind and thunder.

"Hey, you're the one who put together our contingency plan, kid," Ren reminds Leo. "If we got separated, we're supposed to meet at the spot. High ground, right? If we want to meet up, we need to stick to the plan."

"The plan," Leo repeats. Those are magic words to a guy who lives by facts and figures. Follow the formula.

Her argument works. Leo nods. He pushes forth without being prodded further. Ren doesn't have to plow him through the floodwaters again like he's the prow of her personal nerd-yacht. She wants to get away from whatever the hell happened and get out of this murky muck that might have slithering roots reaching and probing.

Did it destroy a whole goddamn city block?

Ren feels it. Like she's being hunted. Like the whole world is in danger. A sense of impending doom. Meteor heading for the planet or a solar flare coming to toast the whole hemisphere or a zombie apocalypse to end life as she knows it…or unexpected pregnancy. Something was always going to come and wreak havoc on her life.

Turns out it's the goddamn Kraken.

That fucking creature wants to get rid of every last one of them.

16"

[Edd]

If Edd had ever had a choice, it'd disappeared a second after he hesitated. When the building had imploded/exploded/deconstructed behind him, he could've reached out and grabbed the stronger, steadier man in front of him. Representative Roquefort probably went to the gym five times a week and had a personal trainer. The last time Edd had done a push-up, he'd looked like a female human/bunny hybrid, and it had been performed in virtual reality. But as Edd lost his footing, he'd refused to grab hold of a lifeline who'd repeatedly dismissed Edd as something worse than the last Kleenex he'd tossed in the trash.

As Edd fell and started splashing, he'd managed to knock down two of his new companions in his attempt to avoid being saved by that political prick. Pride goeth before the failure, as he'd often quipped as Jessiqua online. Famous last words? He couldn't even manage to get his face above water to utter anything profound.

Edd had swept both Cass and the barista off their feet. Cass has started splashing like a toddler in her first bath, and the barista had an arm stuck above the surface like the shark's fin in *Jaws*. The current had carried all three out of the alleyway. Edd had been able to clutch the side-view mirror on a Grand Caravan up to its windshield wipers in flood.

Cass had managed to grab a windshield wiper for a moment. She'd given him a withering glare before the current yanked her away, the wiper blade breaking clean off. Edd hadn't possessed the strength to fight the flood—he had time for a deep breath before being flushed away after Cass.

Edd had managed to surface often enough to avoid drowning. He hadn't been able to get ahold of another anchor, swishing along without a rudder, bouncing off fire hydrants and downed trees and submerged cars. He'd felt the bruises bloom here and there and everywhere. He'd suffered one spectacular crash against a lamppost that might've broken his arm. He'd been too numb by then to tell for sure. Edd had thought he was going to die.

Now, he sits on the second-story balcony of a stranger's house. The water is high enough to cover the entire first floor. He holds his right wrist. It feels broken. But he isn't dead. He'd ridden the rapids and lived to talk about it. But no one wants to hear Edd's story.

"You klutzy motherfucker," Cass insults.

The three of them had survived whatever happened to the coffee shop. Edd, Cass, and the barista sit under an overhang, protected from the worst of the rain. The current had deposited everything to this low point. The wind blows from the other way, giving them a brief reprieve beneath the awning from the relentless storm. They've been thrown several blocks off-course by Edd's ineptitude. Now they're stranded on this deserted island of some stranger's suburban home.

"What the heck happened back there?" the kid in the barista polo asks. "The coffee shop. It like, *dismantled.*"

Edd had glimpsed it as he'd pinwheeled to avoid Representative Roquefort. Like an ant watching some kid take apart a Lego house, Edd had seen brick sections being pulled and lifted away. Parts of the roof and the wall had disappeared into the gray overhead, sections being sucked upward in defiance of gravity. What he had seen was impossible. But this entire day has been impossible.

"It's that thing," Cass says. "The thing Leo showed us on his computer. It's taking the town apart. Piece by piece."

"What're you talking about?" the barista asks.

Cass stares into the wind and rain. She's antsy, acting like she's about to get up and start running. The floodwaters are too deep to even touch the ground.

"It happened at Marcus's house." Cass's voice is cold and dead. "I thought it was the storm, but, of course, it wasn't the storm. That's impossible. But then, everything I've seen lately is impossible. A fucking monster is coming. It's sitting off the coast of Cocoa. Its big tentacles are reaching all the way inland and taking the whole city of Orlando apart."

Edd stares out into the downpour as if Cass is seeing exactly what she's talking about. But of course, it's all in her head. There aren't monsters in the storm. The fantasy world she's talking about only exists online, relegated to places where heroes like Jessiqua can save the day. There aren't any heroes out here in the real world. And there aren't any monsters.

Does he see something move in the storm?

Who's he kidding? Everything is moving out there. The world is in constant motion.

Edd stands up and leans over the balcony rail. He cradles his aching arm. His glasses are no help, spatters making a haze out of what's already blurry. He moves his face forward as if mere inches can make whatever he saw seem clearer. He knows his mouth is moving in a mumble, the motion he makes to cause his mother to bark out, "Quit making like a fish." Yet his wordless lips keep making nonsense.

"Do you see something?" Cass asks, alarm coloring her voice.

"There's nothing out there," Edd says. "Nothing but a fucking storm. Probably made by the military. Or funded by the local government. Bunch of libs who want to make a statement about 'climate catastrophe' by making this thing worse than it is."

"I don't think it can get any worse," the barista says.

"Famous last whirrrrr—"

He didn't see it because it isn't out there. He's right about that. It's *up* there. Like the rain and lightning and clouds above, it's in the sky. Maybe it's also "out there," and maybe it's "under there" in the water, too, like Leo had said. But the part that gets Edd is up. UpUpUp.

Wrapped around his neck, the tentacle cuts off his last word. *It can get a whole fuckin' lot worse, you barista bitch,* Edd thinks as he watches the kid and Cass disappear behind a veil of rain. Disappear *beneath* him.

Another tentacle grabs hold of his busted arm, and if he wasn't being choked out, Edd would've screamed like a goddamn girl. He doesn't feel very Jessiqua now. Because rabbits don't fucking fly. Not even super-hero rabbit/human hybrids with a smokin' set of tits. This is more some Condor Kid kind of shit.

Then two more tentacles come out of the wind and wet. He feels like he's being lifted higher and higher. The world gets brighter as the storm seems to thin, but the lack of oxygen is going to make him black out. Just before unconsciousness claims him, the tentacle around his neck releases, four other appendages wrap around his extremities, bring-ing him still higher as the fifth retracts, perhaps to find other prey.

Lightning crackles around Edd, so bright he can see red even as he shuts his eyes tightly. The thunder rolls so loudly up here he's sure his ears start bleeding. He fears he won't ever regain his hearing, but then he supposes that might not matter.

The clouds disappear. He's higher than the hurricane. Up where the airplanes fly. He surveys his surroundings. The tops of the rolling thunderheads are like the raging waves of a turbulent sea, fingers of electricity running through the waves of clouds. It is so cold. He feels numb. Like his mind has left his body and his soul is looking down as it leaves Earth. He's not the only one. Hundreds and hundreds of other tentacles reach across in the sky, ratcheting higher than the clouds, and none of them are empty. Edd can see what's in their grasp, those close enough. Parts of buildings. Some whole structures. Entire tractor trailers. Chunks of building materials. And people. So many people.

He can see the eye of the hurricane far away. Huge. Far in the dis-tance. Maybe on the coast? Or closer? Miles across. Then the eye blinks.

Edd moves his lips, but no sound escapes. It is gibberish. The air is so thin, he can barely breathe.

A larger appendage comes up from behind and wraps tightly around his torso. The other four tentacles pull Edd apart like a wishbone, quartered at 20,000 feet.

As he dies, he wonders about the spray of red blood squirting from four separate parts of him. It will mix with the wind and rain and fall on the survivors below. He will be one with the hurricane.

He will be the storm.

16.5"

[Rabe]

Robert shouldn't be alive, but here he is. He drags Amaris behind him like she's waterskiing and he's the speedboat. He's always been built like a brick, heavy for his size and dense like stone. Momma had always said he could never keep from sinking while swimming, even with a floatie. Some people lack all-natural buoyancy. His heavy stature now helps him resist the flood's push and pull. Every step on the submerged sidewalk has a firmer grip than anyone else in the group would've managed. Luckily, Amaris had ended up with him as her anchor.

He doesn't want to think about what had happened back at the coffee shop. He'd been the last person inside the storeroom when the walls started falling away. And it hadn't been like the walls were crumbling in or falling into the floodwaters, but rather something had disassembled the structure like one of those videos posted online of someone running the tape backward on "how to make a model cabin" or some shit.

Something had meticulously removed the roof, then pulled open the walls. The wind and rain had suddenly been everywhere. The drone of the storm had drowned out the screams of the people in the main part of the coffee shop. The cluster of the cowardly congregation had certainly saved Robert's ass. They'd acted as a distraction. The bigger meal. Robert had been the small morsel who had managed to get away. A discarded crumb who could be sought out later.

The wall between Robert and the rest of the escapees in the alleyway had simply disappeared. Instead of climbing up the stacks of coffee beans and squeezing through the open window, Robert had simply walked forward. Amaris had been standing right there, reaching out, grabbing hold of Robert while a flailing Edd had splashed against the rushing water, knocking over Cass and the barista before all three were flushed away.

"No!" Amaris had cried as the others disappeared into a curtain of precipitation.

Robert had looked both ways along the alleyway and chose in an instant. The plan had been to go against the current and get to higher ground before moving west. That's the direction Leo had probably led Renata and the rest. But that plan hadn't considered disappearing coffee shops. The roar of disassembly hadn't quit, either. More than the coffee shop had been in the process of being dismantled. Something had been taking apart the whole stretch of connected buildings from one end of the block to the other.

Robert had wanted to get the hell away and as fast as possible. Fighting against the current would've slowed them down too much. And he'd already known which way half the group had gone. He'd waded away from the shop going *with* the current, after Cass and Edd and the coffee shop kid. He hadn't given Amaris a choice.

Now, they've put several blocks between them and the former coffee shop. Robert pays particular attention to any movements in the water, flinching at anything that might be construed as tentacle-shaped. He knows darn well what he'd done to deserve this damnation, but he needs to survive to keep this innocent kid safe. Amaris doesn't deserve this.

"Wait," Amaris pleads. "Hang on a sec."

He pulls her up the slope of a handicap ramp that leads to the entrance of a law firm. The front windows are covered in plywood. Someone had taken the time to staple a laminated flyer on the plywood panel, advertising the firm would love to represent you if you were injured in a car accident. Their favorite clients surely rolled up this very ramp. Amaris leans against the wall and closes her eyes.

"Need a minute," she says, putting her foot upon the handrail and rubbing her long, wet legs. "My muscles are cramping. Lemme stretch it out."

The overhang above them barely holds out against the wind. One end had been knocked loose by a large oak that had toppled against the far end. The thick branches and remaining awning give them some welcome respite from the wind and rain. Robert realizes he aches all over, top to bottom. He has never been so drained.

"I deserve this, you know," Robert says. "I shouldn't even be here."

"If you weren't here, I'd probably be dead right now."

"Maybe a better person wouldn't be holding you back," Robert suggests. "I think I'm in hell."

"This isn't hell," Amaris argues. "It's just a storm."

"We get what we deserve," Roberts says. "I lied to everyone I love. Now I'm left alone to deal with the devil."

"We don't deserve this. Neither one of us. We're going to get out of here."

Robert isn't so sure. There's something out there in the storm. He examines the limited view over Amaris's shoulder, peering into the rain. The world holds dangerous mysteries. Terrible and deadly things. Things Robert needs to face because every step of the way had gotten him from there to here, from then to now, to the future crashing right into his present. He can almost see his terrible fate as he stares into the whipping wind and relentless rain.

The gator erupts from the surface of the water, and its jaws clamp down on Amaris's calf as she props her shoe on the handrail, kneading her thigh. Robert is stunned for a split second as Amaris throws her head back and screams while the reptile reverses, pulling her back toward the water. Her other leg is pulled out from under her, and she goes down, hard, hands flailing for Robert to save her. He's paralyzed with fear.

A fucking *alligator*.

His eyes meet Amaris's terrified eyes as she's dragged down, into the flood, toward certain death. Her hands grab at the slick handrail, slipping, slipping, slipping. The predator must be eight feet long. At least. A prehistoric monster as deadly as anything from the future. Then the gator's back in the water, still pulling his meal along, great jaws clamped down on Amaris's leg.

Robert leaps into action. There's one universal truth in man versus nature—go for the eye. He lands on the gator's snout, the two tangling in two feet of water. The reptile refuses to release the girl's leg. She's an easier victim than if it regroups and tries Robert as prey instead. But Robert is relentless, too. As they get pulled into deeper waters, he finds the gator's left eye socket in the hard carapace of its skull. The sharp hide cuts into his skin and tears up his flesh, but he feels the cold jelly of the eyeball pop as he shoves his thumb inside the eye hole.

The gator releases Amaris.

And targets Robert instead.

The teeth chomp down on his shoulder, and the pain is like nothing he's ever experienced. Like a vice with a dozen knives clamping down on his body. His face is right against the gator's head, Robert staring into the empty socket of the reptile's left eye. Darkness. A certain kind of hell. This was going to be how it ended, then. He'd become some alligator's shit.

His shitty future.

Then the unexpected. The gator had dragged Robert into deeper waters. The animal whipped around its head, keeping Robert off balance. He might be heavy like an anchor, but the thrashing predator wouldn't let him get his footing again. Robert should've been doomed. But the gator's movements had attracted other predators.

A shark.

A fucking shark.

The great white erupts out of the flood. Mouth as wide as the gateway to hell. Teeth and darkness. Certain death. Coming right for Robert and the reptile.

Its jaws clamp down on the belly of the alligator.

For a moment, Robert is in the mouth of a gator in the mouth of a shark.

Then the gator lets go, and Robert is free.

He turns to see an epic fight that could rank with Godzilla versus Kong or Superman fighting Spider-Man—the alligator manages to twist around and bite down on the massive shark's dorsal fin while the shark chomps the gator with its rows and rows of teeth. The reptilian tail whips around and almost decapitates Robert before the shark dives into deeper water and the flood swallows them both. The end of that fight will be underwater, and there may not be a winner. There might not be any winners today.

Robert scrambles for higher ground. His weight gives him a good grip on the submerged pavement, and he finally arrives at the handicap ramp and pulls himself along the handrail. Amaris is crying and shaking and still alive. Her leg is mangled and bleeding badly, but she isn't dead. His shoulder is bleeding, too, but he isn't dead either.

"You saved me," she cries, hugging him, quivering like palm tree fronds in a hurricane. "You risked your life."

"I have some shit to atone for, kid," Robert says. "And you still have your whole life ahead of—"

"Oh," Amaris interrupts.

She looks down at her injured leg. Robert follows her gaze. Wrapped around her mangled limb is a sickly white tentacle. It pulsates like the tongue of a snake. It has wound around her leg several times. The tentacle trails off the top of her hip and behind her, up and up before the unending downpour obscures its end. Robert reaches for the appendage.

Too late.

Like a bungee cord retracting, the tentacle snaps back.

Amaris disappears into the sky.

Gone.

17"

[Leo]

"Something's wrong."

He wishes he could say something else for once. Everything has been wrong since this storm arrived. The whole world is wrong, and it keeps coming, as if wrong is being wrung from the clouds and falling from the sky with the rain. Wrong on the wind, whispering terrible things from the future. Wrong in the water, getting higher and higher and higher, predators slinking about in the tide—things even worse than gators and sharks.

They're sitting inside an abandoned surf shop. Boards and bathing suits and snorkel equipment and everything he never needed surround Leo. The ocean is a vast expanse of experience and experiment, and fools like Carlos spend a lifetime riding over the surface like they're trying to ride a fucking orca. No one's off the coast of Cocoa Beach catching a wave right now, are they? No one's looking to the surfer to save their asses. It's all up to Leo.

Maybe Leo doesn't want to save them. Maybe this is the prophecy finally fulfilled—the plague of humanity is being expunged. This is the goddamn end of times. He's been reading the signs from the past in his study of paleotempestology, and everything has always pointed to the downfall of humankind. It has always been inevitable. Now it's here.

The future is fucking them over.

Armageddon has arrived, but now Leo isn't so sure they still deserve it. He'd once thought nature was the victim and human beings the perpetrators. But those kaiju killing everyone out there are big biological bastards, killing machines no better than the Smiths and Kumars and Wangs polluting the world. The gargantuan size of these monsters isn't going to be any better for the environment than man's carbon footprint upon the earth. This isn't the world taking back what it had given up. Nature isn't peace and harmony but violence and death. This is the further entropy of a system designed for destruction and decay.

"Something's wrong?" Marcus repeats. "That's the damn understatement of the epoch."

"Can you give me a little good news here, Leo?" Renata sighs.

"We're still alive," he replies. He looks at Cass, sitting at the window, keeping watch between two sheets of plywood boarded over the front facade. She'd found them in the meeting place. High ground. She had brought the barista. But Edd had been taken by the tentacles. The world had reclaimed one of them.

And Rabe and Amaris are still missing.

"Give us the bad news already," Marcus demands.

Leo had set up his equipment here. He had meticulously erected his antenna and attached all the cords. Rabe and Amaris each had a battery back-up, but their absence would become an inconvenience only after his primary units went dry. He has a couple of hours of juice left. From his readings, that might be more than he needs. They can't stay here for long.

Edd had been carrying some of the pieces Leo needs to reconnect to the University's drones flying out east. If they're even still airborne or transmitting. Maybe it doesn't matter anymore. Does Leo need to know if the monster is getting closer? If more tentacles were probing inland? If they are indeed more fucked now than they were then, maybe it doesn't matter if he's aware of it.

"The water is too deep," Leo says.

"No shit, kid," Marcus snaps. "That's been the problem all along.

That's not news. That's nothing new at all."

"I mean, this is supposed to be the higher ground," Leo said. "If the water is reaching this high above sea level, then most of the Florida peninsula is already underwater. It's still getting higher. And there's nowhere left to run."

Across the street is the park where they'd previously agreed to meet. This should be the highest part of the surrounding area, but the water is up to the front door. The whole street should be flood-free. They ought to be high enough to avoid being submerged. Instead, the water is still getting *deeper*.

"That's impossible."

Leo glares at Marcus. "What about this situation would you call *possible*, Representative?"

"How can there be enough water to flood all of Florida unless the polar ice caps are melting or something?" Renata asks. "Isn't it a matter of sheer quantity of liquid?"

"Maybe the displacement of the sea creature is of greater mass than the readings indicated," Leo suggests.

Leo pulls up the satellite data and focuses on the turning mass of the hurricane. The shape is familiar to anyone who has ever watched a weatherman get a hurricane-hard-on on CNN. Leo still has enough hardware to connect to the live satellite feed. Its purpose is to monitor the storm, but Leo isn't looking at the storm. The shadow off the coast of Florida is so massive—but the map is 2D. The instruments recording the conditions aren't measuring *depth*. How big is that behemoth? Could it be pushing billions of gallons of water across the whole peninsula? Could it be displacing enough ocean to drown out the state to the Florida–Georgia line?

Leo starts to notice something else as the radar updates every few seconds.

There's a crooked line running north of Apopka. It looks like a boundary on a map designating the separation of counties, but that isn't the shape of the division between Orange County and Lake County. The borderline on his instruments is being picked up by radar.

It's a structure.

Something built a motherfucking wall.

Leo points to the screen. "Look at that."

"Does the satellite map show city limits?" Marcus asks. "Is that the northern border of Apopka?"

"No," Leo exhales. "That's a *structure*."

The shape is a line that roughly connects Lake Monroe to Lake Griffin. The line follows the northern edge of each lake and continues east and west outside the radar's range. For something to show up on the satellite images, it would have to be substantial. Big enough to be picked up by the surveillance system.

The monster had disassembled the coffee shop and the whole structure all along the block. It had meticulously removed the pieces. *Why*, Leo wonders? But then survival had superseded hypothesis and he'd been running for his life. Now, he wonders again. *What would a massive monster need with building materials?*

"It's a dam," Leo says.

The water is still rising because it doesn't have anywhere to flow. The creature is building a dam north of Orlando to stopper the floodwaters and impede escape. The kaiju is trying to drown them all like rats in a barrel. Then it can slurp them all up through a fucking straw.

"It plugged the drain," Renata says.

"The water is going to keep rising until we either drown or are trapped on scattered ships," Leo warns.

"It'll be like bobbing for apples," Marcus realizes. "We're doomed."

Cass turns away from the window and studies the room. Six of them remain. "We need to get out of here. The one way out is going north. We get over the dam. Then we run. And we don't stop. We keep running."

Leo nods. It's the only option. The only plan. They can't go south. Everything's flooded. They can't go east, either. But the north is where there're monsters in Montana. And west is where there are maybe monsters in California. They can't run away from all four points of the compass. Because then they'd just stand still.

Leo worries there's no place to run to.

17.5"

[Renata]

They can't stay. The water is already up to the thresholds on the buildings at the highest point in Apopka. The rest of the city will already be underwater. Marcus insists on opening the door, and when he does, Renata takes a step back. The wake from the waterlogged streets rolls across the threshold in a wave and gushes across the floor. They had arrived a few hours ago in an abandoned neighborhood, but now the streets are full of people. Boats had taken over the area.

The narrow corridor of the street creates a windbreak to dull the worst blasts of the hurricane gusts. The rain eases for a few minutes to give the parade maximum exposure, as if the storm endorses mass exodus. Ren can see the line of watercrafts stretch a block on either side of her before the veil of precipitation conceals the extent in each direction.

Boats of all shapes and sizes clutter the street. Speedboats navigate carefully through the route, cautiously aware of anything underwater that might beach them or puncture a hull. Rowboats and canoes and a couple of paddle boats keep to the right (there's even a "slow lane" in a watery exodus.). One is a big swan-shaped novelty boat someone had stolen from a local lake. Plenty of kayaks. Jet skis. A veritable parade. They come through the veil of rain and wind. Appearing as if from a dream, then fading like they'd never existed at all.

No sailboats. No inflatables. Even the swan boat looks ready to fly at the next gust of wind. The locals have been told all their lives to shelter in place during a hurricane. Yet here they are, out, escape on the mind. This is more than a hurricane.

Ren's whole group stands out on the sidewalk in front of the surf shop in knee-deep water. The sidewalk slopes down a boulevard to a street lower than the storefront by a few feet, making the water deeper along the avenue. A pontoon comes along. Someone captains the ship, and several adults are posted along the flanks, cradling guns. Kids are overspilling the deck, outnumbering the armed adults ten-to-one. The boat sits low in the water. Parents along the route come out of storefronts up and down the street as the pontoon passes and hold up their kids, offering them up to be saved, but the boat keeps going, uninterested, already overloaded.

Not everyone has a boat. Some people swim in the stream or float on toppled trees or detached wood doors or even one floating bathtub where two tweens constantly scooped the rainwater back out to keep afloat. Renata wonders where their parents are and what happened and realizes she doesn't want to know. No parent would leave their kids behind during the end of the world.

Renata feels sick to her stomach.

He comes out of the curtain of rain, revealed by the static of the downpour little by little. He's alone. And Renata's heart joins the sinking feeling in her gut. It's Rabe. He's clutching his arm, injured and looking like absolute hell. And Amaris isn't with him. She meets his gaze. And he shakes his head.

When Rabe gets close enough, he says something, but the words are carried away by the wind and noise.

Words don't matter anyway.

They start following the others engaged in this mass exodus. The water grows deeper as Ren departs from the high ground. Leo leaves behind his heavy equipment so he can stay afloat. He doesn't need to see what's out there anymore. It doesn't matter what's trying to kill them.

It doesn't matter if it's coming from above, below, or out of the rainfall right in front of their face. There's one option—move. Move or die. Maybe move and still die.

The waves threaten to drown Renata as the floodwaters grows continuously deeper. The survivors who have been together since the coffee shop stay together as if they find some sort of lifeline in their familiarity with one another. They use the storefront signage and awnings of the buildings along the route to keep from being washed away. The current pulls Ren this way and that. She bobs and twirls. She sees Rabe trying to stay steady with one good arm. Her leg is giving her trouble, but it still reluctantly obeys her commands. Leo is there, then he's under a wave, then he's back again. Strangers pass them by.

The water gets deeper and deeper as they make their way. The floodwaters get choppier as they start moving away from the downtown area. Suddenly, the water is up to Ren's chin, and the next wave goes over her head.

Renata realizes she's going to die.

This is the end. She isn't ready for it. Before this storm, she'd had a future. A future she wasn't going to let some unexpected pregnancy derail. Now, she is the one being derailed. This is her undoing.

The sea swallows her up.

She's underwater, and she feels entirely helpless. Her fate is no longer in her own hands. Her precious existence could be plucked away at any second. Something in the water wants her dead, and it could be anywhere. Her life is so fragile. It could end at any instant. She's at the mercy of events occurring around her, and she's too insignificant to fight back.

There's something in the water.

She feels it around an ankle. Slithering up her calf. Something yanks her wrist, then lets go. Ren imagines something grabbing her violently and yanking her apart, tearing off a leg or ripping away an arm. Shredding her. Pulling her apart until there's nothing left.

Someone heaves her up out of the flood.

It's the surfer. He's surprisingly strong for an old man. He's got an arm wedged in a sturdy downspout that acts as an anchor. He shouts to be heard over the rain and wind. "Grab ahold."

They're all anchored to a series of vertical spouts. Rabe, Leo, Cass, Marcus, the barista—they hadn't lost anyone else. Renata had almost been swept away but not yet.

The water keeps getting deeper and deeper. They hold onto the downspouts, moving up, passing a marquee advertising this establishment was once a bakery. Renata imagines a thousand soggy treats. And no one left to eat them.

The wind stops entirely, and the rain continues to abate. Renata wonders for a moment if it's over and the storm is blown out. But hope is fleeting, and she immediately fears that the monster has come all the way inland and it's simply so near that it blocks the wind and rain, an open maw about to swallow them all whole.

Is that what happened to Amaris?

Perhaps she'll see...

"Maybe we deserve this," she says to the surfer. "People are what's wrong with this world."

The old man gazes up into the gray sky as rain patters against an ancient face. He looks wise, eyes catching the lingering lightning as it crashes somewhere in the distance. His hoary beard is grizzly and magnificent.

"The whole world's shit, lady," Carlos says. "I used to think it was beautiful and perfect and everything was all right when I was out there on the water. But the water doesn't give a damn about us. People are what's wrong? Those sharks have been swimming around for longer than man has been here. Gators, too. There were hurricanes long before we started mucking things up. The world doesn't give a fart in a windstorm. But at least people can care. Maybe they don't always, or often enough, but they *can*. At least they can try."

The wind remains calm for a while longer. Here and there they see more boats. But no one else wading along anymore in the floodwater. The water is too deep. Renata realizes they've risen to the roof of the building and are nearly out of places to hold on to. There are no more structures to use as an anchor anymore; everything beyond is underwater—full of rip currents and moving boats and dangerous debris. Another foot higher and the roof will disappear beneath the waves.

The boats exiting the street between nearly submerged buildings become fewer and farther between. Marcus points at a longboat gliding like a ghost ship, empty and directionless. Then another one of those paddle boats shaped like a swan, empty. The next is a speedboat going too fast carrying a dozen people, all wide-eyed and terrified.

Something is coming through the storm, a vague shape beyond the veil of rain. The shadow of it slowly takes form. The precipitation makes everything nebulous, so it might be a dragon or a great white whale or Satan himself on a homemade raft. Instead, it's another pontoon, this one with the tarpaulin roof ripped and flapping, snapping like a flag in a tornado. The whole platform is empty. If anyone had been aboard, they were now all gone.

Blown overboard by a strong wind gust. Or taken by the tentacles.

"Go!" Marcus shouts.

And they swim for the pontoon because there isn't any other choice.

There's only one option—move.

Move, or die.

Maybe move and still die.

18"

[Marcus]

Marcus stands over Leo's right shoulder, barking orders like mad Ahab captaining Ishmael. The white whale out there is bigger than any goddamn thing anyone's ever seen, ten thousand tentacles snagging ships and sailors away like a monkey picking nits. Marcus doesn't want to be anything's fucking nit.

A whole squadron of ships sails for the dam. Marcus can glimpse a hull or a stern here and there through the rain, running lights turned down so as not to draw the attention of the terrible tentacles. They are all running blind, ships in every direction beyond the veil of wind and rain. Crashing into one another is preferable to being plucked off the surface like a kid who's done with his bath toys.

They've been sailing for miles. Leo steers the ship into deeper waters, larger ships appearing as they draw closer to the dam. The direction leads to Lake Griffin. Marcus had once fished the area with a Lake County Commissioner who endorsed him for the Florida House. The lake had been shallow. The indicator on the captain's counsel next to Leo now shows the depth hovering around a hundred feet. Most of the lower half of the peninsula must be underwater.

"Starboard side," he bellows as Leo struggles to keep the pontoon from overturning in a gust of hurricane wind. "Get your asses starboard." Marcus even leans in that direction, putting his weight against the wind and rain.

The others slip and slide to the right side of the ship, grabbing any handhold and wedging against any foothold, giving the pontoon as many pounds against the platform as possible so the wind can't catch underneath and overturn them. The pontoon dips lower in the water and denies the gust purchase beneath the prow.

Leo turns against another gust, and the wind lifts them. Marcus grabs ahold of a handle; he fears this is the blast that overturns the boat. If they flip over, they're all dead. The water is crawling with appendages ready to draw them down to drown. Their one chance is to get to the dam and ram the damn thing.

Thank goodness they hadn't left the barista behind at the coffee shop. If they'd been a hundred pounds lighter in their load, the pontoon might've flipped like a poker card. Instead, it settles back onto the floats and they move forward, fast, maybe fast enough.

A yacht appears from the veil of the storm and paces them, an eighty-foot beauty riding low and steady in the storm. It pulls even with the pontoon on the windward side, blocking the blasts of gale-force winds. Leo stays on the leeward side and is able to keep the floats on the water without the storm trying to overturn them. He could manage the wild waves and churning current.

"You know how to sail," Marcus says, clapping the kid on the back.

Leo glares. "All that studying. All those tests. Everything I sacrificed my whole life. And it's driving a boat that saves my ass. I could've spent the last eight years chasing tail and still been able to drive a fucking boat."

Marcus examines the dumpy smart dude. He has acne peppering his face and his outfit looks like he might have stolen it from a geriatric home. Girls at that age are shallow and facile and would be more interested in what's on the outside than the inside—fit bod, cool car, nice style, fresh confidence, fun toys. This guy isn't a heartbreaker in any sense.

Leo wasn't going to get any tail even if the kid had had all the time in the world on his hands. Not even if he'd been the last guy on Earth.

Marcus considers the roiling sea. Maybe Leo *will* be one of the last actual guys on Earth. Probably then he might stand a chance.

If that teenage girl had survived, she might've been impressed with Leo's captaining skills. But she hadn't made it. Renata isn't paying enough attention to care who is saving their asses right now. Cass is closer to Leo's age, but she seems disinterested in any kind of appreciation. Marcus had wanted to bed her the first moment he'd seen her, so revved up and sensual in that tight pink mini dress. Then again, a few hours ago, when he'd been supercharged with adrenaline and they'd shared a moment in the storm. Now, he just wants to live—to hell with love.

When he survives to lead the New-World Order after this unexpected reset of global society, he'll need a new queen to support him. Cass had survived it all alongside him, but he isn't sure anymore that she's the right choice. He needs someone devoted, and Cass has always been disinterested. Even with limited options, she doesn't seem any more likely to choose Marcus than Leo or even Carlos or anyone. Maybe she's really into Renata? Or the barista? Maybe Cass doesn't need a man.

It doesn't matter. He needs to survive first, worry about being a leader among the survivors later. Some women will always be interested in Marcus's fit body, nice style, and fresh confidence. And the fact that he's still living.

"How much farther?" Marcus asks Leo, shouting over the storm.

"We're flying blind. The instruments aren't working," Leo hollers back. "But based on speed and direction, the dam shouldn't be too far ahead."

As if on cue, the yacht that's been sheltering them starts to slow down. Through the veil of rain, Marcus starts to discern shapes from shadows. Other boats are floating in the vicinity, a gathering that rapidly builds to a massive flotilla of ships. The pontoon comes close to a cluster of other boats—a couple of canoes, several kayaks, speedboats, a jet ski, the luxury yacht, a paddleboat (that somehow survived to cross the floodwaters) shaped like a pelican, and another pontoon. The two flat rafts come close enough that Marcus could step across from one to the other with a big step.

"What's this?" Marcus asks the captain of the other pontoon.

The salty ol' sailor points to a shortwave radio wrapped in a clear plastic sack against the driving rain. "They've got a plan."

Marcus feels a twinge of regret that he isn't a part of whoever is making decisions. He should've been one of the leaders on this mission instead of in the dark. He has been stuck with the wrong group of ragtag survivors. He ought to be on a yacht instead of this shitty pontoon.

Instead of asking about the plan, Marcus says, "Who's *they*?"

"Who cares?" Leo snaps, shoving Marcus aside. Marcus glares at the nerd. He doesn't care that they'd all be dead if Leo hadn't goaded them into leaving the coffee shop, or steered them toward higher ground, or discovered the dam, or prodded them to keep pressing northward. He only cares that the little sumbitch has disrespected him. Leo faces the captain of the other pontoon. "What's the plan?"

The captain adjusts his weather-worn hat and stares out toward the east. They can't see anything, but they all know something is out there. Something large and unstoppable. The fucking future is coming for them. But that's not all. There's something else in the hurricane.

"It's the damnedest idea," the captain says.

And he tells Leo exactly what they're going to try. It isn't far off from Leo's original idea. They want to ram the dam. Break through to the other side and escape. But someone came up with a bigger motherfucking battering ram.

Maybe Marcus is fortunate after all that he's not a part of the decision-making. Because this idea could go wrong. But at least he won't be blamed. He can pick up the pieces. And there will be a whole lot of pieces to pick up. Whether this works or not.

Either way, it's going to be something to see.

18.5"

[Cass]

As a reporter, Cass always tries to frame the facts into a compelling story. She covers political stories on the *Blahblahblahg*, and some people think that's drier reading than the nutritional information on a box of rice cakes. She's used to juicing up the narrative and adding flouncy modifiers to punch up the melodrama. She could make the minutes of the county budget committee sound practically Shakespearean.

What a story this situation will make. Cass wouldn't have to add a single flourish. The straight biography of the last couple of days would stand fine as a minute-by-minute tell-all. Every moment lately has been filled with action and high stakes—science fiction has turned into new science facts. The fantastic had settled in as the new normal. Cass could get her Pulitzer. If she lives long enough to put pen to paper.

Even this new plan is like something Bruce Willis would propose at the end of a *Die Hard* movie. The captain of the adjacent pontoon explains the details to Cass and the others as they move into a cluster of floating conveyances along the massive dam. A wall erected by the hurricane monster. The structure is half-obscured by the wind and rain, but Cass could see it stretch up over the water's surface at least another ten yards. At *least*. The top is hidden by the veil of constant precipitation.

178

And what's on the other side? Leo argues the world beyond the dam is their one chance for freedom. He theorizes the beast in the sea built a fence to trap them in and drown them out. To make the prey all float to the top. This is a border wall. Leo argues the tentacles have limited reach, even if they seem to stretch dozens of miles inland. Dozens cannot be hundreds. Cass hopes to hell he's right.

Success is contingent upon a damn crazy idea.

Hundreds of ships depend on the success of this plan. There's no way to know how many people have arrived, but Cass can see ships passing them through the rain, and the chatter of the Captain's short-wave radio on the pontoon-next-door updates as more and more boats gather. The shortwave radios remain the last communication devices still operational. The future hasn't figured out a way to jam something so archaic. And the shortwaves weren't dependent upon downed radio and cell towers or blocked satellites.

There are hundreds of boats. *Thousands.* All fenced in with one viable way through the wall. The bonkers plan.

The rain and wind occasionally subside as if they have finally reached the outer bands of the storm and benefit from some rhythmical reprieve. If the monster is the eye of the hurricane, then maybe this differs from other storms—a sentient stationary weather pattern that will exist in one place until the beast decides to move on, maybe along the coast, gobbling everyone within reach as it heads north toward New England or south before crossing the Caribbean.

Either way, the only safe escape is to head *away* from the oceans.

"So much for the idea we were going to be able to ram this dam in this tiny boat," Marcus says, staring up thirty feet to where the structure disappears into the rainy sky. This is one of those brief respites from the relentless weather. "This thing looks as sturdy as Hoover Dam."

"It has to stretch for miles to contain all of this water," Leo calculates. "I would have said such a structure would be impossible."

"I wouldn't blame you, kid," Rabe says. "This *is* impossible."

"Yet impossible is right here in front of us," Cass sighs. "The last thing between being food or sweet freedom."

"Freedom..." Carlos repeats as he stares at the dam. He seems to think otherwise. Maybe he believes there is no escape.

"This plan gonna work?" Renata asks Leo. Despite his missteps, he has gotten them here. No one else could've brought them this far. The group still defers to the brainy kid for answers. Leo seems more apt than anyone else to steer them in the right direction.

"It has to," Leo says.

This plan. The captain of the adjacent pontoon has been in radio contact with other vessels. The calvary is coming. When Cass had first heard what was going to happen here, she had to check herself. It was like those news stories she'd been told by some crazy person where she knew the facts were twisted around or the shit was straight-up made up. But the world had been turned on its end, and monsters are hunting them in the hurricane. She had believed the captain when he told them what was coming.

"There are three of them left," the captain had said. "It started as more, but a few ran aground or got moored in a low spot between the coast and here. Now they're fifteen minutes out. Taking it slow. Until they get close. Then they'll open it up and ram right through this fucking wall."

Fifteen minutes had become five.

Now the survivors become quiet as the captain on the pontoon next to them turns up his shortwave radio. Someone somewhere at the far perimeter of this flotilla of ships marks the passing of the calvary—three cruise ships, as big as they come, heading straight for the dam. Like battleships on a kamikaze mission, they're going to punch right through the barrier.

A voice across the airwaves narrates the situation— "Oh, fuck. Fuckin' fuck. The ship... The Daisy Princess got ripped in half. God, oh God, the tentacles of the thing are like snakes the size of freight trains. This is pure fuckin' evil. This is the end of the wor—" The radio cuts out or the captain switches the channel. Cass doesn't ask, and it doesn't matter.

"There are still two more ships," Leo says. His hands are folded as if in prayer. The man of science suddenly clinging to faith.

Then the sky clears for a moment, clouds in a small circular opening like an eyelet on a camera's shutter. The gray and white mix turns in a wheel, the iris as blue as any sky Cass has ever seen. The rain subsides for a second around them, maybe a hundred yards in every direction. Sunshine comes through the opening, a warmth that seems like it's been gone for years instead of hours.

Cass notes how strong and thick and secure the dam appears. She can't imagine anyone climbing up one side and scaling down the other, the jagged, wet debris giving so few places for purchase. The only way is for those massive ships to—

Fly right overhead.

The shadow plunges them into gray like some unexpected lunar eclipse. But it isn't the moon passing over and blocking the small aperture allowing sunlight. One of the cruise ships passes directly overhead, as high as an airplane moments after takeoff. As the rain returns, Cass realizes the sprinkles are dripping from the hull of the cruise ship directly above them. Suspended by multiple tentacles as big as oil pipelines, she imagines the ship falling, coming right down on their heads. What a way to die—squashed by an ocean liner falling out of the sky. That would be a story.

But the cruise ship passes overhead like history's heaviest dirigible. The tentacles extend far overhead and reach into the distance. A moment later, an explosion sounds off like the whole world on the other side of the dam has detonated. The monster's arms seem stretched taut, maybe at their limit. Leo had been right. They need to get over this dam and far enough away. Out of reach.

But the tentacles are done carrying the ship away. They'd dropped the ocean liner on the other side. And now the appendages have enough time to pluck smaller boats off the surface of the flood. Or stop the last ship...

19"

[Carlos]

Carlos wonders if the monster got all three ocean liners. Their best chance had been for one of those ships to punch a hole out of this prison. Even if he could manage to scale up one side of the barrier and descend the other, the smaller tentacles out there in the storm would pluck off anyone going over the dam as easily as sanderlings plucking up creatures living beneath the surface of the beach at high tide.

The hurricane subsides for a moment on one of the regular troughs of wind and rain. It's like riding waves of weather. Carlos can see a hundred yards back the way they'd come and all along the stretch of endless wall. Ships clutter the water's surface like an island of ocean trash, the garbage of humanity all clustered in a last-ditch flotilla. Then at the edge of as far as Carlos could see, it appears. Somehow, it has evaded the tentacles. A ship the size of a small town. It says Royal Rose on the hull, and it's the most beautiful thing Carlos has ever seen.

Then it rams right into the fucking wall.

The noise of the explosion of the other ocean liner had been louder than the clamor of the crash, but this sound is *denser*, the thrum of a massive amount of metal against the construction materials of disassembled structures and reconstituted building materials. Carlos hasn't studied science in decades, but he knows about how big-ass things in motion tend to stay in motion.

The ship smashes through.

Then the weather returns, concealing the situation in a veil of wind and returning rain. The clouds seal up the aperture overhead, and they're plunged back into wet gloom. Carlos braces for the wave from the ship's impact to arrive. Wisely, the pontoons have anchored to each other and the rafts around them, one massive flotilla with too much surface area to capsize.

That doesn't mean it won't buck the sailors like a wild bronco. Carlos had never been on a horse, but there was a mechanical bull down at the seaside bar where he'd used to go when he still felt the need to feed his carnal desires. It had always been easy pickings among the tourists for a salty surfer when he felt the urge for a quick fuck. This must be what it had felt like to ride that animatronic bull.

Four survivors fly off. He sees Cass somersault like a gymnast doing an Olympic tryout. She hits the surface of the churning sea in a form nothing like a championship diver. The barista slides along the deck, scrambling for a grip on everything along the way, pulling loose a gathered coil of rope and some tie-downs and a life vest right before she pitches over the side. Rabe dances like the worst contestant at a competition, shuffling right off the end of the pontoon and into the floodwaters. That prissy prick politician has a firm grip on the starboard railing like the metal handlebar is the only thing between him and death—and it probably is—but the two pontoons get smacked together so violently it causes the handrail to crumple, and the bolts come loose. Marcus and the handrail go over together, the prick's grip not loosening a bit.

Leo has the intelligence to brace himself effectively for impact. Renata has the street smarts to survive whatever life throws at her. And Carlos has ridden the gnarliest waves to ever break a Florida beach. The pontoon comes up and down like the trustiest of surfboards.

"Cut the tethers!" Carlos cries as the pontoons settle back on the floats.

Renata unfastens a carabiner from a leash joining the pontoons as Leo and Carlos pull the sailor's knots loose. The current carries them toward the spot along the wall where the ocean liner had punctured through. The water pouring through the hole in the dam would be pulling every ship in the vicinity toward the gap. A waterfall cascading through the new opening would carry a whole shitload of debris along in an irresistible current.

"We can't get there too fast," Carlos shouts. "The first ships are going to get pulled through and over by the initial gush through the wall. We have to work against the current and let as many other ships go through before we do."

Leo points the boat away from the hole in the wall and opens the throttle. They still move in the direction of the breach in the dam but more slowly. Other ships pass them, bumping in and knocking them around. Their partner pontoon has disappeared.

Marcus reappears at the edge of the pontoon. The handrail he'd been holding is still attached to the deck by a couple of bolts, dragging the rail along like a prop. He looks like a drowned rat, and Carlos figures any politician would look the same. Rats know how to survive. The other three survivors who went overboard are all long gone.

The other ships being pulled toward the opening in the dam shove the pontoon aside. Their race to the hole in the wall would take them through and plunge them over a high waterfall. The sound of crashing water and smashing ships is a cacophony in the background, the wind and rain of a hurricane not even enough to hush the horrors. But the line of boats going by are nudging the pontoon closer and closer to the wall.

"We can't get caught on the wall," Carlos cries out over the caterwaul of chaos. "Grab something!"

Carlos and Renata and Marcus use metal poles unstrapped from the remaining rails to push the pontoon away from the wall as Leo tries to steer away. The wake of all the ships and the tide slapping against the wall and the wind and the rain makes the effort impossible. Carlos can't keep them from crashing against the dam any longer. Leo decides to steer away, turning into the stream of ships and letting the current take them toward the hole in the wall.

Carlos hopes they've waited long enough. His legs brace to go over the edge of a waterfall even though he knows he'd never survive the fall.

They crash into the side of a yacht that perhaps had once been owned by someone very rich but is now full of foreigners dressed in tourist t-shirts. The pontoon gets wedged between the yacht and a group of speedboats captained by an assortment of kids, none older than the trunks Carlos is wearing.

The congregation of boats has clogged the drain, like a backed-up toilet. Perfect.

Then he sees the white tentacle—the big one that had carried the ocean liner over their heads. It's remaking the dam. A huge chunk of wall featuring a logo indicating it had once been part of a tech head-quarters dropped into place in the hole, crushing a half-dozen boats already crashed against the dam.

Smaller tentacular appendages pluck people right off the decks of random boats. Carlos watches a half-dozen tourists disappear into the sky. Other wriggling tentacles come up from the water, wrapping around some of the unsuspecting kids in the speedboats and pulling several of them overboard. Even if the dam isn't blocked again before they get through and they manage not to be swept over the other side by the waterfall, then the tentacles might get them anyway.

Carlos isn't going to survive this by staying in one place. He'd stayed in Florida too long already. He should've left a long time ago, but he couldn't leave the water. And now the water doesn't want him to go.

Carlos considers the other survivors. He's the better swimmer. He could maybe grab Renata and help her stay afloat. Leo has a long life ahead of him if he can make it through the next few minutes. And Marcus…aw, fuck Marcus.

Fuck 'em all.

Everyone for themselves.

Carlos dives over the edge and swims for the opening.

There's one way out.

He's going to find out if he can swim faster than the future.

Then his wrist is snagged by something behind him. It feels like sea-weed. He's too far from the sea. The underwater grip on his wrist tight-ens. Carlos knows it's one of those anemic tentacles, and he tries to scream, but a wave hits his face, and water gets in his mouth. He sput-ters, but rain fills the place where his spit makes room.

He isn't fast enough.

Then the grip on his wrist relaxes. Carlos turns to face his ending. It isn't a tentacle after all. It's not a what but a who. People. A lot of people swim in the choppy surf. Someone else grabs an ankle. Then an arm wraps around his waist. Another around his neck. People grabbing him. Drowning people. Trying to latch on to the better swimmer like he's going to save them.

Carlos tries to throw them off, but there are too many. Grasping. Pulling. Dragging him under. He can hold his breath longer than any one of them, but there are more than one. There are too many. One after another trying to make him save them. But he can't save them all. And they seem to think it's all of them or none.

He's drowning. When one lets go, another grabs him. Again. Again. The monster isn't killing him. It's people. It's the goddamn people.

Maybe people *are* the real monsters.

Carlos curses one last time, and the water enters his lungs. It's over. Fucking humanity was the end of him, after all.

He wishes it had been the monster instead.

19.5"

[Rabe]

Robert manages to swim the short distance to where the flood-waters meet the dam. The barista has followed him through the flood-waters. He always manages to pick up a young sidekick like he's fucking Batman. His lame arm almost leaves him a drowned man. They arrive at the wall made of pieces of houses and smashed vehicles and sections of stores and pylons from bridges and concrete slabs of former parking lots. Cass is already here, hanging on to the edge of a billboard advertising a new breakfast burrito. So far they've avoided drowning, but they've also lost their ride out of this storm.

"Now what?" the young barista screams over the sound of nearby destruction, holding onto a piece of rebar while getting battered by waves slapping against the stacked debris.

Robert doesn't know "now what." Does he look like fucking Bear Grylls?

"Now we get the hell out of the water," Cass says.

Ten feet from where they hold onto the pieces of the dam, some-one zooming by on a jet ski gets plucked off the machine by a tentacle that pops out of the flood. Beneath them and behind them are millions of gallons of water, most certainly containing those alien appendages in endless abundance. Robert doesn't want to get pulled into the depth by those creepy white tentacles.

"Up and over," Cass says.

Robert doesn't have a better idea.

His arm is still useless from being chomped by an alligator. He'd tried to save Amaris and had instead ended up with an injury that might get him killed. If he'd let nature take its course, Amaris would still be dead and he would have an arm strong enough to get him up and over this dam. His conscience might be the thing that gets him killed.

The barista climbs fastest. Robert loses sight of the kid in the downpour. The wind gusts feel like they might lift Robert up and away like he's a kite. Cass seems to be slowing her pace to let him keep up, and she's smart enough to hug her body closer to the wall to keep the wind from giving her trouble.

If Edd had survived this long, he wouldn't have made it over the wall. If Leo had blown off the deck—maybe he had and hadn't made it as far as Cass and Robert—the nerd wouldn't have had the stamina for this. At least these three have a chance.

Others are attempting the same feat. An older woman struggles as Robert overtakes and passes her. Even with one good arm, he has a chance and she doesn't. He sees her eyes flash as lightning rips open the sky, a plea for help, but Robert has already learned his damn lesson when it comes to helping. He isn't going to atone for the sins he'd committed against his wife and family by helping strangers. He must get back to them so he can apologize in person. The only person who can make amends is Robert.

He needs to get his life back together, and the one way to do so is to say he's sorry.

Dead men can't apologize.

He catches a flash of white like the lash of a whip and watches the older woman disappear into the rain. She's screaming, but he can't hear her over the roar of thunder. She's reaching out to him, but Robert doesn't even try. If he pauses to help her, it might be him being secreted away into the hurricane.

He reaches the top of the dam. A dozen others are peering over the opposite end of the apex. Cass is among them. The barista is gone, either already descending the other side or snatched away by the tentacles before she reached the summit. Robert crouches beside Cass. She gazes at him through the rain, and her eyes don't show the need for help. She knows as Robert does—it's everyone for themselves.

"See you at the bottom," Roberts says.

"Be careful," Cass offers. It's all she has to give.

Cass and other climbers start to descend. Before Robert follows, he looks along the length of the dam. More people are arriving at the summit. A constant stream. Maybe enough will survive to make a new go of it. Maybe this is the great escape, like Moses leading the oppressed out of Egypt. But a dozen tentacles strike like cobras from the veil of rain, attacking the escapees, pulling them back over the other side of the wall. So many victims. The sea would run red.

Robert starts to descend the outside of the dam as quickly and carefully as possible, trying to temper the fear of getting snagged by those albino snakes against slipping and falling to his death. His injured arm is going numb. Blood loss? Tissue damage? Shock? He doesn't know, but he does know it isn't good. He loses his grip. Almost falls. Slips again. This time the wind grabs him and nearly sucks him away. So much for the dam acting as a windbreak. The weather is everywhere.

Cass is waiting for him. They can't even be halfway down. He wonders if she'll offer to help him, but she weighs less than half of what he does. If she provides a helping hand and he slips again, they'll both be dead. He knows from his attempt at saving Amaris that trying to save someone isn't worth it. Besides, Cass isn't waiting to help. Not help him survive, anyway.

"Just in case," she says, never a good start to a sentiment, "do you want me to tell anyone anything?"

Robert pauses on his descent. He's wasting their precious little time. He considers sending a message with Cass for his wife and kid. "Tell them I'm sorry" or "Tell them I love them." But they already know how he feels, and it's better if his wife never knows why he really came to Florida. Maybe he won't say anything if he makes it back, and everything will go back to normal. The old normal is better than what this new future has in store...

"No," he says.

Cass nods and resumes her descent. Robert realizes he never even offered to take a message in case *she* doesn't make it. But she's not the one Cass is worried about.

His arm is completely dead. If he tries to move down, he's going to take the express route to the ground. Cass had known he is done.

He doesn't want to get snatched by a tentacle.

He doesn't want to know what's on the other end of those white worms.

A teenage boy scaling downward beside him flashes Robert a glance full of pity before a tentacle appears from above and entangles around the kid's neck. Gone. Robert exhales. He could be next. At any minute.

He knows that he's not going to be able to make it down to the ground, but he also knows he isn't going to wait here and get plucked like a ripe berry. He came down here acting like a mothafucka, and he's going to die like one. He uses his good arm to dangle from a section of concrete and finds a foothold on a repurposed windowsill.

His hand slips, and he manages to kick out with his left foot, stopping his plunge by shoving his sole against the outcropping of an IHOP sign. He's able to snag the door handle of the restaurant's entrance door with his good arm, luckily dead-bolted in preparation for the hurricane before its unconstruction. His face stares right at the hours of operation and an advertisement for sunrise stacks of buttermilk cakes on sale through the end of the month.

The handle is wet, and Robert is getting weaker. His grip is slipping. Losing hold. His fingers begin to release...

Someone climbing down from above uses the IHOP door handle as a foot grip. Smashes all the fingers on Robert's hand. The climber is wearing cleats, certainly useful for scaling cliffs but a bitch on Robert's knuckles. The pain is excruciating, but it's all that keeps him from plunging to a deadly end. He wants his hand free, but he wants the pain to go on a little longer because this is his last moment.

Then the climber is gone. He doesn't descend past Robert but reverses, yanked skyward by a tentacle. And so the boot is gone, and Robert falls. Falls. Falls.

At least he'll die on the ground instead of the water. At least he'll die of impact rather than as a snack. At least his death will make sense in a world that doesn't make so much sense anymore.

20"

[Leo]

The clog in the drain got worse. Carlos had abandoned the ship without a word. Leo isn't confident enough in his swimming ability to follow. Marcus goes to the edge of the pontoon platform and seems to consider it. Leo doesn't know what Marcus sees to make him change his mind, but Leo could guess. But hell if Leo isn't going to prove his hypothesis. He doesn't care about the scientific method anymore. He wants an answer. To explain this fuckery.

He needs to know—by any goddamn means necessary.

Renata takes the opposite direction of Carlos. The pontoon had rammed a yacht before a dozen more ships had proceeded to smash into the back of them. More and more vessels pile up as the current pulls them forward toward the hole in the wall. A few yards away, the gap through the dam empties gallons of water into the other side.

"The wall," Renata mouths.

Leo shakes his head. They can't all make it up and over. Maybe Marcus could. He's fit enough. But they'd be easy pickings for the tentacles plucking people away.

Renata motions. She makes legs of her index and middle fingers and shows like she's planning on climbing up and over. She shakes her head, raindrops flying from her soaked head. Then she makes the fingers follow the length of her arm. Not over. Along, and through the gap.

Leo nods. Marcus volunteers to lead, of course, and Renata will bring up the rear. She's slow because of her injured leg and refuses to slow them down.

Leo follows Marcus off the pontoon and onto an outcropping in the dam's wall. Slowly, they make their way closer to the opening created by the ocean liner when it rammed the wall. The largest tentacles, the ones that had sent the ocean liner sailing through the sky, are working diligently to repair the damage in the dam. Leo knows enough about basic engineering to realize how a dam should be structurally shored up, and the creature seems to know as much as Leo. He hasn't yet ascribed an intelligence to the monster, but certainly, the thing could hunt and trap and defend by instinct.

Maybe the thing is as smart as Leo.

Smarter?

The way Leo is going to survive this situation is if he's smarter than whatever that thing is.

Leo stops Marcus as he approaches the breach in the wall. The roar of the waterfall makes Leo's bones shake. Leo waits until the creature finishes work to plug this end of the broken dam. Through the rainfall, Leo sees signage indicating the debris comes from a former high school. The tentacle disappears after placing a large section of the wall. Leo spurs Marcus forward.

Marcus leads the line of humans precariously scooting along the ledges and surfaces of the dam of debris like ants parading from a picnic. They move through the gap some ten feet above where the water still cascades past the opening in the wall in roaring rapids. Leo has seen a documentary on the fools who would walk a tightrope over Niagara Falls. Now he's the fool. They manage to make it through and around the backside of the dam, moving away from the breach before the creature drops another section to repair the hole.

The top of the dam is fifty feet above them, and the ground is fifty feet down. Halfway to dry land. Or drier land, at least. Leo tries to calculate how much water has burst through the dam and where it is collecting at the base of the wall, but he shuts down his calculations. The numbers aren't going to solve the problem. The figures aren't going to explain what's happening.

The future doesn't make sense.

But Leo can't accept that. He must make it make sense.

Leo follows Marcus as they descend. He's aware of Renata above him, but he doesn't look up. He knows she has a bad leg, but he can't help her. She'll either manage or she won't. Marcus is using a zigzag pattern to find ways downward, taking them away from the breach in the dam. Smart. Whatever mess is caused by crashing ocean liners and the dozens of ships that followed it over the waterfall, Marcus wants no part of it. In this place, the dam curves severely so that they round an arc away from the pile of debris.

Leo's mind tries to grab hold of logic even as his slippery hands grab ahold of pieces of former homes, offices, schools, jails, hospitals, businesses. An entire town had been broken down and reconstituted to trap them all. The idea of it boggles his mind. He can't wrap his thoughts around it. It's too big.

Here and there, water leaks through the dam in little streams, like the trickle of tap water when he doesn't turn off the faucet all the way. Or the slow fill of a toilet tank petering forth. The dam is dozens of feet thick, but there should still be holes enough to let water through. There ought to be sprays and jets of floodwater gushing forth on the backside. Instead, there are minor leaks no worse than a pinched urine stream.

That doesn't make any sense. He recalls the old story of Hans Brinker putting his finger in a hole in a Dutch dike to save a village. Leo pauses. He doesn't want to think; he doesn't want to know, but he *needs* to. It's how he's wired. He peers into a crevasse where there should be a leak. Lightning flashes, briefly illuminating the shadows within the crack. He sees something in the fissure, plugging the hole, a white finger that is not Dutch and isn't a boy. The *monster* is plugging the holes. Hundreds of thousands of holes. Beneath the water, there must be an endless web of appendages like some grotesque root system.

Horror wriggling within the wall, like demons weaving their way through the gate of some futuristic Hell.

Then it's the last five feet before he touches the ground.

Renata is at his elbow. They're standing on a large slab of concrete elevated the last few dozen inches off the ground. It might've once been a wall, or part of a parking lot, or a section of a bridge. Now, it acts as the platform where Leo can say goodbye to the absolute clusterfuck of his recent life.

"C'mon," Renata says. "I've had enough of this hurricane."

"Yeah," Leo agrees.

Marcus is already on the ground. He helps Renata down off the concrete slab because of her injured leg. "You're next, Leo. Let's go. You got us this far, kid. Let's take it across the finish line."

Leo nods. He takes a step to the ledge of the concrete, and his knees go weak. This is the moment in the horror movie where the hero gets so close to the end, and the bad guy gets him right before he's safe. Snagged right out of the air as he leaps that last little bit. Hauled away right at the precipice of success.

"What's the trouble, Leo?" Renata cries over the wind and rain and thunder. "This is it. Jump!"

Marcus steps up, and Leo recognizes the look on his face. He's a politician. He's going to give some grand speech and inspire Leo to action. If there was the prow of a Navy ship among the debris, you can bet Marcus would stand on the hull and inspire the masses. Instead, he looks like Romeo giving a soliloquy to Juliet.

"Save the fucking speech, Marcus," Leo says. He jumps down, feet squelching in the mud at the base of the dam. No tentacle pulls him back into the storm. The monster doesn't care whether Galileo Enomoto lives or dies. It isn't the devil trying to chase him down for whatever evil deeds, and it isn't God who guided Leo to this place, safe and sound. It was his intellect. His mind.

He outsmarted the fucking future.

Leo swaggers forward. He lifts both of his hands and extends two middle fingers behind him. Fuck all the fuckers who couldn't make it. And the fucking monster who ate them all. Survival of the fucking fittest. Sometimes the good guy survives.

20.5"

[Marcus]

Marcus Roquefort plans on being the next great president of whatever remains of the United States of America. Leo says Montana is getting ravaged by snow and another monster, and Florida is obviously off the board, and there might be something causing quakes out in California that's tied to the hurricanes and blizzards—but the rest of the country? Marcus is ready to lead the ragtag remnants of the nation back from the brink of Armageddon.

The next chapter of America.

The sequel is always better than the original.

"All right, genius, what's next?" Marcus calls over the caterwaul of the waterfall and falling rain, over the wind and rolling thunder.

Leo looks back over his shoulder. Marcus hopes he isn't going to flip his middle fingers at the wall again. He had looked like a dipshit the first time he did it. Instead, Leo appears a little more cautious, as if he'd poked a bear and is having second thoughts about it.

"We gotta get some distance between us and the dam."

No shit, Sherlock. If this is the kind of insightful intellectual assistance Marcus can expect from Leo, maybe he doesn't need the genius on his team. But he agrees they need to get the hell away from the wall.

There's something about the dam. Marcus follows the line of Leo's gaze. It's like the wall is looking back.

Renata has already turned and started away from the dam. Marcus follows. He looks back to see if Leo is coming, and the kid saunters along right behind him, not six feet away, the smirking swagger of someone who got up to some shit and got away with i—

A white tentacle lashes out from the face of the dam and wraps around Leo's neck. Another length of white appendage ensnares Leo's ankles. More entangle his torso, forearms, thighs until the wet, white roots cover Leo like a mummy. Only his face remains exposed. Marcus takes a step forward and reaches out, but he stops his feet before he gets close enough to take Leo by the hand. Leo mouths something. *Help me? Hell no? He'll see?*

Renata appears at Marcus's elbow. Marcus hasn't even realized he's screaming until he understands the sound coming out of his mouth was what had gotten Renata's attention. However, she's no more of a hero than Marcus. Neither has a machete or a samurai sword. They are ill-prepared for self-defense against the kaiju.

"What do we…?" Renata starts, but she doesn't finish.

There isn't anything more to say.

Marcus doesn't take a single step forward. Renata keeps her feet planted right there beside him. Leo's lips move to mouth one last word, but Marcus can't tell what it is. His eyes bulge, and he turns blue. The wind blows the stink of shit wafting from Leo as the tentacles lift him off the ground, holding him out to Marcus and Renata like the creature is saying, "See? This is how you die. Scared and shitting. See?" It isn't pretty. Death is ugly and messy. Leo's swollen tongue pops out between his purple lips. Marcus closes his eyes.

There's no helping Leo.

There is only giving him a less lonely death, and neither Marcus nor Renata wants to volunteer for suicide. The white appendages retreat into the wall, so fast and so strong. They retract back into the hidey-hole they'd emerged from. They don't release their hold on Leo. The tentacles constrict like some super-powered python and squish Leo's meat and bones into a thin rope, making the scientist into slivered sausage links, pulling all two hundred pounds of Galileo Enomoto through a fissure the size of a post office box. Leo's head pops off like the top of a dandelion and lands face-first in the drink. It rolls once, so a single eye remains above the waterline, staring up at a sky that had forsaken Leo on every level.

And that was the end of Leo.

Marcus turns and stumbles away from the wall. Renata finds his hand. She has suggested she has disliked him ever since they met, but he's still alive, and he's the one she knows and she doesn't seem to be ready to let that go. Marcus holds tight. He doesn't want to let her go, either.

They run.

He doesn't know how long he runs. He doesn't remember if it was night when he'd started or daytime. He only realizes the rain eventually dissipates to a sprinkle, and the wind starts to press at his back, pushing him along.

Renata had let go of his hand a long time ago, but she still jogs alongside, keeping pace despite a pronounced limp.

There are others. Hundreds. Hundreds and hundreds. A crowd fleeing from whatever horrors are back there in the hurricane. They find a highway, then they keep moving farther away. Eventually, they find a roadblock manned by the military.

Finally, Marcus feels safe. Fi. Nal. Ly.

"Who's in charge?" Marcus asks the first soldier who looks like he might not run away from his own shadow. Even tenured combat vets are scared shitless about this. The situation is unprecedented, but Marcus Roquefort has walked away from it. He *survived*. He's going to make sure everybody in Florida knows that.

The soldier points to a command center.

Marcus marches up to the trailer and makes the guard fetch him the commander. The officer onsite outranks anyone who'd ever endorsed Marcus on his previous campaigns. But this time out, he's going to be a lot more pro-military. He's suddenly a big fan of big, fucking artillery.

The bigger, the better.

"I'm Representative Marcus Roquefort," Marcus says. "I'm running for the US Senate. Is there an evacuation plan for important officials?"

"I'm General Reed. Two days ago, I'd say your idea of 'important' is overblown, Representative," the officer insults, "but as far as I know, you're the highest-ranking politician from Orlando we've seen escape."

"The mayor? The deputy mayor? The other members of the city council?" Marcus asks.

"Some tried to hunker down inside Orlando. Others may have tried to evacuate. None are accounted for. All dead, as far as I know," General Reed says. "The mayor tried to escape the city in a helicopter transport. The creature took it down. We sent in a squad to retrieve the deputy mayor, but I had to listen to the screams of my men as something took them out."

"Nobody else important has made it out of the city?" Marcus asks.

"Plenty of people more important than politicians, sir," General Reed says. "But my opinion is secondary to my superiors'. They seem to want someone who saw some shit to help with policy. I'm here to evacuate as many citizens as possible. By my orders are to expedite any politicians that wash up."

Marcus nods. He doesn't demand respect. He doesn't throw a diva fit. That was the old Marcus. The one who wanted the fame and the glory and the perks and the power. Now, he knows he could make a better decision than anyone who hadn't been there. He's seen some shit. He's survived a lot. He knows what the enemy is like. Now Marcus thinks he would make a damn good leader.

Marcus wants to save the world.

"So why aren't they blowing that son of a bitch sky high?" Marcus asks.

"Targeting systems are FUBAR. Missiles can't track in that shitstorm. Can't fly any aircraft over to drop traditional munitions. They tried to shove a MOAB up its ass, but it got swallowed like a bitter pill and digested by the sea. It's too big. Can't fight fucking Mother Nature."

"I might have a couple of ideas," Marcus says.

"The rest of your kind are gathering out west." General Reed looks like a man left to clean up someone else's mess. "Kansas."

"I'm going to put a plan together. We're going to come back and reclaim Florida."

"Right," General Reed dismisses. "Take a transport out back. One of the Jeeps. I can't spare a man. I know you understand. Sir."

Renata is waiting outside the trailer. Marcus holds up a set of keys. He smiles his megawatt grin that has already won him three elections and will win him the next. He'll be the leader of the free world before the last chuff of this storm puffs.

"Want a ride?" he asks.

It's time to get away from the future. He's ready for tomorrow.

21"

[Cass]

Cass and the barista stick together. Maybe after the impromptu funeral for Rabe, they're bonded in a way neither wants to let go of quite yet. Rabe had fallen from the sky with the rain and landed right on his face as Cass had stepped off the last section of the wall. The sound of his breaking neck had been louder than the racket made by a dam being constructed or the rumbling thunder. Cass couldn't stop and bury the dude, but she could at least drag him out of the rain. The barista had carried his feet. They'd tucked him under an overhang to protect him from the worst of the weather. It was the best they could do.

Cass had survived. Cass and the barista.

She doesn't even know the kid's name.

The winds gradually lessen and the floods subtly subside, and soon they've left the worst of the weather behind. They march across the Florida marsh with hardly a thought about snakes or gators. There are worse fates than either one of those out in the world. They have already survived it. Bring on any namby-pamby reptiles any day.

They aren't alone. Thousands of survivors trek across the field. After hours of a seemingly interminable hike, they arrive at a military encampment. Red Cross tents are filled with EMS workers tending to the injured.

Rabe might've been able to sew up his gator bite if he could've made it this far. But the endings of any life are oftentimes unexpected, and one never knows where any day might take them.

Cass wants the day to take her anywhere else but here.

For so long, Cass had been obsessed with the future. Always trying to make today into tomorrow instead of only appreciating the present. Now, she wants to live *this* moment. This precious second. Because the next one might not even come to be.

She sees a crew from Channel 2 News. She doesn't recognize the reporter. Anyone with a familiar face must still be back in Orlando. Flooded out and dead by now. This wasn't news *for* the people of Orlando. This is about letting everyone else in the world know what had happened *to* Orlando.

Orlando has been lost.

The reporter is giving a eulogy.

Cass takes a step forward to volunteer to tell her story of what had happened inside the metro area. She's wanted the Big Time for as long as she can remember. Since she was a young kid standing in front of a makeshift camera phone and recording the daily gossip of the neighborhood. Now, she has her chance to be in the limelight. This is her shot.

And Cass doesn't care one bit. None of it matters. Because if these assholes think it isn't coming for the rest of them, they have another think coming.

Cass listens for a minute. The reporter introduces herself as Chelsea Chesney (as alliterative of a moniker as any journalist could hope for). She updates the viewers at home—rescue teams have been deployed. *Bullshit.* The situation is under control. *Bullshit.* This is an unprovoked attack by a biological weapon. *Bullshit-ish.* A counterstrike is imminent. *Big-time bullshit.* If the military were going to respond, they would've already bombed the hell out of the kaiju.

Cass approaches the little geek who is certainly the producer. "What's this drivel?" she whispers out of the corner of her mouth. "This is some propaganda shit."

Chelsea keeps spewing mistruth.

"This is the only thing we can say." The producer looks too young and appears shellshocked. He wouldn't know the truth if it wrapped its clammy white tentacles around his balls.

"This isn't the news."

The producer snaps out of his funk for a moment. "What we do—that hasn't been the news in a very long time."

"You could try," Cass suggests.

"For what? What's the purpose?" The producer holds his thumb to his mouth and mimics the facile falsetto of his star reporter. "'Hi, this is Chelsea Chesty, and we're all fucked. Kiss your ass goodbye because there's a big monster out there that's going to turn you into a heaping steamy pile of kaiju shit.' Like that?"

Cass nods. She gets it. Bad news is all the news there is. But this is beyond bad. This is the end of the news.

"The future is here, lady. I don't need to tell anyone anything. They have to wait around, and this story is going to land on their front porch." The producer stares at Cass, and there is truth in his eyes. A terrible, terrible truth. "You don't think this is the only one out there, do you?"

Cass thinks about Montana. About California. Maybe more. Certainly more.

Cass leaves the reporter, who is still talking about how things are looking up. Cass wants to leave it behind. The barista has waited for her while she spoke with the producer. Now they're going to hit the road and try to thumb a ride off the Florida peninsula. Cass wants to get as far away from the ocean as possible.

"Cass!"

It's Renata. Cass doesn't know why, but she's never been so happy to see anyone in her whole life. She had assumed everyone else was dead, and she hadn't even taken it hard. She hadn't known these people very well. But the fact Renata had survived beyond all odds gives Cass some thin spark of hope.

Cass runs over to where Renata gets her leg stitched up in one of the Red Cross tents. Cass leans over the very handsome EMS dude, and the two women embrace. Cass realizes the barista had come over too and wrapped her arms around the two women. Marcus stands beside Ren. He survived. Like a cockroach. He's got a set of keys in his hand. Marcus claps Cass on the back. They'd come a long way since they'd first met. She never thought she'd be here at the end of the road with Marcus Roquefort.

"We have a ride," Marcus says. "You gonna tag along?"

"Where are you going?" Cass asks.

"Do you care?" he retorts. "It'll be north. Isn't that all that matters?"

Renata thanks the EMS attendant as he finishes and hands her some gauze with a bottle of painkillers. Ren takes Cass's hand. "Come on."

They all start walking toward the vehicles parked out back of the camp. Marcus unlocks one of the black SUVs. He starts toward the driver's side, and the barista puts a hand on his shoulder.

"You don't look like the kind of guy who usually drives himself around," the barista says. "What say you hop in the back?"

"I'm being bossed around by a coffee shop barista? The future President of the United States?" Marcus asks with his patented "Aren't I cute?" smirk.

"I'm here to save my own ass," the barista says. "Besides, I voted for the other guy."

Marcus grins even wider. Genuinely. He passes the keys to the barista.

"By all means, Vega, pilot us out of this Godforsaken swampland."

Cass gets in the front with the barista, and Renata climbs in the back with Marcus.

"Your name is Vega?" Cass asks. Vega nods. "How did Marcus know?"

"He asked," Vega says.

And Cass looks in the rearview mirror. Marcus surveys the many people milling about like shellshocked survivors after a surprise attack. Cass considers how they ought to bring as many as they could to escape, but maybe there's no escaping. Maybe they're going from the mouth of one beast straight into the maw of another.

Epilogue
[Renata]

They've driven for twenty-four hours straight in shifts. They left the storm far behind, but that didn't mean they left all the trouble back there.

They listen to reports of other monsters. Not only Montana. Not even only Montana and California. All over the world. And as the monsters roam, the worst in humanity bursts forth. There are monsters in each of us, and they've broken free. As Ren and the other three survivors had passed through the metropolitan areas between the south and the Midwest, they'd seen wild looting, outright anarchy, unchecked crimes, and sheer panic. Horrors in the street before any monster had even shown up.

Some routes north and west had been entirely jammed with others attempting exodus or roadblocks mandated by panicked local officials trying to keep order in the face of inevitable chaos. Renata and her companions had managed to get around with the all-terrain SUV. The radio had worked sporadically, here and there where the signal hasn't turned to static yet. What little news they'd heard was a constant stream of terror. Eventually, Cass had shut off the radio, and they'd driven in silence.

They had taken turns behind the wheel. The whole back of the vehicle is an auxiliary fuel tank and the engine is a hybrid, so they had managed to get halfway across the country without refueling. And halfway is all the way they plan to go. Kansas. Maybe they can find some safe respite in Kansas.

Renata never thought she'd be relocating to the Midwest, but the coasts have gotten a little too intense. Scant reports coming out of any place south of the dam stretching across Central Florida indicated the whole bottom half of the peninsula is now underwater. Miami, Orlando, Tampa had all gone the way of Atlantis. And there had been reports out of Jacksonville. That the monster is moving northward. Or had another creature arrived from the future?

Renata had expected Marcus Roquefort to ditch them at the first hint of new American leadership regrouping anywhere along their route west and north, but they'd passed near Atlanta and Nashville and Marcus had given no indication he even considered staying behind. Renata thought maybe the camaraderie of the survivors had given Marcus reason to stay with them, but he'd finally told her his grand plan when they were outside St. Louis: "You're going to have everyone with an ambitious political bone in their body vying to step up and be in charge. We caught bits and pieces of their agenda over the airwaves on our way by Atlanta and Nashville. They're arguing to stay and fight. Those with ambitions of power all jumped right up on the soapbox at the first chance. But it doesn't matter if you're the first. Those people are still in the danger zone. They won't survive the coastal chaos long enough to lead anything. First, you have to live through it. Then you're poised to pick up the pieces."

"Kansas, then?" Renata had asked.

"We put the pieces back together there. Like a puzzle. You and I and the others—we're a good start. We'll build the resistance back up from the foundations. In Kansas."

Marcus hadn't sounded like a politician anymore. This effort wouldn't get him accolades or political influence or the perks of an office. This would be dangerous and tough and relentless. He wants to lead a rebellion against an overwhelming enemy. Marcus Roquefort has a different future today than he'd had yesterday.

Now here they are, crossing the border into the land of Dorothy and tornadoes. Renata will take a good, old-fashioned twister after the fucking week she's had. Then she thought about some impossible kaiju stalking the flyover states while in the eye of a tornado. Why not? That could damn well be the next thing...

Are they safe anywhere?

Vega pulls into a small town called Lawrence. She glances at Marcus in the rearview mirror, and he nods. "This is as good a place as anywhere."

"You think we're safe here?" Cass asks.

Marcus shrugs. "We're a thousand miles from Orlando. As far from the Pacific."

"And the thing in the north? The snow monster?"

Marcus doesn't know, but you don't have to know to decide what to do next. "Let's hope it's warm enough this far south. Any closer toward Texas is too close to the Gulf."

"Not south, not west, not north. Certainly not east," Vega says. "Right in the middle."

Marcus heads off to find someone he can lead. Renata thinks he might have a shot. No one else in Kansas has seen what he's seen. He's stared the beast in the eyes and survived. Who better to lead them? Anyone else who might have firsthand experience is probably back east, like Marcus said, and would be dead before anyone could become a leader. Maybe they needed a President Roquefort.

"All right, ladies," Cass says. "What about us?"

It's cold. There are fingers of snow on the ground, and Renata shivers. It isn't the first time she's seen snow, but it's the first time in a long while. The way Vega nudges it with the toe of her shoe, she guesses it's the first time the younger woman has encountered frozen precipitation. Renata considers the reports of the snow monster and shivers. Maybe they're still too far north after all...

"Let's find somewhere to get warm and get some rest," Renata suggests. "I've been tired and wet for days now."

They trudged down the avenue toward the row of storefronts along Main Street. They aren't the only ones who have made the trek to Kansas. Some may be staying the night and moving on. Others are surely thinking the same thing Renata and the rest of the Floridians are thinking. This place is maybe as safe as anywhere.

There's a Red Cross tent set up between a local cafe and a coffee shop. Vega eyes the coffee shop like it's manna from Heaven. "You two go on," Ren says. "I'll catch up."

Cass looks into Ren's eyes, and she understands. Renata isn't so sure she's as safe as can be. Maybe there's no safe place anymore. But she must check. Renata turns north, and as she moves against the steady flow of people walking toward the town center, she touches her belly. She's come this far. She needs to keep them safe going forward. They've survived too much to become complacent and end up like Leo and Amaris and Rabe and Carlos and Edd.

She's lost enough. Time to hold on to whoever she has left.

She finds the northern edge of town, and cars come in from here or there. She scans the license plates—Michigan, Minnesota, Iowa, lots of Nebraska, and several from the Dakotas. She wanders around the makeshift parking lot that had until recently been an open field. There are hundreds of vehicles all askew, and more arriving in a steady stream from routes north.

Renata shivers.

The wind is picking up.

She studies the sky. Steely gray clouds seem to warn of something wicked. There's a scent in the brisk air that smells like danger. Maybe far. Maybe too nearby.

Renata has always thought of the future as so far off she couldn't even touch it. Some day that's always in the distance—amorphous and indistinct. Always easy to push away. Today is all that had ever mattered, living for the now and to hell with tomorrow. But the future is here. Now. It had busted through, and it's closing in on her from every direction.

She can't run anymore.

She must make a stand.

Here better than anywhere. With Cass and Vega. Even with Marcus.

But if you're going to stand up to the forces against you, it's best to know what you're dealing with. She might've been wrong avoiding her future for all her past, but Ren's mettle in plowing through anything in her way might prove advantageous in the present. She knows how to deal with what life throws at her. Renata confronts the problem and makes a plan.

Someone arriving at the makeshift parking lot features the thing she's been looking for. It's an Expedition with Montana plates. It parks in the back, and the doors open. Renata recognizes the look in the eyes of these newcomers. It's like staring into a mirror. They've seen some shit. They know what's out there. They've seen the monsters up north in the white.

They are other survivors.

ABOUT THE AUTHOR

Edward Newton won the Robert L. Fish Memorial Award for Best First Short Story from the Mystery Writers of America. He has published *Horrorfrost*, the sci-fi novel *The Infinite Minute*, and the fantasy novel *Truth to Light*. He lives in beautiful Central Florida.

|

HORRORFROST

EDWARD NEWTON

def. hoarfrost
hoar·frost
ˈhôrˌfrôst/
noun
a grayish-white crystalline deposit of frozen water vapor formed in clear still weather on vegetation, fences, etc.

0°

Hoarfrost covers the glass in the small cabin, concealing the world outside. A fire licks the air inside, tasting the cold, snapping and snarling at the precipitous drop in temperature. A storm moves in, wind howling against the walls and whispering through the cracks and crevices of the old place. Snow falls from the sky in big, fat flakes, shushing and scraping against the pinewood logs of the foundation. It was just morning moments ago, but now darkness falls as the thick precipitation blots out the universe beyond.

Roman Carver doesn't even ponder the resort town at the bottom of the mountain slope, let alone the universe beyond it. Twenty years ago, he'd been a successful banker in a big city in the flattest part of Texas. In any given week, he could foreclose on a family home, bankrupt a small business, and deny loan after loan after loan, sending working folks into a financial spiral. He had been connected, corporate, and cold.

Then one day he unplugged. He stood up in the middle of an afternoon in December and walked to his floor-to-ceiling window in the corner office on the top floor of a downtown high-rise. It never snowed in this part of Texas, yet an errant snowflake drifted outside the plate glass, dancing like it did not have a care in the world. Roman had watched as it did some sort of natural ballet in the sky, a frosty kiss that broke a spell he had not even realized he was under.

There'd been a conference call playing on a speakerphone on his desk. His desk had been half the size of the room where he'd spent the past two decades of his life. He'd walked away from the desk, out of the room, and off the conference call without signing off, an urgent "Mister Carver? Mister Carver? Are you there?" following him all the way down the hall to the elevators. He'd owned a million dollar penthouse in the Renaissance district, but Roman did not even bother stopping at home before he left town forever. Six months into a relationship with a stockbroker from Austin, he never even bothered calling to tell her it was over.

Roman Carver had left Texas and came to the mountains of Montana.

He'd built this cabin with his own two hands. A man who had become successful entirely on his own, rising through the ranks to run a multimillion-dollar corporation, he had not asked for help on this new endeavor. Trial and error. His initial supplies had consisted of a flint lighter, some how-to books on survival, a first aid kit, a bowie knife, some tin pots and pans, fishing line and hooks, and a compound bow with complimentary arrows. The first month, he had almost starved. The first winter, he had almost froze. The first spring, he'd gotten so sick he thought he was going to die. That was all twenty years ago.

Roman is still alive.

He sips a mug of hot coffee cupped in calloused hands. Steam issues off the black surface, further obscuring the view out the window. Not that he needs to see snow. This high in the mountains, a storm could easily yield a foot of new powder overnight. Nothing to do but hunker down and wait out the worst. He stares at the fire. There is no electricity in the cabin. No television. No phone. No electronics of any kind. Roman had left it all behind.

A noise outside sounds like a tree giving under a load of snow, the burden beating the ground with a solid thump. The surface of the coffee in his mug ripples like a pond disturbed by a pebble. Roman had not seen a movie in twenty years, but he knew *Jurassic Park*. He is fairly sure he does not have to worry about a t-rex, but the rippled-java effect was certainly not caused by falling snow. Nothing short of an avalanche.

"The hell?" he mumbles, his voice dry and scratchy from irregular use.

Roman has not gone down to the town in the two decades since he arrived from Texas. He did not need supplies. No news. No gossip. He crossed paths with an occasional hiker in the warm months and a skier every once in a while during the winter, but he never stopped for more than a "Howdy-do." When he had come up into the mountains, Bill Clinton had been president, Elway had gotten his Super Bowl ring, and "Mmmbop" had been driving him crazy. He never asked what happened after that.

No one ever comes up here in anything big enough to cause a noise like that. Roman glares at the opaque pane. *What is out there?* He ponders for a while until curiosity finally outweighs the cold.

His coat is bearskin, a grizzly he'd taken ten years ago. Boots are sheepskin. Gloves rabbit. Before he'd left Texas, he'd been a regular contributor to PETA, and now he looked like some creature the organization would seek to protect. Ethical treatment of animals is using every part of the kill, the spirit of the beasts living on by helping Roman survive. He had never had such respect for the creatures of the wild when he'd been using them as a charitable tax deduction.

Maybe it was an animal that made the noise? A moose that bumped into a nearby tree?

Roman opens the front door and a small hill of snow crumbles into the cabin. He pushes through a drift as high as his waist, then pulls the door shut behind him. The wind cuts as sharp as the knife strapped to his waist, ready in case some winter-starved predator dares attack. The white is absolute, the driven snow like a wall that might be solid but for the shifting grains moving before his eyes.

He pushes through the snow. The cabin is in a clearing, and his home disappears behind him after he takes just three steps. He knows these woods like the back of his hand in the dark, but the blowing snow is disorienting. Better off blind than mesmerized, Roman closes his eyes and forges forward. He marks his way by putting a hand on the old tree ten yards from his front door. From there, the denser forest blocks some of the blizzard.

Roman moves in the direction of the sound, forward, forward, until he finds what he is looking for. It is a blue spruce, snapped in two, as big as any other tree in the woods. Boughs heavy with the season's snow must have sounded like an earthquake when it broke. But the weight of the snow could not have made the tree trunk crack in half. Something broke it off. Something big enough to snap it mid-section, some sixty feet up.

"The hell?" Roman says again, the wind whiting out his words.

A gust brings snowy blindness, suddenly obscuring everything. Whatever did this is still out there somewhere, in the white. Did a small plane crash in the woods? There is no other evidence. A meteor? Maybe. Something else? Something else covers a lot of possibilities. Roman has largely ignored the developments of the modern world these last two decades, so maybe they had invented something that could do this kind of damage. After all, man is always inventing new ways to destroy nature.

Another trembling bass, this one thrumming through the soles of Roman's sheepskin boots. Like an explosion deep within the earth, but the sound carries across the winter air, muffled by the thick snow. The origin is back the way he came, from the direction of his cabin.

Roman stares into the white before rushing off. Deliberating. He knows the dangers of this world. He has crossed every type of animal that lives in these mountains over the last two decades, sometimes as predator, sometimes as prey, sometimes as passerby. It feels like something else. There is something else on his mountain. Something new. But he cannot see anything through the snowfall, just a shifting white curtain that conceals everything beyond.

Roman moves back toward his home. He gets to the old tree and stops again, eyes straining against the static of the snowstorm. He cannot pick out a stationary object within all the turgid swirl of the scene. No hint. Nothing he can separate from the constant white noise.

He can't see anything out in the clearing. The blowing snow erases everything. He steps forward, one foot in front of the other. The clearing is about fifty yards in diameter, his cabin at the center. If he loses his way in the disorienting blizzard, he will find more trees. Another step. The snow gathers in drifts now nearly to his shoulders. Forward, forward, forward. Right to his front door.

Or where his front door ought to be.

The walls are all flat, smashed to the ground and nearly covered already by fresh snow. Everything he ever had has been pummeled, flat as the pancakes he made just that morning.

Something squashed the cabin as easily as Roman might flatten a pill bug under his heel.

Whatever it was could be as close as his fingertips, concealed by the white.

And the wind rises, the temperature slips another degree, and Roman Carver shivers.

It has nothing to do with the cold.

-1°

Trevin Mendoza sits on the edge of the bed. Behind him, a tussle of pink hair peeks out from beneath a rumpled bed sheet. The head does not belong to his fiancé. It is someone who had been just a friend before last night. Trevin watches the ice creep up and across the glass of the patio door that leads to the suite's balcony. It is cold outside. It is cold inside.

Maybe he is not ready to be married. That's what Alex had told him last night, before things got out of hand and went too far. Those words had made sense a few hours ago. Glancing back at Alex's pink bangs sticking out from the tangled bedding, they still make sense. His mother had always told him he wasn't the marrying kind. He hates to admit his mother is right about anything, but the evidence still hangs in the air like Alex's musky aftershave.

This is supposed to be a bachelor party weekend. The engaged couple came to Enchanted Point Ski Resort together, with an entourage, ready to celebrate the last days of bachelorhood before tying the knot in Vegas next week. Alex is supposed to be the best man at the ceremony. Yet somehow Alex had ended up in Trevin's bed. And bad things had ensued.

Such deliciously bad things.

Shit.

Trevin stands up, considers pants, then snorts. What goddamn difference did it make now? He walks naked to the icy patio door and peeks out the small corner not yet covered with frost. Outside, snow blankets the small town of Zukunft Falls, Montana. From what Trevin can see of the balcony, the railings look like lumps under a sheet. Like a lover concealed beneath the blanket of sin.

Trevin sighs. The breath turns to condensation on the glass, then freezes, crackled ice radiating out from the edges of the pane toward the center. It looks like broken glass. One more broken thing. He turns away.

Alex is sitting up in bed, watching him.

"You look like someone caught you with your hand in the cookie jar, Trev," Alex says.

"Don't call me that," Trevin says. "Only David calls me that."

"I bet he might call you something else when you tell him about this."

"Who says I am going to tell him?" Trevin challenges. "It would ruin everything."

"The only reason you did this is so you can tell him. You *want* to ruin everything."

Trevin looks away. Modesty has never been part of his personality, but standing here naked in front of Alex, he feels ashamed. Alex is right. He did this so that there could be no turning back. If he simply told David that he did not want to get married, David would try to talk him out of it. David would succeed in talking him out of it. But this?

There is no talking out of this.

"You want me to tell him?" Alex asks.

Trevin glares. Passions can flare between two people, dangerous emotions both dark and bright. So often the extremes occur on opposite sides of night.

"I'll tell him," Trevin says.

"When?"

"Tomorrow," Trevin responds, postponing the inevitable.

One last day together.

Trevin and David have been a couple for more than four years, ever since they'd met online shortly after David moved to L.A. from Nebraska. He'd been an ingenue, and Trevin was a seasoned SoCal social superman. Trevin had introduced David to everything fantastic, and David had showed him what it meant to take a step back and appreciate those fantastic things.

David had told him on their fourth anniversary that he wanted to move forward or he was going to move on. Trevin proposed. And for a while it had been fine. Exciting. A new adventure. But then they'd started planning this trip and reality started to solidify. It got hard to see the future. Then it started to show cracks.

Now, it is in pieces.

"Why wait 'til tomorrow?" Alex presses.

"Tomorrow is as good as today."

"That is the thing about tomorrows, Trev. They never get here."

"Get dressed," Trevin snaps. "Get out."

Last night they couldn't get enough of each other. Now Trevin has had enough. This is the other side of the coin.

Somewhere outside the translucent window, the world gray and gloomy despite the midmorning hour, comes the sound of thunder. Alex, pants up and shirt half-buttoned, turns to the patio door. Trevin, still without a stitch on, approaches the balcony. Another boom. Louder. Closer.

"What was that?" Alex asks.

Trevin steps into a pair of Calvin Klein sweatpants that were crumpled in a corner. He pulls on the white and blue Bogner ski jacket he wore on the slopes yesterday. There are a pair of Hestra mittens that must be Alex's tossed not far from pink bikini briefs that also do not belong to Trevin. He pulls on the mittens. Stepping into his ski boots, he opens the glass door; the quick flick of cold takes his breath. Yesterday had been sunny and perfect; this morning is like nothing a SoCal surfer has ever seen. Trevin likes his water in waves instead of flakes.

The white is absolute. He remembers seeing the white sand of

Coronado Beach for the first time and telling his boyfriend at the time that it must be like walking in snow. Nope. It is nothing like snow. This is endless, oppressive, unstoppable. Trevin feels like he is staring into oblivion, and if he looks into it long enough, he might go blind.

Somewhere in the white, another boom. Trevin cannot be sure with the swirls and eddies of the snow, but he thinks the sound made the flakes *vibrate*.

"That is not thunder," Alex says from right beside him, making Trevin jump. "It sounded like an explosion."

Alex had donned a pair of spare gloves, hat, ski goggles, as well as his own jacket and boots. He looks ready to survive a blizzard. Well, if he wasn't going to leave willingly by the main hotel room door...

"Go check it out," Trevin goads.

Alex gives him a face. "Why don't you go?"

"You're dressed for it," Trevin says. "Goggles and everything. I wouldn't be able to see a thing out there in that blizzard."

They stare out into the suffocating snow. The wind gusts and Trevin cannot see more than two feet in front of him. For one excruciating moment, he imagines David, unseen, in front of him, looking back as Trevin looks out, yet they cannot see each other. Close enough to reach out and touch, yet separated by an insurmountable distance. The space between them is too great to erase.

"Scared?" Trevin taunts.

Another boom.

"Yes," Alex says.

Instead of forward, both men take a step back. Retreat. They close the frosted door and stare at the pane veiled with hoarfrost. Snow had sneaked in while they'd been staring down the storm, tendrils like tentacles winding away from the closed door, quickly melting, fingers of water leaving wet streaks on the gray carpet. Outside, the sounds of more explosions, like someone had declared war on this resort town.

Then the lights go out.

-2°

Rhonda Phelps stares into the mirror. Was that another wrinkle? Another line? Shitshitshit. They popped up lately like weeds in a garden. Every morning. Festering like an infection. Of course, the stress over each one likely caused the next, a snowball rolling down a hill gathering momentum. Her mama, God rest her soul, might hate her for it, but Rhonda plans on going under the knife as soon as she gets back to Rochester.

She had dyed her hair for the occasion, a professional job that she'd driven an hour out of town to get done, far enough away from anyone who might have known her. She has been doing the same thing since the first errant strand of gray arrived some fifteen years ago. She had her regular local hairstylist, and then her secret one, who existed out of town, for coloring, like she was married to one and cheating with the other. All to keep up the illusion. Everything to stave off the realization of time running out.

This trip was a bust. She had been dating Howard online for the last few months. They arranged a face-to-face for a week of skiing in the middle of nowhere, Montana. They'd met for the first time ever in the lobby of the community lodge to kick off the vacation with some drinks and an introductory meeting. Well, Howard's online profile picture was from a good fifty pounds ago. And as he had pointed out before leaving for home five days early, Rhonda's was from a good two decades ago.

She had lied about her age. She has been lying about her age since forty snuck up and stole her future. For a few years, it had been easy to get away with. Perpetually thirty-nine, she looked it until just recently. Something had changed in the last year. Like the borrowed time she had used up on lying these last ten years had all piled on at once, advancing too fast. The woman in the mirror is not thirty-nine. Tomorrow, Rhonda turns fifty.

He had left her the birthday gift he'd brought. It is a gray scarf the color of hoarfrost. She picks it up now and wraps it around her neck. It covers up some of the waddles and wrinkles that seemed to appear overnight. Like her body knows fifty is only a day away.

There is another reverberating bass in the distance, like a drumbeat loud enough to make her bones ache. Thunder? Some local phenomenon? An artificial annoyance?

The old woman in the mirror disappears into darkness as the lights flicker and fail. Like candles blown out on a birthday cake.

Howard had left, but Rhonda had decided to stay. The suite is prepaid through the end of the week, and she was not prepared to go home to New York and face her family and friends about the shitty reality of her romantic vacation. Certainly, Sheila would arrange a night out with the gang for Rhonda's birthday. None of them believed she was still thirty-nine. That had turned from a cute joke to an awkward obliviousness over the last couple of years. No one would be surprised she is turning fifty.

None of them except Rhonda herself.

She had such plans. She had wanted to be married by thirty, two kids by thirty-five, and by now she had expected to be cheering at a high school football game or giving a standing ovation at the state spelling bee. Instead, she looks like a grandmother with no grandchildren to show for it.

The dark is a brief blessing.

Then she feels her way out of the suite. Dim light leaks in from the terrace doors flecked with crystalline frost, a gray ambiance that reminds her of the strands that populate her black hair, more and more and more. Before she had her coif colored for this trip, she'd plucked enough gray weeds to make Barbie's granny a wig.

The light is just bright enough to separate objects from the pathway, barely illuminating the route to the front door of the suite. Rhonda opens the door with the number 438 on the front. In the hall, emergency lights cast everything in a dull red glow. Other occupants stand in doorways and gather in small groups.

"What's going on?" Rhonda asks a woman who looks like she is maybe twenty-five and does not have to lie about her age. Little blonde thing with hair all tussled like she just woke up and still looks as pretty as if she spent hours on her face. The girl obviously exited her suite without putting on a bra, the nip in the air ensuring it is not the only nip noticeable. What is not noticeable is any sag whatsoever.

Little bitch.

"The lights are out," the girl answers, like Rhonda had just asked the stupidest question ever. She does not even look up from the phone she is on, texting away like some stenographer transcribing their conversation. The blonde did not have to ask anyone in the hall what is happening; her phone is the only companion she needs.

Someone ought to slap some sense into the girl, but that someone is not Rhonda. Not today. Instead, she turns away from the nubile youth and walks across the room to a woman who makes Rhonda look young in comparison.

The occupant in the room across from Rhonda's looks like she is in her sixties, a slight, sprightly white woman wringing her hands like she is applying lotions and pissed about it. She is wearing colorful leggings over a fit form and a sweater that looks as trendy as anything the idiot blonde might wear. The older woman at least has the sense to wear undergarments.

Closer now, Rhonda notices the sweater is on backward. Under other circumstances, Rhonda would have honored the sisterhood code and notified the lady—Rhonda is not shy about boogers hanging from noses or a piece of spinach caught in someone's teeth—but there seems to be something more important to discuss than turned-around tops.

"Do you know what's happening?" Rhonda asks.

"No," the woman answers with a worried expression, not wasting words with a stupid reply. "Clarice went down to the lobby. She was concerned after the explosions started. No nonsense, that one. She scooted off before the lights went dark. I hope she isn't stuck in the elevator. With her arthritis, she never takes the stairs. Do you think they have an emergency backup for the elevators?"

"I'm sure they do, ma'am," Rhonda replies. She has no idea.

Someone with a flashlight sweeping the hall left to right starts coming down the corridor. It is a resort employee with a name tag that says "Conner." Conner looks the same age as the blonde still standing braless in the doorway of her suite, the glow of her phone casting shadows across her shirt, highlighting twin nubs that keep getting pointier. Conner gets an eyeful, pausing right between Rhonda and the girl.

"You have some answers for us, Conner?" Rhonda asks.

"Just stay inside your suite, ma'am," he answers without looking at Rhonda, absorbing an eyeful of the blonde's perky bosom.

It's like Rhonda isn't even there. Age has made her invisible. There had been a time when she'd been the one who had caught the boys' attention. Now, she is the incessant buzz in the background.

"Have you seen my friend?" the old woman asks Conner. "Her name is Clarice Otter. She went down to your lobby to find out what this is all about."

"What?" Conner stutters, distracted by delectable tits. Then he finally turns, the task at hand finally resurfacing. He looks at the old woman. "I didn't see anyone on my way up. She might still be in the lobby. She shouldn't be wandering around without a flashlight."

"Why did the lights go out?" Rhonda asks.

Conner looks as clueless as the blonde across the hallway. "For your own safety, please return to your suite until the electricity comes back on." He is reciting the company line, like an automated message repeating on an intercom.

Another explosion sounds outside. Closer. The maid's cart parked under the emergency light two doors down rolls a few inches up the hall from the reverberation, a bottle of cleaner shaking off the edge of the cart. Rhonda grabs the door jamb to steady herself, her other hand cupping the old woman's elbow to make sure the senior citizen does not topple over.

"What the fuck is that?" Conner swears, eschewing company protocol in favor of stark fear.

The blonde looks up from the glowing screen of her phone like she has just witnessed someone murdered right in front of her face. "I lost my signal."

Conner pulls his own electronic device from the pocket of his resort uniform. "Me, too." In the pale light from his screen, he looks like a ghost. "The tower must be down."

"No Wi-Fi, either," the blonde adds.

Another explosion shakes the entire building.

"My last message," Conner whispers, reading, professional mission now entirely abandoned. "It's from my buddy who works out at the lifts, up the mountain. He says there is something in the snow."

Rhonda looks over Conner's shoulder and reads the last text message on his screen from someone called "Doobie," a dubious eyewitness account from someone named after a marijuana cigarette: "cant see it jist shadows theirs somethng trrble in the white."

The bass sounds again, this time shaking Rhonda so hard she stumbles forward, almost knocking into Miss Braless Blondie. *There's something terrible in the white.* For so long, she has dreaded turning fifty. Wished tomorrow would never come. But now, Rhonda Phelps wants nothing more than to see just one more day.

Press
Presents

With barely a moment to rest after wrapping up his last case, Jasper O'Malley is handed another assignment that sends him and his partner, Amelia Rio, to the Big Apple. This time around Jasper's been hired to find a missing person, one Ray Armstrong, a former associate of his.

The trail eventually leads Jasper and Amelia into the tunnels beneath the city, where the case takes an unexpected turn when they stumble upon a desiccated corpse. As much as Jasper would like to believe there's a logical explanation for the condition of the body, all evidence points to one thing…

There's a vampire prowling the city and preying on its citizens.

Now, in addition to locating Armstrong, Jasper needs to track down and destroy the creature sucking the city dry in typical O'Malley style. God help New York City.

Midnight.

The Witching Hour.

But the creatures of darkness are not
confined to the shadows of the night.
Lonely stretches of highways…
Bustling college campuses…
Quiet suburban neighborhoods…
Pricey, upscale day spas…
They're everywhere.

Earl and Dale, a pair of burly truckers,
seem to be drawn to those that dwell in the darkness.
Monster hunters by default, they
confront the evil fearlessly—and with just a bit of humor.
Vampires, werewolves, half-human spider demons,
and those that prey on the innocent…
All will realize they've met their match
when they go head to head with…

The Midnight Men

THERE WAS SOMETHING WRONG WITH THE MARTINS' BABY.
IT LIVED.

What's Wrong with the Baby?

Vincent Courtney

THE FEAR IS GROWING

From the moment he saw the ancient castle rising out of the picturesque Scottish countryside, filmmaker Dan Martin knew he'd found the ideal location for his vampire horror movie. And nothing could make him leave. Not the eerie legends of soul-stealing beasts of the night...nor a bizarre series of freak accidents. Not even his pregnant wife's tragic miscarriage.

THE TERROR IS BORN

Except that now there is another fetus growing in Vicki's womb. But little Darian is not going to be a normal baby. The Martins' adopted ten-year-old son Marty will soon find that out. In fact, Marty will soon know exactly what his new brother really is.

Shrouded in Mystery
The locals call it *Isla de los Perdidos*.
Island of the Lost.
According to the legends, those who venture onto the shores of this cursed island never return.

Abandoned
Valarie DeNola and her sister Julie have chosen to ignore the legends and the warnings. They have been selected to lead a team of explorers to the island to discover the mystery surrounding it. But once ashore, they become cut off from the outside world, and what they discover is something they could never have prepared for.

Inhabited by Death
Now they must fight against an unknown presence that is picking them off one by one. No one can be trusted, and when even nature rises up against them, all seems lost. Their one hope is the extraction team they know is coming.

But will any of them survive to see it arrive?

If you can't run with the big dogs...

It was supposed to be a corporate retreat and a series of morale-boosting exercises. It was a weekend Shawn Biltmore nearly didn't survive.

There was something else playing in the woods that night, something other than a bunch of corporate drones with paintball guns.
And it had chosen Shawn as its new chew toy.

...rip 'em to shreds.

The local authorities chalked it up to a bear attack.
So did the doctors.
Shawn knew the truth, however, as much as he wanted to deny it.
But when one of his coworkers is viciously killed,
Shawn must face the truth...
He's a killer who needs to be put down.

Or is he?

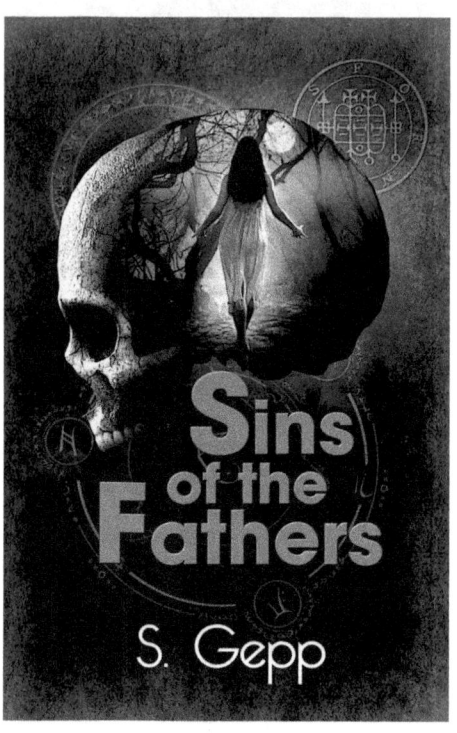

Sins of the Fathers

S. Gepp

They called themselves The Round Table. Seven friends, a bunch of nobodies in high school—until they learned the art of manipulation and how much influence they could wield with the right bit of knowledge. After years of being bullied, they had their first taste of power…and they wanted more.

In college, they found their power had faded. Their petty blackmail schemes no longer made others eager to do their bidding…and that just wasn't acceptable. But the Darkness offered them everything they could possibly want—for a price.
A price they were all too willing to pay.

And now, twenty-one years later, married with children and successful careers, their past is coming back to haunt them and threatening to take everything they hold dear. How much will they lose before they can placate the spirit of the dead?